To Greg,

DANCE

Never forget how
to Dance!

TEODORA KOSTOVA

Teodora Kostova xx

ISBN-13: 978-1497407251
ISBN-10:1497407257

Edited by Kameron Mitchell
Proofread by Charmaine Butler and Midian Sosa

Disclaimer

This is a work of fiction. All names, places and incidents are either the product of the author's imagination, or are used fictitiously.
This is not an actual representation of the musical theatre world. Even though an extensive research has been made, all facts, details and information have been transformed to fit the plot.
This is a love story, not an encyclopedia.
Enjoy!

To everyone who, like me,
believes in love at first sight

"Dance, when you're broken open.
Dance, if you've torn the bandage off.
Dance in the middle of the fighting.
Dance in your blood. Dance when you're
perfectly free."
~ RUMI

CHAPTER ONE

Fenix

Poison was moving to Queen Victoria!

Finally.

Fenix was beyond ecstatic. Queen Victoria had always been his favourite London theatre, ever since he'd seen his mother, the great ballerina Evelyn Bergman, dance on its stage fourteen years ago. A nine-year-old Fenix had watched in awe and clutched his dad's hand tightly as they sat side-by-side in the front row, and had been forever captivated by the iconic London theatre.

It was because of that moment that right after he'd graduated from Juilliard, Fenix had accepted the offer to move to London and play the lead in a brand new musical called *Poison*. He could have stayed in New York, only to fight tooth and nail pursuing his dream to be on Broadway. And he knew he would have, sooner rather than later. He had inherited his mother's grace and talent. But while Evelyn could not sing to save her life, Fenix had a voice that could fill stadiums. His mother always joked that her greatest fear was that he'd choose to become a rock star instead of a dancer. And Fenix had always replied that Broadway was a much nicer place for effeminate gay boys than the rock and roll world.

In a way, he had become a rock star. *Poison* was a show based on the rock *band City of Shadows*'s music, and Fenix's character was the lead singer. He played a rock star every night, a very convincing one at that. He'd put on eye liner to accentuate his pale blue eyes, style his long blond hair in a messy way, put on the leather pants and a tight, black t-shirt and pour his heart out on stage. That was what Fenix lived for and it showed.

Poison was based at a small London theatre, but Fenix saw the potential the moment pre-production had started. Obviously, everyone else saw it too. After just four months of performing on the barely-large-enough stage of Cutty Sark theatre in Greenwich, *Poison* got an offer from Queen Victoria. It was going to be their main event, with four scheduled shows per week. Queen Victoria was hosting another musical – *Of Kids and Monsters*, but it was aimed at a younger audience and started at 4:00 pm, five days a week. The show was hugely popular ever since it had opened at Queen Victoria about a year ago. It had started as a small production, created by a couple of kids with nothing better to do while they studied at LAMDA – The London Academy of Music and Dramatic Art. Steven Hamilton, a notorious West End producer, saw the show one night at the small amateur theatre and had been immediately interested. Long story short, *Of Kids and Monsters* and its creators had become one of those incredibly lucky, overnight success stories. The show was offered the matinee slot at Queen Victoria the moment it got a little makeover. Fenix imagined Mr Hamilton's influence had played a great role in the offer, but it really didn't matter. He'd seen the show and he knew it deserved all the success it had gotten so far, and then some.

Of Kids and Monsters had been playing at Queen Victoria for almost a year and it was still sold out weeks in advance. Fenix knew the lead, Jared Hartley, had a lot to do with that. He was one of the original creators, and the man's charisma and stage presence made the musical what it was today. Sure, the script was great, the story well thought out, the songs were beautiful, and the whole production was lavish and entertaining, but the moment Jared stepped on stage, the atmosphere in the whole theatre changed.

Nobody was able to look away. Fenix was sure that was exactly what Steven Hamilton had seen that fateful night at the small, amateur theatre. He'd felt Jared's presence, fallen under his charm and, like the good businessman that he was, he'd known that man would make this show a hit. And would make *him* lots of money.

Fenix had a slight crush on Jared ever since he'd gone to see the musical a couple of months ago. He'd seen his picture in the magazines before, and had always thought the guy was gorgeous, but seeing him in person was a whole other experience. And now Fenix was going to share Queen Victoria with Jared! It wasn't Broadway, but this was almost as perfect.

The next two weeks flew by. Fenix had been in a constant happy daze. The final performance at Cutty Sark the night before had been an emotional one; the audience all stood, cheering for ten minutes straight. The theatre staff had thrown the cast a small farewell party, and everyone had shed a few tears, including Fenix. Yes, he was extremely happy he'd be performing at Queen Victoria from now on and he'd be within touching distance of Jared Hartley, but still. He'd had a good time at Cutty Sark – it had been the first stepping stone in his career and he'd always remember it fondly.

Fenix looked at his watch as he chewed his sugar-free, oat cereal, floating in soy milk. In about half an hour he had to move into his new dressing room at Queen Victoria. Everyone else had decided to go on Monday when the theatre was closed to the public, and while it would have been generally more convenient, but Fenix couldn't wait. He wanted to see the dressing rooms, the rehearsal room, backstage... Thankfully, the staff manager had agreed to meet him on a Saturday – considering the weekend was the busiest time for the theatre – and to show him around.

Finishing his breakfast and rinsing his bowl in the sink, Fenix went to his bedroom to get dressed and pack a small bag with essentials for his dressing room. As he put on jeans and a t-shirt, he thought about his current living arrangements. He lived in Greenwich because Cutty Sark was right across the street. But he couldn't keep living here now that he was performing at Queen Victoria. He wanted to move somewhere closer to the theatre, but the rent in that part of London was impossible to afford right now.

Unless he shared with someone.

Fenix pondered that for a moment. Joy, his co-star and love interest in the musical, was a possible candidate. She was the closest thing to a best friend Fenix had ever had. He'd never been very sociable, and he'd never had many friends, but Joy was cool and they got along pretty well. Unfortunately, she needed to have her own space and she'd rather commute for an hour from her downstairs apartment than share with anyone. Fenix had already tried to convince her to move in together with him to save money on rent, but she flat out refused.

Another person he sort of liked was Benedict, or Ned, as everyone called him. He played *City of Shadows*'s drummer in *Poison,* and Fenix knew him pretty well, since they'd spent so much time together. But those past few months were precisely why Fenix was reluctant to share an apartment with the guy. Ned had to be taken in small dozes otherwise it just got too much. Everything around Ned was constantly changing – his opinions, his hair, his style, his boyfriends, his mood. It was a non-stop whirlwind of emotion that Fenix found fascinating but could not imagine having in his home twenty-four-seven.

Fenix didn't know anybody else well enough to live with them. Besides, the rest of the *Poison* cast were all either married or already living with someone or he knew he wouldn't get along with. Fenix ran his fingers through his hair, which didn't do anything to tame the mess it was right now, and sighed. Commuting an hour to work it was, then.

"What do you mean I have to share with Jared Hartley?" Fenix squeaked when Gary, the staff manager, escorted him to the dressing rooms. They were standing in front of a door with Jared's name on it and Fenix was too stunned to move a muscle.

"Everyone shares, man. We don't have enough dressing rooms to fit all performers individually," Gary explained.

Wait, did he think Fenix was complaining?

Fuck no.

If Fenix believed in God he'd be on his knees right now, thanking him.

"I understand. I meant, isn't he going to mind?"

"Nah," Gary said. "Jared is a cool guy. He used to share with one of the guys from *Cult,* but when they moved to the Barbican, their places opened up." He eyed Fenix curiously and frowned before saying, "Look, if you really don't want to share with Jared, I'm sure we can re-arrange the set up and fix you up somewhere else. Nobody has shown up and moved their stuff in yet, so it won't be a problem..."

"No!" Fenix yelled in alarm. Gary startled and his frown deepened.

Great. Way to make a good first impression, moron.

"Sorry," Fenix apologised, giving Gary his most charming smile. "I didn't mean to sound so dramatic," Gary rolled his eyes, murmured 'actors' under his breath and moved in to open the door. He walked in and Fenix followed him.

The dressing room was large enough for two people to share comfortably. It had two huge vanity tables with three-part mirrors, a wardrobe, two sofas, a coffee table, and a big window overlooking Piccadilly Circus.

"This is pretty much it," Gary said, walking to the centre of the room and spreading his arms wide. "You've got a bathroom through that door," he continued, pointing to the left. "When you meet Jared, he'll tell you where to put your stuff."

Fenix thanked Gary before he left the room, and flopped on the sofa. Smiling slowly he pondered how quickly his life had changed, and wondered what else was in store for him.

"Hi," a voice said, startling him. Fenix had been daydreaming and hadn't even heard the door open. Looking towards the owner of the voice, he saw his new dressing room mate.

Jared.

Jared Hartley was standing a few feet away, a pleasant smile on his handsome face. The man was even more beautiful up close – he was probably no taller than Fenix, but didn't have Fenix's lithe dancer's body. His shoulders were wider and the arms peeking under his t-shirt were bulkier. His dark hair was tousled, curling under his ears and falling into his eyes.

"Hi," Fenix replied as he exhaled the breath he was holding. Jared quirked an eyebrow and Fenix realised he must look like an idiot sitting there, staring at the guy. "Hi, sorry. I just got here and I'm still a bit overwhelmed." Jumping to his feet, he offered Jared his hand. Jared took it in his own, his dark blue eyes never leaving Fenix's icy blue ones. The touch of Jared's warm skin as his elegant, soft fingers wrapped around Fenix's palm sent shivers up his arm and his skin erupted in goosebumps. "I'm Fenix Bergman," he said quietly.

"I'm Jared Hartley. Welcome to Queen Victoria, Fenix," Jared said smoothly, letting go of Fenix's hand. "I have to admit I haven't seen your show. But judging by all the excitement it's caused around here, it should be pretty good." Jared inclined his head to the side studying him. Fenix felt exposed under the man's inquisitive gaze but couldn't look away. There was something about Jared – you didn't just dismiss him and avert your eyes. You stayed captured in those navy blue depths until he took pity on you and released you.

Since Fenix had apparently lost the ability to speak, he just grinned while Jared proceeded to show him around. He showed Fenix his vanity table, his side of the wardrobe and where everything was. There was a small fridge Fenix hadn't noticed before where water and energy drinks were usually kept. The dressing room wasn't too big so the whole orientation lasted no longer than a few minutes.

"So, any questions?" Jared inquired. Fenix shook his head and stuffed his hands in his pockets, starting too feel claustrophobic in the small room, considering Jared's presence took so much space. "I have some time before I have to start getting ready. Do you want me to show you around the theatre?"

"That'll be great, thank you," Fenix said as they headed out of the dressing room.

Jared led him through a maze of corridors, twists and turns, pointing at doors bearing names, little nooks with coffee machines, restrooms, and yet more doors. He showed him the rehearsal room, which was bigger than the main stage at Cutty Sark. Fenix couldn't wait to put on his dancing gear and try it out.

"Is there some kind of schedule to use the rehearsal room?"

"Usually, no," Jared said, raking a hand through his hair. A few strands fell immediately back into his eyes. Fenix had to suppress the urge to reach out and push them gently away, caressing Jared's cheek along the way. "Both shows have very different time schedules, so there was no need for that. You guys would probably use it more often, especially if you've made any changes to your show. We don't use it that much anymore since *Of Kids and Monsters* has been running for a year and we pretty much know it in our sleep." Jared chuckled and Fenix let the sound envelop him like a caress. Jared had a beautiful voice – low and smooth and comforting. Fenix wondered what it would be like to fall asleep listening to that voice. What it would be like to hear that voice whispering his name.

"Fenix?" Jared asked, frowning slightly. "You OK?"

"Yeah," Fenix replied and blushed.

Great, just great. Keep giving him the impression you're some awestruck aspiring performer.

"I said that you could use the rehearsal room any time you want. I know you probably dance daily, so it's OK to do it here."

"Thanks. I'll keep that in mind."

"Do you wanna see the stage?" Jared asked and smiled wickedly.

"God, yes!" Fenix exclaimed and beamed. Jared's stare turned from polite and friendly to something... else for a second. His eyes flashed and he licked his delicious lower lip. Fenix zeroed in on that pink tongue sliding across Jared's mouth and had to force himself to look away. If he didn't, he might do something extremely stupid.

Like kiss Jared until they were both flushed and panting and grinding against each other.

Yeah, extremely stupid.

"Lead the way," Fenix croaked the words past his dry throat. Jared nodded and headed down yet another corridor.

CHAPTER TWO

Jared

Jared knew he was screwed the moment a pair of pale blue eyes fell on him.

The man was exquisite! Jared stared at him, captivated – he was sprawled on the sofa in his, or rather *their* dressing room, his head dropped back on the cushions, lost deep in thought. Jared had never in his life felt such instant attraction to anyone. He'd never, *ever*, wanted to tackle someone, rid him of all his clothes, feel every inch of his skin under his tongue and fuck him until they both dropped of exhaustion, without so much as a 'hello' first.

"Hi," Jared said and smiled. There. The 'hello' was out of the way. Could they move on to fucking now?

After an awkward introduction and tour of the theatre during which he tried to remain as polite and unaffected by Fenix as possible, Jared excused himself and headed back to the dressing room. He needed to start getting ready soon.

"Hey, Fenix, have you seen *Of Kids and Monsters*?" Jared asked, stopping midstride and turning back to face Fenix.

"Yeah, a few months ago. I wanted to see it again because I loved it, but it's sold out for weeks in advance..." he trailed off, his blond bangs falling in his eyes adorably.

Bingo.

"You're not officially in until Monday, right?"

Fenix nodded. Jared knew everyone was supposed to move in on Monday and was quite surprised to see Fenix in his, *their*, dressing room today. "Come, I'll get you a backstage pass for the weekend until you get your own on Monday."

Fenix beamed as his eyes lit up like a child's. Jared's chest felt tight and uncomfortable, and he rubbed it absently. What was this guy doing to him?

Whatever. He was not going to analyse it. He liked Fenix, and he felt pleasant warmth spread all over his body as the man caught up to him, excited grin still in place, and they continued walking side-by-side again.

Jared felt different performing that night. He always gave his all on stage – he might be saying those exact same lines for the hundredth time, but for most people in the audience, it would be the first time they'd seen the show. He loved the reaction he got from the kids every single night – their laughter, their excited squeals, their applause. It was what made the show what it was, and what inspired everyone on stage to act as if it was their first time.

But tonight... Jared could feel Fenix's eyes on him the whole time. He knew the guy was backstage. Jared had seen him right before curtain call. He knew Fenix was absorbing every word, every movement, every dance move. It was a bit unnerving because Jared had heard that Fenix was an amazing dancer. He hadn't had the chance to see *Poison* for himself, but if Queen Victoria had gone out of their way to get it, it must be pretty damn good.

Of Kids and Monsters was Jared's project, his baby. He'd teamed up with his best friend and fellow classmate at LAMDA, Adam Fischer, and they'd created it in their spare time just to gain some experience. They'd done everything – the script, the songs, the decor, the auditions. It had been a gruelling, yet incredible experience. Of course, ever since it had been commissioned for Queen Victoria, the show had gotten a makeover in terms of better songs, lavish decor, professionally created and fitted costumes, more experienced actors... But in its core it had stayed the same.

Every line, every song, every dance move was ingrained in Jared's very being. And yet, tonight, with Fenix watching, he felt nervous. Unsure.

He needed to get a grip. This was ridiculous.

Jared shook his head subtly to get rid of thoughts about Fenix and cleared his mind of everything but the performance. It was almost time for his first solo song and he needed to get into that head space. Taking a deep breath and feeling all the lights but the one trained on him die out, Jared began singing, his strong, clear voice filling the hall:

Looking back in time
I don't know how it started
But it doesn't really matter
'He's fearless,' said my mama
'He's reckless,' said my dad.
'He's brave,' she kept saying
'We'll see,' was all he said
I'm not a kid anymore, but I believe in monsters
Fear is overwhelming
It will rob you of your freedom
How do you fight the monsters under the bed?

The kid that played one of the lead characters, Sean, ran on stage just as the music started dying down. A light found him and lit up his steps until he collided with Jared. He put his arms around the kid and tried to calm him down. Sean was shaking and distraught – man, that kid had a bright future in acting. At ten years old he performed that demanding role to the T every single time.

"How do you know?" Sean whispered, turning his huge brown eyes on Jared. "How do you know about the monsters under the bed?"

"Because I used to be one," replied Jared, and began singing softly:

When all is said and done
When you don't want to fight anymore
You'll see the monsters are not under the bed
The monsters are inside your head

By the time Jared got home that night, he'd made up his mind. He needed to do something about Fenix. He'd known the guy for barely a day but he couldn't stop thinking about him. When the show had ended tonight, Jared found himself incredibly disappointed when Fenix hadn't been backstage. He wanted to talk to him, ask him what he thought about it, just... be in his presence. But he hadn't been there and, frustrated, Jared had gone straight home without even taking a shower.

Home. Right now, home was an almost entirely empty studio flat on the fourth floor of an old building, just off New Bond street. Jared had seen the 'FOR SALE' sign when he'd gotten lost one day, about four months ago, looking for a pub where he was supposed to meet some friends. Something about the old, but well-maintained four-storey building caught his eye and drew his attention. The apartment was close to the theatre – a fifteen minute walk to be exact, and Jared moving out of Adam's place had been long overdue.

Adam might be his best friend, but they'd been roommates ever since their first year at LAMDA. They both needed a change, especially considering their history. Adam had been Jared's first and they'd dated for a while. Although dated wasn't the correct term. They'd been friends and roommates and they fucked occasionally. But they'd always been friends first, fuck buddies second. Jared loved Adam, but he'd never been in love with him. He'd never been in love with anybody, actually.

So, this flat had seemed like the perfect opportunity to move out; to give Adam his own space and stand on his own two feet for the first time in his life. The studio was in bad shape and in desperate need of renovation, but it was large with high ceilings and great potential. Nobody had lived there for years and it showed. The owners – an elderly couple with no children to leave it to – wanted to get rid of it as quickly as possible and spend the money on travel and little luxuries. However, their plans had turned south when the property had been on the market for over a year with no interest from buyers. This was a very expensive part of London, but when nobody showed any real interest, they were forced to lower the price. Considerably. When they met with Jared, he managed to charm them into lowering the price even further. On top of that, it turned out they were massive theatre fans, had even seen his show, and when he offered them as many free theatre tickets as he could get, he had himself a deal.

And it was a great deal. He would have to invest a lot to make it habitable, but it was worth it. Jared spent all his savings, including what was left of his father's life insurance to buy the place, so he had nothing left for renovations. All he could manage were the essentials – a cheap bed, a second hand wardrobe, and sofas that didn't match, and an Ikea coffee table and kitchen utensils. Some rugs, curtains, sheets and towels. Thankfully, the kitchen was intact with decent cupboards, a washing machine, and an oven that actually worked. The electricity probably needed rewiring, but it worked for now, so did the gas boiler and the plumbing. There was damp everywhere – on the ceiling and on the walls, which definitely needed replastering.

It was a huge project Jared had neither the time nor money for. But he'd get there. He was thinking of taking out a loan, because he could not live like this much longer.

Jared flopped down on his bed, which creaked under the assault. He hadn't had a guy in here ever since he'd moved in almost two months ago, and he doubted the bed would hold if he decided to invite someone over. Thinking of inviting someone over reminded Jared that he was horny as hell. He hadn't had sex since... Jesus, he couldn't even remember. He'd gone home with a guy he'd met at a bar probably about three months ago. No wonder he was so taken with the first attractive guy he'd met since then. Jared needed to get laid. Pronto.

He got up, took his clothes off and headed for the shower. It was 8:00 pm. He had plenty of time to make plans for tonight.

In about an hour, freshly showered, dressed and fed, Jared took out his phone and dialled Adam. The guy never stayed home on a Saturday, even though they had a show the next day. They arranged to meet at the Mai Tai Pit for drinks, and then go to Lono's for dancing and, hopefully, finding someone for a long, satisfying fuck in his creaking bed.

CHAPTER THREE

Jared

"Who is that?" Adam asked, his eyes fixing on someone over Jared head. By the hungry look in his eyes, Jared could tell whoever it was, he'd end up in Adam's bed tonight. Jared turned around to see the object of Adam's fascination and was startled when he met Fenix's eyes across the crowded dance floor. Lono's wasn't big, but it *was* one of the most popular gay bars in London. Jared, Adam and their friends frequented the place and knew the staff, which was a bonus since they usually got to jump all the queues. The bass of the music that played at the moment was fast and loud, and Jared's pulse involuntarily synced with it. Out of all the clubs in London, how was it possible that Fenix, and obviously some of his friends, had decided to come to Lono's tonight?

Fenix waved at Jared and gave him one of his disarming smiles. Adam grunted behind him.

"You know him?"

"Yeah."

"How?"

"Didn't you see him backstage today?" Jared waved back and turned to face Adam again. Adam shook his head. "He's the star of the new headliner musical. And," Jared leaned in closer to Adam and had to crane his neck to speak in his ear, "my new dressing room buddy."

Adam jerked back in surprise. The look on his face was so comical that Jared had to laugh. His big brown eyes were round with shock, and his mouth curled down in disappointment.

"Fuck. Why do you always get the hot ones?" Adam shook his head, frowning. "First Cade, now this guy? I'm always stuck with the ugly or straight ones. It's not fair." Adam pouted and Jared laughed harder. The pout did not fit his six-foot-two friend at all. Jared was just about to comment on that when he felt a warm hand on his lower back. Turning his head, he saw Fenix standing right behind him. His pale blue eyes looked colourless in the dim light of the club. Even so close, the man was perfect. Jared felt the familiar pang in his chest and flutter in his belly.

"Hi," he said, smiling at Fenix, who awarded him a lopsided grin in return. Adam cleared his throat and Jared was just about to introduce them when Mark, who played a Monster in the show, appeared out of nowhere, flushed and exhilarated from dancing, and enveloped Fenix in a hug. Jared couldn't help but notice that it was a long, full body hug. Every part of Mark was touching every part of Fenix, and Jared saw red. He wanted to burst between them, separate them, and push Fenix behind his back and out of reach.

But he didn't. He slowly sipped his drink, patiently waiting for the hug to end.

"So glad you could make it, darling," Mark drawled in his usual pretentious manner. "Did you bring any of your friends as you promised?"

"Yeah. They're here somewhere," Fenix said and his eyes started scanning the dance floor. "That's Ned," he pointed to a very attractive guy dressed in leather pants and a tight t-shirt, with dark hair falling past his shoulders in messy waves. "He plays *City of Shadows*'s drummer."

"Ah, perfect. I love drummers. They have rhythm like no one else," cooed Mark and headed straight for Ned.

"He does realise Ned *plays* a drummer, right?" Fenix asked as he leaned closer to Jared to speak in his ear.

Jared shivered.

He wanted this man, right now.

He wanted to pull him into his arms and never let go.

The feeling was so strong that it stunned Jared. His insides were melting at Fenix's proximity and he knew he wouldn't be able to control himself much longer with Fenix so close.

"You OK?" Fenix asked, his face a breath away from Jared's. It was impossible not to lean in and...

"Hi, I'm Adam. Jared's co-star," he interrupted and thrust his hand between them, taking Fenix's and shaking it.

"I know who you are. I'm a fan," Fenix said smoothly as his eyes met Adam's. Jared felt the loss of Fenix's undivided attention like a punch in the gut.

What the fuck was wrong with him? He didn't even know his body was capable of such reactions to another human being.

"I'm Fenix," he continued, still holding Adam's hand. Adam wasn't in a hurry to let go, apparently.

"So I've heard," Adam flirted.

"You wanna dance?" Jared whispered in Fenix's ear, impatient to get him away from Adam. Fenix claimed his hand back and turned to Jared.

"Sure."

"Go ahead. I'll be right behind you," Jared inclined his head towards the dance floor.

"I hope so," Fenix said and sauntered away.

"Back. Off," Jared said through gritted teeth when Fenix went out of earshot. Adam stared at him in surprise.

"What?"

"I said, back off. He's mine." Jared gave Adam one last warning look and followed Fenix to the dance floor, leaving Adam to gape behind him.

Fenix must have been on the dance floor no longer than a minute, but by the time Jared found him, he was already crowded by admirers. No wonder – the man could move! It was like the music flowed *through* him. Fenix had his back to Jared, his ass jiggling deliciously to the rhythm, his tight jeans not leaving much to the imagination. Jared snuck behind him, wrapped his arms around his waist and glared at the guy dancing with Fenix until he took the hint and bounced off. Fenix turned his head slightly and smiled when he saw Jared. He raised his arms over his head and brought them down behind Jared's neck in one graceful movement. Jared's mouth was an inch away from the skin on Fenix's neck and the temptation was too much.

Losing all rational thought at Fenix's closeness, Jared brought his lips to his warm skin and tasted it. It was sweaty from the dancing and the heat of the crowd, but also hot and sweet. Addicting. Immediately, Jared wanted to taste more. He ran his tongue up Fenix's neck to his jaw and bit his cheek gently. He felt, rather than heard, Fenix moan as he dropped his head backwards on Jared's shoulder, silently asking for more. Fenix's hips never stopped moving and his ass was grinding against Jared's crotch. There was no doubt in Jared's mind that Fenix could feel his erection through his jeans.

Gladly accepting Fenix's invitation, Jared nipped his way up his neck and sucked on his earlobe. He could see Fenix biting his lip as his hands came to rest on Jared's. His palms were sweaty as his fingers entwined with Jared's and squeezed.

The man was a walking sex addiction.

Jared nuzzled his temple and inhaled his scent. Fenix smelled amazing, and his blond hair felt so soft on Jared's face. He groaned and pressed Fenix harder against him. Fenix's eyes snapped open, and with one elegant movement he turned in Jared's arms, smashing his lips over Jared's.

The shock of the sensation startled Jared. Fenix's lips were soft and sweet and gentle as they glided over Jared's, and he'd never craved a kiss so much in his life. The club, the music, the crowd, the *world* disappeared around them as Jared opened his mouth wider and invited Fenix in deeper. Fenix wasted no time – his tongue explored Jared's mouth with such uninhibited urgency that Jared could not hold his moans back any longer. His hands travelled all the way up Fenix's back and tangled in his hair as he pressed his head firmer against his lips.

Jared wanted to devour him, right here in the dance floor. He wanted to feel Fenix, all of him, learn everything about him, and make him come ten different ways. The need to posses this man right here, *right now*, was so strong that momentarily Jared was lost in it. He felt Fenix whimper, then yelp alarmingly, and the sound snapped him out of his trance.

Fenix's eyes were frantic as he brought his finger to his lower lip and touched it gingerly. It was red and swollen, and Jared could already see the stubble burn that was starting to appear all over Fenix's face.

Jesus, what the hell is wrong with me?

Fenix looked like he'd been mauled by a wild animal.

"I'm sorry," Jared whispered, meeting Fenix's eyes and feeling the blush of embarrassment creep up his cheeks. Fenix looked at him in surprise and inclined his head to the side, his bruised lips slowly spreading into a wicked smile.

"Don't be," he said, almost shyly, before he leaned in and whispered in Jared's ear, "I like it rough."

The combination of the innocence in Fenix's eyes and the dirty words that came out of his mouth made Jared snap. He grabbed Fenix's hand and dragged him off the dance floor, through the crowd in front of the bar and into the toilets. Fenix didn't resist. Jared's vision tunnelled as they walked into the dimly-lit restroom and headed straight for one of the empty cubicles, banging the door shut behind them.

Fenix's arms were around Jared's neck the second he turned the lock. Their lips met once again with urgency, their gasps and moans clearly audible in the small space. Jared pushed Fenix against the wall and grinded against him. Fenix gave as good as he got, pushing his hips against Jared's, his hands tangling in Jared's hair. Jared hooked one arm under Fenix's knee, bringing his leg up with ease, his dancer's body pliable and flexible under Jared's touch. His other hand slipped behind to grab Fenix's ass. Fenix gasped and moaned wantonly.

"Jared..." he whimpered urgently against his lips, his eyes wild as his hips continued to snap against Jared's, despite the awkward angle. Jared let go of his leg and snuck his other hand behind Fenix, grabbing his ass with both hands, simultaneously squeezing and pulling him even closer. Fenix sucked Jared's tongue deep into his mouth and the hands in his hair tightened painfully. When he released his tongue, Jared bit and sucked all the way down his neck to his collarbone, making sure he left visible marks behind.

Fenix loved the onslaught. He cried out as Jared sucked on his Adam's apple and pulling on his hair, guided his head back up. Their lips met again in a painful, urgent kiss.

Jared could not resist this much longer; he was agonizingly hard. He needed to come right now or he was afraid his cock would snap in half.

As if reading his mind, Fenix groaned against his lips and said,

"Jared... I'm going to come. Please, don't stop..." He gasped as Jared pumped his hips against Fenix's cock, hard. Fenix's whole body shook and he made the sexiest sound from deep inside his throat. Jared pulled back and watched him as he succumbed to his pleasure.

He was beautiful.

Even with his lips swollen and red, with his skin flushed and his blond hair sticking to his head, Fenix was beautiful. His gorgeous eyes snapped open after a long moment, but they were so much darker than before. Jared felt a jolt pass through his whole body as Fenix kissed him again, slow and languid, savouring his taste, teasing his lips instead of bruising them. Fenix's hand snuck inside Jared's jeans and as his fingers brushed the head of his cock, Jared thought he was going to explode. It was too much. Fenix, gorgeous and coming undone in his arms; his touch, his taste, his scent... All that swirled around Jared in a blur as Fenix wrapped his hand firmly around his dick, squeezed and tugged. The dry pull was nearly painful, but it only added to the pleasure of Jared's already too sensitive body. Fenix sleeked his palm with the precome leaking from Jared's cockhead and the next few slides up and down Jared's shaft were exquisite.

Jared came so hard his knees gave out. He was vaguely aware he shouted Fenix's name as he held on to his shoulders for support. Fenix whispered in his ear, but Jared could not understand what he was saying. All he knew was his voice was soothing, and Jared rode out his orgasm until the sensation dulled out.

Once he was back in his body, Jared pulled away slightly from Fenix as he studied his face. He was looking for remorse or detachment, or even rejection. It wasn't every day that he dry humped a guy in a club's bathroom, and he was willing to bet it wasn't a usual occurrence for Fenix either. Despite that, he didn't really know the guy, did he? He didn't know what to expect once the urgency and sex crazed fog dissipated.

Jared didn't see any of that on Fenix's face. His eyes were warm and back to their usual pale colour, and his cheeks flushed. The marks Jared had left behind were stark red against his pale skin. Fenix's full mouth transformed into a grin and Jared felt the weight on his shoulders fall off. He'd have been so disappointed if Fenix had rejected him and ran out of the stall.

"You look like you're going to apologise again, even though I told you that's how I liked it," Fenix said, cheeky grin still in place.

Jared shook his head. He was not sorry for anything that happened tonight. Hell, it had been the best sex he'd ever had, even if they were still fully clothed.

"No. I'm not going to apologise," he said gently as he traced Fenix's jaw with the tips of his fingers. He leaned in and kissed him tenderly, resting his forehead against Fenix's. They were both sweaty and sticky, and Jared's jeans were wet and uncomfortable, and yet he couldn't bring himself to care. The only thing he cared about was Fenix and the fact that he didn't want the night to end like this.

"Come home with me," he said quietly. Fenix hesitated. "Please. I...," he pulled back to look in his eyes. "I want to make love to you in a bed. Not that this wasn't great, but fast and hard in a club's toilet is not my idea of romance."

"I wasn't aware we were looking for romance," Fenix replied, his voice teasing.

"Well, now that you are aware, will you come home with me?"

Fenix nodded, and Jared felt butterflies erupt, not just in his stomach, but in his whole body.

CHAPTER FOUR

FENIX

The cab ride to Jared's place was short yet extremely uncomfortable. Not just because of the sticky mess in Fenix's jeans. The air inside the car was charged with the sexual desire between them, but they sat as far away from each other as they could, concentrating on the traffic outside the window. Fenix knew that if Jared looked at him with those dark blue eyes the way he'd done just a while ago in the club, he'd throw all caution to the wind and maul him right there in the back of the cab. That would not go down well with the middle aged, male driver, and Fenix would rather spend the night in Jared's bed than explaining to the police why he was caught with his pants down in public.

Jared looked as eager to get out of the car as Fenix, and when they finally stopped in front of his building, he threw a couple of notes at the driver, murmured his thanks, and jumped out of the car, followed closely by Fenix. The driver sped away, shaking his head.

Jared started patting his pockets, looking for his keys when he met Fenix's eyes. They were alone in the middle of the deserted, dimly lit street. Fenix took the few steps separating them and collided with Jared in a fierce kiss. Jared had to take a step back, losing his balance for a moment, startled by Fenix's attack. He quickly recovered and put his arms tightly around Fenix's waist.

"Let's get inside," he murmured against Fenix's lips. Fenix nodded but kept kissing Jared. He couldn't pull away. Didn't *want* to pull away.

Jared laughed softly as he detached himself from Fenix gently. Grabbing his hand, Jared tugged him off the street and towards the entrance. He unlocked the front door quickly and they climbed the stairs to the fourth floor in record time. Jared thrust his key in the lock, his hand shaking slightly, and let them in. Once inside, Fenix plastered himself to Jared once again, pushing him against the door as it banged shut. For a while, all that could be heard in the dark, quiet room were their lips smacking together and their harsh breaths as they got acquainted with each other's bodies. Fenix grabbed the back of Jared's t-shirt and pulled it over his head, dropping it to the floor. It was too dark to see clearly, so Fenix traced his fingers over Jared's abs, his ribs, chest, neck, feeling the warm skin prickling with goosebumps. Jared made a pained, strangled sound. Fenix could just see the outlines of his face – he was biting his lower lip, his eyes closed and his face was taut.

Smiling wickedly, Fenix dropped his head and sucked Jared's nipple into his mouth. Jared jerked and his fingers weaved in Fenix's hair, tightening as Fenix increased the pressure on the sensitive bud. Jared swore quietly and tugged Fenix's head back up roughly, slamming his mouth over his.

"I want you so fucking much," Jared whispered as he kissed his way along Fenix's jaw to his earlobe. "But I want to do it properly this time." He pulled slightly back to peer into Fenix's eyes. "OK?"

Fenix nodded, afraid that his voice wouldn't hold if he spoke. Jared's hands left Fenix's hair and slid down his arms. He entwined their fingers and led Fenix further inside his home, switching a soft light along the way. The flat was a large studio with high ceilings and huge windows. It was also in a desperate need of renovation.

"Sorry about the..." Jared began, making a wide gesture around the apartment. "Mess. I just bought the place a few weeks ago and ran out of money. I'll fix it up soon..." he trailed off, a slight blush creeping up his cheekbones.

Fenix found it endearing.

"I don't care about the mess," he said softly, placing a kiss on Jared's neck. "Where's your bed?" he whispered.

"It's over there, behind the partition. I wanted to create a little privacy, like a bedroom, otherwise it's like a whole big space."

Fenix smiled and started tugging Jared towards the makeshift bedroom.

"Wait," Jared stopped him. "Let's get you out of those jeans and put them in the wash." He pulled Fenix back into his arms and kissed him. "And then, maybe we can take a shower together."

"That sounds so good," Fenix groaned. "I can't wait to get rid of these dirty jeans and boxers!"

"Me too," Jared said with a wink.

They took their clothes off and put them in the washing machine. Jared poured some liquid detergent, snapped the door shut and pressed a couple of buttons until the machine started spinning softly. Then, he focused his full attention on Fenix, who was standing naked in the middle of the room, starting to feel a bit self-conscious. Jared was staring at him, his mouth slightly open, and his eyes dark. The man was built like a Greek god! Fenix could not stop his eyes roaming all over his body, drinking in every little detail – the shape of his nipples, the pronounced V on his hips, the toned, flat stomach, the long, slightly curved fully erect cock...

Fenix inhaled sharply as the desire to climb inside Jared took over his whole being.

Jared was on him then, kissing and stroking, biting and licking every inch of skin he could get his hands, and lips, on. His strong fingers wrapped around Fenix's cock and he started jerking him off with slow, sensual movements, bringing him on the edge of orgasm and then slowing painfully down.

"You're so beautiful, Fenix," Jared said in a hoarse, desperate voice. "Perfect."

If his vocal cords still worked, and if he could actually summon enough brain cells to form a few words, Fenix would have returned the compliment.

Jared was the perfect one.

Fenix opened his mouth to say it, but as he did, Jared took both their cocks in his fist and started jerking them off together with fast, strong movements. All that came out of Fenix's mouth was a hoarse cry as he came all over Jared's stomach and hand. Jared followed not a second later, his whole body convulsing as he surrendered to his pleasure.

They held each other, trembling in the middle of Jared's home, panting. Fenix brought his hand to Jared's chest, right over his heart, and he could feel how fast it was beating. He turned slightly and placed soft kisses on Jared's neck, gently pushing his fingers through Jared's wild hair. They stayed like this until both their hearts resumed the normal human heart rate, but even then neither of them moved.

"What happened to doing it properly?" Fenix joked.

Jared laughed softly.

"You stripped," he said, pulling back to place a long, sensual kiss on Fenix's lips. "And I couldn't resist you."

Fenix beamed as Jared's words filled his chest with unexpected warmth. Jared kissed him again and said,

"How about that shower?"

"Lead the way."

The shower lasted until all the hot water ran out. They explored each other's bodies, nothing hidden in the harsh bathroom light. They kissed, soaped each other and whispered sweet words. Fenix was overwhelmed with desire for this man. He had come twice in less than an hour, and yet he was fully erect once again, unable to control the urge to be with Jared. He'd never wanted someone so much that the need to be close to him overrode all intellectual thought.

"Fuck," he groaned as Jared squeezed his ass and traced his crease with two fingers. He pushed Jared against the opposite wall and dropped to his knees, swallowing his whole cock in one movement.

"Holy shit," Jared cried out, his head bumping the wall behind him loudly.

Fenix took that as an encouragement and sucked Jared's cock earnestly, bobbing his head, swirling his tongue over the sensitive head, and massaging his balls with the other hand. He let it slide out of his mouth with a pop and fisted the shaft, tonguing the slit and tasting Jared's precome. Jared moaned loudly and Fenix looked up to find him staring down at him, his eyes half closed and shining with lust. Pure, hungry, carnal lust.

Fenix licked at the head leisurely, still watching Jared, teasing him, provoking him. Jared took the bait and grabbed Fenix head, pushing him down on his cock. Fenix smiled and sucked the whole length in his mouth again.

"Fuuuuck," Jared groaned and started thrusting his hips into Fenix's willing mouth. Fenix hummed around Jared's cock, grabbing his thighs, encouraging him to move faster. He sneaked one hand behind Jared, grabbing his ass cheek and sliding one wet finger inside him.

"Ahhh," Jared gasped and his movements became erratic. Fenix gently pushed his finger in and out of Jared's hole, finding his prostate and massaging it. "I'm gonna come. Don't fucking stop!" Jared begged. Fenix obliged. He added another slick finger, just as Jared pulled him off his cock and started pumping it with his hand. It took three fast strokes before Jared was coming all over Fenix's face. He cried out Fenix's name and he felt Jared's hole contracting around his fingers. The expression on Jared's face was pure bliss. He came in a wave after wave of pleasure and Fenix felt so satisfied that he was the one who did this to him.

Had someone else ever made Jared come so hard, three times in an hour?

The thought died in his mind as Jared pulled him up and licked his face clean. They kissed and Jared's taste felt so good on Fenix's tongue that he immediately wanted more. His cock was still fully erect and he hadn't touched himself even once as he was sucking Jared off. He grabbed his own shaft and slid his fist up and down a few times before Jared swatted his hand away.

"No," he said firmly as he turned Fenix around. Fenix propped his hands on the wall as Jared dropped to his knees, forced Fenix's legs wide open and spread his ass cheeks apart. Fenix felt Jared's tongue dart between them and he almost lost his balance.

"Oh, God!" he whimpered as Jared pushed his tongue inside Fenix's ass. It felt incredible! Jared's tongue was wet, warm, skilful. He licked the crease slowly all the way from his balls to his spine and repeated the movement several times until Fenix begged him to tongue him again.

Jared hummed, more than happy to oblige. Fenix was so turned on he thought he might spontaneously combust if he didn't come right now.

"Please... Jared, I need more, please..." he begged, too far gone to feel ashamed.

Jared snuck one hand around in front of Fenix and took his cock into his hand. He jerked him off in the same rhythm as his tongue worked his hole. Fenix felt his balls tighten as his stomach clenched, and he was coming so hard that for a long moment he lost track of time and space and direction. He didn't know if he was lying down or standing up, or if he was even still breathing.

Jared's arms around him and his warm breath on his neck brought him back to reality. He was saying things like, 'I've got you' and 'Shh, it's OK' over and over again and Fenix realised he was shivering violently. His body was still in shock from all the pleasure.

With Jared's help, Fenix finished rinsing off, and walked out of the shower. Jared gave him a fluffy towel to dry off with and guided him towards the bed. Fenix's body felt boneless. He was so tired that he felt like he would topple over any second. Flopping down on Jared's bed, Fenix threw the covers around himself and Jared followed. He wrapped Fenix securely in his arms and kissed the top of his head. Fenix voiced the last thought that went through his mind before he fell asleep:

"Has it ever been like this for you?" His voice was almost inaudible, his words slurred as if he was drunk.

"Never," Jared whispered, and that was the last thing Fenix heard before he fell in an exhausted, dreamless slumber.

CHAPTER FIVE

Jared

The bright sunlight streaming through the windows woke Jared up. Closing the curtains had been the last thing on his mind last night and now he was paying the price. The light didn't seem to bother Fenix though. He slept peacefully in Jared's arms, his head tucked under his chin. Memories from the previous night, or rather early morning, assaulted Jared's tired consciousness. Had all that really happened? It seemed like a dream, a distant memory, even though it had been just a few hours ago.

Jared was by no means a virgin. He'd been with lots of men, all of them attractive and experienced. Yet, he'd never felt like *that* before. Last night had been a first for him, in a lot of ways. He'd never before invited a guy he'd just met back to his place, for example. Granted, Fenix wasn't some random guy – they'd met and talked at the theatre and they were going to work together, sort of. But still... Jared shook his head slightly.

He could sit there and analyse his behaviour, his feelings, his need for this man all he wanted, but it wouldn't make any damn difference. Jared wanted Fenix here, right here in his bed, and he'd wanted, no – *craved* – everything that had happened last night. But what was more, he wanted it to happen all over again tonight, and the night after that. He wanted to wake up with Fenix sprawled on top of him tomorrow and the morning after.

Was that realisation scary? Hell yes.

Jared's only sort of a relationship until now had been with Adam, but he'd never felt that way about him. He'd never needed Adam so much that he wasn't willing to let him out of sight, even for a second.

Despite all that, despite the fact that he'd known Fenix *a day*, despite all rational thought and reason, Jared decided that he was not going to stand in his own way. He was not going to sabotage whatever this was, overanalyse and obsess over it. He was going to be honest with himself and with Fenix, and he'd take one day at a time.

Fenix stirred in his arms, sighing softly as he turned on his back. His long bangs fell in his eyes and he swatted them away sleepily. He looked so cute, so young and sexy and gorgeous. Jared's heart flipped inside his chest and he felt a sharp stab of tenderness. Unable to stop himself, he leaned over Fenix, cupped his cheek and kissed his lips gently. Fenix frowned and pouted, but didn't open his eyes.

Jared smiled. Just when he'd thought Fenix could not get any cuter, he pouted in his sleep. Those plump lips were made for pouting. And kissing. And they looked incredibly hot around his cock.

Jared kissed Fenix again, this time a bit firmer, parting his mouth with his tongue and sucking his lip into his mouth. Fenix reacted on an instinct it seemed, because his eyes were still closed and he didn't give any indication that he was awake. Opening his mouth, he took all of Jared's tongue in and kissed him back languidly. Jared trailed his hands over Fenix's warm, naked body, feeling every muscle, every perfect part of him, until he reached his cock and realised he was fully erect and leaking already.

"You'd better be awake or you're gonna get molested in your sleep," Jared murmured against Fenix's lips. Fenix smiled and opened one of his eyes. "Good."

Jared slid down his body, placing kisses and licks and little bites all over it, paying special attention to his nipples. Fenix groaned and arched his back asking for more. Jared teased him, sucking on the skin in the crease between his thigh and groin, slowly blowing over his cock but never touching it. He played with his balls and his ass, still not touching what Fenix wanted most.

"Jared!" Fenix shouted in frustration, thrusting his hips up.

"Yes?" Jared asked innocently. "Did you want something?"

Instead of biting the bait and indulging Jared in his teasing games, Fenix gave him a wicked look, licked his palm slowly and wrapped his elegant fingers around his shaft. He started jerking himself off, his back bowing off the mattress, his eyes closing in bliss. He moaned in the most seductive way possible and slid his thumb over the wet head, smearing the precome for better friction.

It was the hottest thing Jared had ever seen.

He was half tempted to let him finish himself off, but reconsidered. Jared wanted that cock in his mouth, badly. Grunting, he removed Fenix's hand forcefully and took his cock all the way down his throat.

"Jesus!" Fenix cried out and bucked his hips involuntarily. Jared deep throated him again and swallowed around the head. "Oh, God! This feels so good!" Fenix mumbled.

Jared had to agree. It felt incredible.

He palmed his own erection and started jerking off, never losing the rhythm on Fenix's cock. Fenix was whispering incoherently, thrashing on the bed and bunching the sheets in his fists. Jared increased the speed on his cock and felt the orgasm starting to build up in his belly.

Fenix tapped him on the shoulder lightly and said hoarsely, "I'm gonna come, baby..."

Jared did not need the warning: he wanted everything Fenix had to give. The moment the first drops of semen hit his tongue, Jared felt his own orgasm explode. It was an intense feeling –

tasting Fenix as he came, giving him such pleasure as he experienced it himself.

When Fenix's erection stopped pulsing in his mouth, Jared let it flop out and climbed back up Fenix's body. He hovered over his mouth, wanting to kiss him, but unsure if Fenix would like tasting himself on his lips. Sensing the hesitation, Fenix hooked his hand behind Jared's neck and pulled him down for an eager, wet kiss.

"Mornin'," Jared murmured against his mouth, before lying down next to Fenix, pulling him closer.

"Mornin'," he replied and curled around Jared, resting his head on his chest.

"What are you going to do today?" Jared asked as he played with Fenix's silky, blond strands of hair.

"I don't have any plans. It's Sunday, and I don't have a show, so..." Fenix shrugged.

"How about I make us breakfast, and then we go to the theatre? You can watch the show again backstage or just hang out. I finish around six, so we can go to dinner or a see a film, or whatever you feel like," Jared suggested.

Fenix propped his chin on Jared's chest and studied him with those impossibly blue eyes.

"Yeah?" He smiled that charming smile of his, and Jared brushed his fingers over his cheekbone, trailing down along his jaw.

"Yeah."

The truth was he didn't want to let Fenix go yet. He wanted to spend time with him not having sex. Get to know him. Buy him dinner, take him to the cinema and introduce him to all his friends.

"I want to go home at some point, change into some fresh clothes and pack a bag with some more stuff I'll need to take to the dressing room, so that I don't have to go to the theatre tomorrow when everyone will be moving in."

"Perfect. I don't have a show tomorrow either. We can spend the day together. It doesn't make any sense for you to go back to... Where do you live?"

"Greenwich."

"Greenwich. You can pack an overnight bag and stay here again tonight..." Jared trailed off when his eyes fell on Fenix's puzzled expression. He realised that while he'd made peace with the fact that he didn't want to let Fenix go, even though they'd met a day ago, Fenix might not have reached the same conclusion. It might have been just a fling for him. "I'm sorry... I'll shut up now."

Fenix laughed, his eyes twinkled in the brightly lit room.

"No, don't shut up. You're cute when you ramble."

"Cute? Me?" Jared pointed at himself in mock surprise. "I'll give you cute!" he roared and tackled Fenix, tickling him. He straddled his hips once Fenix was on his back, forced his arms above his head and held them there as he leaned down and kissed him.

"OK," Fenix said breathlessly as their lips parted.

"OK? To what?"

"Everything. I'll pack a bag, spend the night here and hang out with you tomorrow."

Jared's smile was so wide his cheeks hurt.

Jared tagged along with Fenix as he went home to pick up his stuff. He lived in a small flat, cluttered with cheap furniture. Fenix explained his landlord was a hoarder and cheapskate who didn't like throwing stuff away. Seriously, who needed three coffee tables in a one-bedroom flat? The carpet used to be beige once upon a time, but now was a weird, faded colour that depressed the hell out of Jared.

"Sit down, make yourself comfortable," Fenix said and pointed towards the ugly sofas that didn't match. "I won't be a minute." He disappeared towards the bedroom and left Jared alone in the living room.

He sat down and a heaviness settled on his chest. Fenix lived in this dump, then he stayed in a similar dump with Jared. He deserved so much more.

Tomorrow, Jared was going to go to the bank and apply for that loan he'd been planning to get ever since he bought his apartment. He didn't want to wait to *save* the money anymore. He wanted to hire the contractors by the end of the week and have a cosy, clean, fully furnished home by the end of next month.

Fenix appeared out of the bedroom, two duffel bags in hand. Jared stood up, grabbed one of the bags and they headed out.

Jared was styling his hair and Fenix was putting his stuff in his part of the wardrobe when there was a knock on the dressing room door.

"Yeah?" Jared called, his eyes never leaving the mirror.

Adam opened the door and walked in, his eyes fixing on Fenix as he frowned.

"Hi," he said to nobody in particular.

"Hey," Fenix greeted him with a smile as he continued to arrange his belongings meticulously.

"Can I talk to you for a sec?" Adam turned to Jared. "In private?"

"Can it wait? I really need to fix my hair and head to the costume shop."

Fenix stopped what he was doing and closed the wardrobe door.

"I'm gonna go get a coffee. You guys want something?"

"Fenix, you don't have to go. Adam and I will talk later. I don't have any time right now anyway." Jared protested.

"No, it's OK. I'm finished. I feel like a cup of coffee. I'll catch you later," he said with a smile and kissed Jared on his way out. "Nice to see you, Adam," he said as he brushed past him. Adam grunted something unintelligible in response.

"What the fuck is the matter with you?" Adam said the second Fenix was out the door.

"What do you mean?"

"First you have a go at me last night at the club, telling me to back off, and I quote, 'He's mine'." Adam made air quotes with his fingers. "Since when are you the possessive, caveman type? You've never done that, not even when I seduced that guy you liked right in front of you." Adam spread his arms wide in exasperation.

"Which one?" Jared asked, sarcastically raising an eyebrow. Adam was not picky when it came to his bed mates, but he especially loved to steal the ones Jared liked. It had never bothered Jared. Not until now.

"And then," Adam continued, rolling his eyes as he ignored Jared's last comment, "you almost fuck him right there on the dance floor, disappear into the toilets no less, and then disappear altogether! I tried to call you, but I got your voicemail every time!" Adam's voice rose with every word and he looked furious. He was right though, none of that was the way Jared usually acted. The last time he'd had sex with someone in a club's toilet had been over a year ago when Adam hadn't been there.

"I'm sorry, I should have told you we were leaving. I didn't mean to worry you," he apologised.

"That is not what worried me! You're a grown man, you can go and do whatever and whoever you like! But this is not like you, Jared. What the hell is wrong with you?"

Jared grinned when he met Adam's angry eyes in the mirror. He couldn't help it. Just thinking about last night made him act like an idiot.

"First, I wanted to warn you that I'm seriously interested in Fenix, because knowing you, and seeing how you looked at him, I knew you'd go after him. Second, the guy is so hot that I couldn't wait until we got back to my place, so we had round one in the toilets. And third, my phone must have died while I had the best sex of my life all night long."

Making Adam speechless was not an easy task. And yet, he was gaping at Jared in the mirror, unable to think of a come back. He opened and closed his mouth a few times before he finally said,

"OK. Just..." he ran his hands through his hair, "be careful. And next time we go out together, you better let me know when and with who you're leaving. I need to know you got home safely." Adam pointed a finger at his reflexion in the mirror.

"Yes, Dad," Jared joked.

"Whatever, asshole," Adam muttered as he strode out the dressing room not bothering to close the door behind him.

CHAPTER SIX

Jared

"Where the hell are you?" Joy screeched as a greeting when Fenix called her.

"At Queen Victoria," Fenix replied vaguely, knowing it would irritate her.

"You've been at Queen Victoria since yesterday morning?" her voice dropped down in a quiet fury.

"Not exactly."

"Fenix!" He could imagine her green eyes narrowing in frustration.

"My phone died, I just found a charger and switched it back on. Sorry."

"What exactly are you sorry for? That you disappeared for two days without a word? That you didn't come home last night and I had no idea where you were? That you forgot about our plans to have dinner ? What exactly are you sorry for, Fenix? Because I almost called the police. It's not like you to drop off the face of the Earth, to not pick up your phone or at least let me know you won't be able to make it to dinner!"

Shit. He'd completely forgotten about dinner. They were supposed to watch a movie at her place, have a quiet night in before all the *Poison* craziness encored.

"I'm sorry, Joy. I really am. I should have called, but..." But the moment Mark had invited him to Lono's, he'd mentally dropped everything else but the thought of Jared dancing pressed against him. Fenix knew it wasn't fair and he knew he'd be worried too if their roles were reversed. "I have no excuse, I really am sorry."

Joy sighed loudly. Fenix knew she'd closed her vivid green eyes and her elfin features were scrunched in a frown. He also knew he'd be forgiven.

"Just... call me next time you bail on me, OK?"

"OK," Fenix said simply, meaning it. Joy was his best friend and she was looking out for him, he knew that.

"So, where have you been?" she asked, curiosity seeping in her calming voice.

Fenix relayed the events of the day, and night, leaving out the more graphic details. Joy inserted the occasional 'Oh my god' or 'Are you serious?' as Fenix spoke, but didn't otherwise interrupt.

"So he's performing right now and I'm talking to you in the dressing room instead of watching the show backstage. You realise the lengths I'll go to prove how sorry I am, right?" Fenix joked, finishing his story.

Joy laughed, all the anger and worry forgotten. That was what Fenix loved most about her – she was easy-going and didn't hold any grudges for long.

"When are you coming back tonight? We can open a bottle of wine and you can tell me all the juicy details that you left out."

"Actually, I'm not coming back. I'm spending the night at Jared's place."

Silence.

More silence.

"Joy?" Fenix looked at the phone screen to make sure the call was still connected.

"Yeah, I'm here. I'm just... surprised. I was trying to remember the last time you spent the whole night in a guy's bed, let alone two nights in a row. He's that good, eh?"

"It's not like that. We're going to dinner and to see a movie... first." Joy laughed when Fenix paused before 'first'. "But yeah, he's *that* good."

They talked and joked a little more, and Fenix promised to catch up with Joy tomorrow evening before disconnecting the call. He was scrolling through his other missed calls and unread texts, when he noticed his mom had tried to reach him. Fenix dialled her number.

"Hi, sweetheart!" his mom's melodic voice rang in his ear. He smiled involuntarily.

"Hey, mom. Sorry it took me so long to get back to you."

"It's OK, darling. It's not anything urgent, I just wanted to see how you've been. I know you'll be very busy the next few weeks so I wanted to catch you at a more convenient time."

Fenix was so lucky he had parents who knew the theatre business inside out, and understood his life without him ever trying to explain. They talked for a long while, Fenix sharing his excitement about Queen Victoria and *Poison*'s success. Evelyn listened thoughtfully, saying all the right things, encouraging him to talk.

"I'm so proud of you, honey," she said, and Fenix was suddenly acutely aware how much he missed his mom. They hadn't seen each other in person ever since he'd arrived in London over a year ago. Right now he desperately wanted to hug her.

"I miss you, mom," he said in Swedish. He was fluent in his mother's native tongue. Some things were easier to say in a language that connected him to his mother in a more personal way.

"I miss you, too, darling." Her voice sounded thick, and Fenix felt guilty that he'd probably made her cry, so he changed the subject.

"I met someone," he said abruptly.

"Oh?"

"Yeah. I really like him."

"Oh?" Evelyn repeated.

"Are you going to say anything else besides 'oh'?"

"I don't know what to say. You've never told me of any of your relationships, Fenix. So I'm wondering how to react so that I don't scare you off and you tell me more."

Fenix laughed.

"There was no one I wanted to talk about until now, mom. I haven't been withholding information, there was just nothing to tell."

"And there is now?" she asked cautiously.

"Yeah."

"OK..." Evelyn laughed softly. "Do I have to take out my interrogation tools or are you going to tell me voluntarily?"

"We met... yesterday. And I know you're going to tell me it's stupid and nobody can feel something for someone they'd just met, but I do and I wanted you to know that," Fenix rambled without pausing for a breath.

Evelyn was silent for a long moment, and Fenix dreaded what he might hear next. His parents had always been supportive of him – of his desire to follow in his mother's footsteps – even though they both knew how hard that life was – of his career choices, of his sexuality. He knew his mom wasn't going to laugh at his naivety, but still... he wanted her to approve. He wanted her to like Jared just as much as he did.

"I wasn't going to say any of that. Nothing you feel is stupid, sweetheart. What goes on in our heads is not something we can predict or explain, it just is what it is. I know that from experience, and I stopped looking for reasons a long time ago," Evelyn said soberly.

Fenix nodded even though his mother couldn't see him. After a pause she continued, more cheerfully,

"So tell me more about him."

And Fenix did. He told her all about Jared, leaving out the 'juicy details' as Joy had called them. He knew his voice sounded giddy. He'd have been embarrassed had it been someone else on the other side of the line. But his mom shared his enthusiasm and even giggled a few times as he told her the story of the last two days.

He was just finishing his conversation with 'Bye, mom, I love you too,' in Swedish, when Jared walked into their dressing room. He was wearing his stage clothes – not so much of a costume since his role didn't require any elaborate costumes – and he looked yummy. His eyes sparkled with the post-show adrenalin, he was sweaty and breathless. Fenix disconnected the call and stood up from the sofa. Jared devoured the distance between them in a few long strides and kissed him.

"That sounded very sexy. What language is it?" Jared said, separating their lips.

"Swedish," Fenix replied and smiled at Jared's puzzled expression. "My mom is Swedish. She moved to the States when she was eighteen to pursue her dancing career."

"So that's where you got those cheekbones from!"

Fenix laughed and kissed him again. Jared pulled abruptly and stared at Fenix in disbelief.

"Oh my god! I'm such a fucking idiot! I just connected the dots!" He grabbed Fenix's shoulders and took a step back, looking at his face as if he was seeing him for the first time. "Your mother is Evelyn Bergman!" It wasn't a question. Fenix grinned.

"Yep."

"Why didn't you tell me?"

"I told you my name when we met. I don't usually add, 'Evelyn Bergman's son' after it," Fenix joked, but Jared kept staring at him, mouth agape. Was it that big of a deal? Would that change anything between them? Fenix didn't think it should, but Jared was still staring. "Jared? You're freaking me out. Quit staring at me like that!"

That seemed to shake Jared out of his stupor and he ran a hand along his face.

"Sorry. It's just... I'm a huge fan of your mother's. She's a prima ballerina, a legend... What happened to her was so tragic..."

"Let's not do this now," Fenix cut him off, a bit more forcefully than he intended. He closed his eyes for a second. "Let's get out of here. I'll tell you everything you want to know over dinner."

Giotto's was not very busy when they arrived. There were many tables available, so Jared requested a secluded table near the windows overlooking the garden. Once they were seated, they ordered their drinks and food quickly, both of them starving. Fenix hadn't eaten anything since the late breakfast Jared had cooked for him, and he supposed Jared was even hungrier, considering he'd performed earlier that day. If anyone knew how much energy went into performing, it was Fenix.

The waitress brought their drinks and lit the candles on their table, smiling warmly and wishing them a pleasant night before she retreated.

"So what do you want to know?" Fenix asked, sipping his freshly squeezed mango and guava juice.

"I want to know everything about you, Fen," Jared said, pinning him with those blue eyes that looked almost navy in the candle light. Fenix raised an eyebrow at the nickname. Nobody had ever shortened his name like that before. He liked it.

"There's not much to tell, really."

"I doubt that."

Fenix sighed.

"I don't like it when people realise that I'm Evelyn Bergman's son," he began, looking away.

"Why?"

"Many reasons. They either expect me to be as good, which is impossible considering mom is one of the most talented ballet dancers ever born, and I myself am not a ballet dancer. Or, they expect me to want special treatment, throw her name around to get what I want." Fenix dared to look at Jared again and saw that he was watching him with interest. Jared nodded, encouraging him to continue.

"I've never used my mom's connections. She knew I wanted to choose my own path and never even offered. The only thing I ever accepted was her good friend Cathleen O'Riley's representation. Cat is an incredible agent, she understood what I wanted and never pushed me to use mom's name to further my career. She got me the lead in *Poison*," Fenix smiled at the memory. "She said, 'This will be the role of your life, darling. Trust me. This part in a small London theatre will get you to Broadway faster than anything you will be offered in New York.' I'm starting to think she was right."

"Is that what you want to do? Perform in a Broadway musical?" Jared asked.

"Yeah. Who doesn't?" Fenix laughed nervously. Jared didn't comment on his rhetorical question. He took a sip of his drink and said,

"How is your mom? It was horrible what happened to her."

Seven years ago Evelyn Bergman's career had abruptly ended when she fell during a show. She'd been hanging over the stage in an elaborate production when her harness broke off and she fell down. She'd badly injured her spine and could not perform anymore. Most days she couldn't even walk.

"She's good. She's in a wheelchair most of the time. The doctors said three of her vertebras were irreversibly injured and even surgery won't be able to fix them. They suggested she keeps off her feet as much as possible, and since my mom is not one to spend all day in bed, she's moving around in a wheelchair. They may have crushed her dancing career but they'll never crush her spirit. My mom is one strong woman."

Jared looked puzzled.

"What do you mean 'they'?" he asked.

Fenix paused. He'd never discussed this with anyone outside his family. Was it OK to share their suspicions with Jared?

"Well... That show had been on for almost a year and there were never any problems with mom's harness. It was checked before every performance. And that night, the thick straps just snapped clean off. My parents were convinced it was deliberate. Dad wanted an investigation, wanted to get the police involved."

Jared's eyes widened.

"Really? That's terrible! She could have been killed, she dropped like a stone from, what, ten feet?"

Fenix wasn't surprised that Jared had obviously seen the footage of his mother's accident. It had been on the news and could be easily found online.

"Yeah, about ten feet. Broadway is merciless, Jared. My mom was the best in the business and she took nobody's crap. I bet there were a lot of people who wished she would have retired early. I mean, she gave birth to me and was back on stage in three months! Nothing could stop her. Well, almost nothing."

"Bastards," Jared swore. "So what happened? I never heard of an investigation of foul play. It was ruled an accident."

"The producers paid her off. They didn't want an investigation, and frankly, they didn't think the bad press would be worth catching whoever was responsible. My mom was out of commission and she was not coming back. They had enough problems with finding a suitable replacement to worry about the police snooping in."

"I'm sorry," Jared said, shaking his head. "I bet it would have made a difference for your family if they had found out what had happened exactly."

"I guess. But it turned out OK in the end. My mom was devastated that she couldn't perform anymore, but with all the money they got, my parents didn't have to worry about their financial future anymore. With mom home, they reconnected. My dad had been on the verge of leaving numerous times – my mom's greatest love had always been *dance* and she compromised her personal life for it. I think he stayed for me," Fenix said thoughtfully as his mind drifted off to his dad. He remembered how all his childhood, it had been his dad who had taken him to school, helped him with his homework, gone to bake sales and sports days. Evelyn had always been dancing.

Jared reached out and took his hand in his over the table, entwining their fingers and squeezing reassuringly. Fenix cleared his throat.

"So anyway, they managed to fix their relationship and do stuff they had never been able to do before, like travel and visit friends more often. Hell, even going out Saturday night had been out of the question when my mom was performing."

Conversation slowed as their food arrived and they tucked in. After a few bites, Fenix spoke again.

"Tell me about your family."

Jared didn't respond for a few long moments, silently eating his wild mushroom risotto. Finally, he took a sip of his drink and said,

"My dad died when I was sixteen. I'm an only child and I was all mom had left. Losing my father devastated her, but she found some solace in the fact that she still had me. She always said I look so much like him." Jared smiled sadly. "I came out to her just before I left for college. She... didn't take it well." He paused and looked away.

"What do you mean?" Fenix asked softly.

"She said my dad would have been ashamed of me, and for the first time since he'd died, she was glad he was dead so he wouldn't have to witness this." Jared blinked rapidly a few times and Fenix knew he was reliving the moment as vividly as if it had happened yesterday. Jared's hand shook a little bit as he picked up his drink. "I haven't talked to her since."

"What? Seven years?" Fenix asked, unable to believe a mother would not seek out her child even once in seven years.

Jared nodded. He swallowed hard and picked up his fork again.

"I'm sorry," Fenix said softly and touched Jared's knee under the table reassuringly. Jared waved him off but didn't look up to meet his eyes.

"It's OK. I've made my peace with it."

Fenix shook his head but didn't comment any further. He'd never understand how a parent could cut their child out of their life like they never existed simply because they couldn't accept them for who they were.

"Tell me about Adam," Fenix suggested in an attempt to shift the conversation in a more cheerful direction. "You seem pretty close. He's one of the creators of *Of Kids and Monsters*, right?"

"Yeah. We met in LAMDA. We were roommates and hit it off straight away." Jared looked at Fenix and there was a glint in his eye that told Fenix there was more to the story.

"Just roommates?" he asked on an impulse. He didn't want to pry into Jared's personal life so much on their first official date, but he couldn't help it. He wanted to know everything about Jared. And besides, the conversation had been really personal from the beginning.

"No. We... There was undeniable attraction between us and we hooked up."

Oh.

"Hooked up?" Fenix raised an eyebrow. He hated the pang of jealousy he felt. Jared and Adam had had sex, but they were still close friends. Which meant their connection ran much deeper than just sex...

"He was my first," Jared said, interrupting Fenix's thoughts. "We were in a relationship for a while, but it didn't work out in the end."

"But you're still friends seven years later?"

"Yeah. We were always better at the friendship thing than the sex thing. Not that the sex was bad, on the contrary, but our relationship was based on friendship."

If Fenix had felt a pang of jealousy a minute ago, now it was a full blown punch to the gut. However, he was determined not to let it show on his face – it was unnatural to feel that way about a guy he'd known for two days. Right?

Fenix didn't ask anything else about Adam and Jared didn't offer any more information, so they left it at that. Fenix thought the conversation needed a lighter topic after all the intimate details they had revealed in the last hour.

So they talked about books and movies, theatre gossip and music. By the time dessert arrived, both Fenix and Jared were in much better spirits than they'd been at the beginning of dinner. They paid the bill and walked out of the restaurant into the warm London evening.

"Do you wanna go see a movie?" Jared asked as he draped his arm over Fenix's shoulders and tugged him close. Fenix shook his head and looked at Jared, biting his lower lip to suppress the smile that threatened to betray his thoughts on exactly what he wanted to do right now. Jared must have read his eyes correctly because he smirked and said, "Let's go home then."

CHAPTER SEVEN

FENIX

There was no urgency this time. This time, they explored each other's bodies leisurely under the moonlight seeping through the windows in Jared's bedroom. Fenix couldn't decide what he liked more – touching Jared or Jared touching *him*. The combination of both was mind blowing.

Fenix lay on his back with Jared on top of him, his brain completely empty save for the sensations he was experiencing right now. The soft, warm skin under his fingers; the scent of soap and skin and arousal; the feel of Jared's hands roaming all over his body, touching every inch of skin, finding all his sensitive spots; the wetness of Jared's tongue as he licked his nipples, his collarbone, his lips, his neck, his cock...

"Ughhhh," Fenix groaned as Jared sucked the head of his dick into his mouth, circling his tongue over it. Fingers involuntarily fastening in Jared's hair, Fenix buckled his hips, desperately seeking more of that incredible, hot mouth.

Jared chuckled and pulled off, tracing Fenix's body with his tongue, lips, and fingers all the way back to his face. He kissed him slowly, not pushing his tongue inside, but licking his lips, searching Fenix's tongue out, sucking on it gently.

Christ, it was too much! Fenix felt like he wanted to climb out of his own skin. He needed *more*, he wanted it *harder*. The need for release was clouding all his other senses as Fenix snuck his hand between their bodies, trying to get hold of his cock. If he didn't relieve the pressure building inside his balls, his *chest*, any time soon, he was going to explode.

"No," Jared gently removed Fenix's hand and brought it over his head, pinning it to the mattress.

"Please... Baby, I can't take this anymore," Fenix whimpered, his whole body trembling. Jared chuckled softly again and said,

"I love it when you call me 'baby'. It sounds so hot," he ground his hips against Fenix's and their cocks mashed together. Fenix arched into the movement, hoping, *needing* it to be enough.

He knew Jared was toying with him, taking him to the edge and then keeping him there, not allowing him to jump and enjoy the freedom, the ecstasy of the fall. But that knowledge seemed too distant, too far away, unreachable.

"Jared...," he managed to grind out. "Baby," he amended himself and smirked when Jared's eyes, dark and intense, fell on him. Jared was on the edge himself, Fenix realised. "Fuck me," Fenix whispered, not looking away from Jared. Good thing he didn't because hunger and lust and something almost primal flashed in them, and spurred Jared into action. He rummaged through the bedside drawer and found condoms and lube, tossing them on the bed. His kisses became harder, his hands more urgent, his breathing uneven.

Fenix drowned in the feeling. He loved how gentle and caring Jared had been, and he enjoyed the sensual caresses. But this... this was what he needed, what he *craved*. Jared losing control and wanting him so much that his hands shook as he opened the lube. He slicked his fingers and brought them to Fenix's hole. Circling the sensitive entrance, Jared slid a finger inside. Fenix cried out. It was so good! He could not remember a time when just a single finger inside his ass could bring him on the verge of coming without even touching himself. Jared appreciated the encouragement and added another finger, and then a third one. He probed and stretched Fenix, preparing him, ghosting over his gland, until Fenix could not wait a second longer.

"Baby..." he whispered urgently, thrashing on the bed, twisting his hips, bowing his back, clenching the sheets with trembling fingers.

Jared removed his fingers, put on a condom hastily, and slicked himself. A moment later Fenix felt the tip of his head at his entrance. Jared pushed in, slowly, and stopped once the head was inside. He lowered his body over Fenix and started kissing him, those sweet, languid kisses that took his breath away and made him yearn for more all at the same time. Jared pushed deeper inside as Fenix breathed through the initial discomfort of the stretch, but his body was so relaxed and so pliable that it quickly passed, and all he felt was pleasure. Mind-numbing, exquisite pleasure.

Jared propped himself on his elbows and started moving faster, with long, precise strokes, all the time kissing Fenix and whispering unintelligible words in his ear. Fenix fisted his cock and wrapped his legs tighter around Jared's waist, encouraging him to move faster, harder.

His orgasm spread like wild fire from his toes to the tips of his hair.

The world could have ended right then and Fenix wouldn't have cared. All he felt was incredible pleasure melting every single bone in his body. Jared's rhythm became erratic, uncontrolled, desperate. His body convulsed as he shouted Fenix's name and came, his cock pulsing inside Fenix. He collapsed on top of Fenix, his heart beating so fast that even in that blissful, unaware state he was in, Fenix could feel it thudding over his own chest.

They lay like that for a few long moments before Jared pulled out gently, disposed of the condom, and used his earlier discarded t-shirt to wipe Fenix off. Fenix could not move to save his life. Jared pulled the covers over them, tucked Fenix safely in his arms, kissed the top of his head, and they slept.

Fenix woke up to noise coming from the kitchen – pans and pots banging, something... boiling? Frying? He groaned. His whole body felt weightless. He didn't want to move and more importantly, he didn't want Jared to move. He wanted Jared's warm body around him when he woke up.

It didn't help that Fenix genuinely disliked mornings. Daylight, noises, waking up... none of that was particularly appealing to him. Never had been.

Something clattered to the floor with a loud thud and Jared swore colourfully. Fenix smiled.

"Need some help?" he yelled over all the noise. A moment later Jared appeared behind the partition. He was wearing only black boxers and a grin. He looked gorgeous! Fenix stared at him and his mouth went dry. The morning wood he was sporting took interest in Jared's demigod form as well. Fenix stretched seductively under the sheet covering his body, hoping it would be temptation enough for Jared to abandon whatever he was doing and come back to bed.

"Oh, don't you start that. I'm making breakfast," Jared scolded him with a stern look. It only spurred Fenix on – Jared was so damn hot when he scowled.

"Can it wait? I'm not hungry," Fenix said and raised an eyebrow. "For breakfast."

Jared shook his head 'no'. Fenix slid his hand down his body and under the sheet, palming his straining erection and giving it a few slow strokes. "You go ahead, finish whatever you're doing in the kitchen. I'll be right there," he said, the last words coming out huskily as his arousal built even more.

"Dammit," Jared muttered and disappeared. Fenix gaped after him, unable to believe Jared had just turned down the opportunity for morning sex. He hadn't even finished his thought when the commotion in the kitchen grew quiet and Jared came back, sliding under the covers next to him. "You do not get to do this without me anymore," Jared murmured as he snuggled next to Fenix, wrapped his arms around his waist and hoisted him on top of his chest. Fenix yelped in surprise and laughed as he straddled Jared and settled his bare ass over Jared's groin comfortably. He flung the duvet off his shoulders and quirked an eyebrow.

"Any requests?"

"Yeah," Jared rasped, his eyes darkening. "I want to watch."

A shiver ran through Fenix's body as Jared's words, spoken in that seductive voice, aroused him even more. He bent down and kissed Jared slowly, biting his lower lip before pulling away. Jared gasped and instinctively followed Fenix's mouth, trying to prolong the kiss. Smirking, Fenix pushed him back down with a firm hand to the chest as he stretched over him to reach in the bedside drawer. Taking out a condom and the lube, Fenix did a quick job of sheathing Jared's cock before he slicked his fingers and reached behind to prepare himself.

Jared stared at him, his mouth slightly open, his eyes completely dark and his skin flushed, already glistening with sweat. Running his hands along Fenix's thighs, Jared groaned as Fenix lowered himself on his cock and started moving. Fingers digging in his hips, Jared met Fenix halfway with every thrust. Fenix palmed his cock and started stroking himself in rhythm with the movement of his body, his eyes never leaving Jared's.

"God, Fenix, you're so hot!" Jared said, his voice strained and hoarse. "I want to devour you. Possess you. Make you a part of me."

Fenix moaned, the hand on his cock speeding up. Jared shouted a curse and pumped his hips vigorously several times, slamming into Fenix's ass and leaving bruises where his fingers dug into his skin. Fenix felt Jared coming inside him as he arched off the bed, closing his eyes in ecstasy.

Fenix kept jerking himself off leisurely, leaving Jared to ride out his orgasm. When he calmed down and managed to open his eyes again, Fenix bent down to kiss him.

"My turn," he whispered against Jared's lips before he pulled back up and started working his cock in earnest.

Jared's dick was still half hard inside him and Fenix moved slowly, finding the angle he needed. He leaned back and propped his hand on the mattress between Jared's legs as he jerked off with the other.

"Jesus, Fenix..." Jared gasped. Fenix felt Jared's hands roaming over his thighs, his stomach, his nipples, his back... Everything they could reach.

"Jared..." Fenix whimpered helplessly as he came in waves all over Jared's stomach.

"What's this?" Fenix asked as he lay half on his side, half on top of Jared, caressing a mark on his skin just below his belly. "Is it a birth mark?"

"Yeah," Jared replied quietly. "My mum used to say that it looked like a horseshoe and I was branded as lucky even before I was born," he continued and entwined his fingers with Fenix's over his stomach. Their fucking had left them both tired and drowsy, but there was additional heaviness in Jared's voice. It was there every time he talked about his family.

"I think she was right," Fenix said and propped his chin on Jared's shoulder to look at him. "You *are* lucky. After all, you've got me."

Jared's laughter filled the room and Fenix leaned in to kiss him.

When they eventually managed to drag themselves out of Jared's flat, it was past noon. Jared insisted they go to the bank first and get the most important job out of the way.

"It's going to take about an hour," Jared told him when he finished talking to the receptionist. "Would you like to wait here in the lobby or take a walk outside?"

"Yeah, I'd rather go for a walk, browse the shops. The thought of sitting here for an hour without anything to do terrifies me," Fenix said. Jared raised his eyebrows in a silent question. Fenix sighed and explained, "I have mild ADHD."

Jared nodded slowly and Fenix was glad he didn't see any pity or ridicule in his eyes. He brushed a strand of hair off Fenix's cheekbone, brushing his thumb over it.

"Go then. I'll call you when we finish here and we can go furniture shopping."

Fenix walked out of the bank and strolled down the highstreet. It was Monday so it wasn't too busy. He browsed through a few shops, not really looking for anything, but it gave him something to do. His mind kept wondering back to Jared as he looked through the racks of clothes. Fenix was astonished at the strength of the feelings he had already developed for Jared. He'd never been one to rush into things. He'd never even had a relationship because he'd never felt like this with anyone before.

What goes on in our heads is not something we can predict or explain, it just is what it is.

His mother's words echoed in his mind. She had been right – it was what it was. Fenix could not force his heart to stop beating a little faster and his chest to stop feeling tight and warm at the mere sight of Jared. He didn't want to.

A faded blue t-shirt caught his eye and he took it off the rack to examine it closer. His phone vibrated in his pocket and Fenix put the t-shirt back to answer it.

"Hey," Jared said cheerfully. "Where are you?"

"In Topshop. You sound happy. Did they give you the loan?"

"Yep. I'll have the money in my account by the end of the day."

"Great. Congratulations."

"Thanks. Now let's go to Zone. There's a leather corner sofa and a vintage coffee table with my name on it."

Zone had everything anyone could ever need when furnishing their home. The best part was that there was something for everyone – high-tech sound systems, soft cotton sheets, black-out blinds, silverware... The price range, model, and design also varied. From vintage chest of drawers to electric recliner sofas and old school movie posters, there was something for everyone.

Jared was like a kid in a candy store. His face lit up with excitement every time he saw something he liked. Fenix could not keep the smile off his own face – Jared's enthusiasm was contagious. He ended up buying the cherry red leather corner sofa he'd wanted, as well as the coffee table, Egyptian cotton sheets, a fluffy new duvet, a colourful rug for the living room, and a Broadway musical poster Fenix had fallen in love with. Jared arranged for everything to be delivered to his flat in two weeks, and they left the store.

"We'll come back next week after the contractors start. We need to choose a whole new kitchen, light fixtures, and a ton of other bits and pieces I'm sure I'll come up with. Oh, and a new bed!" Jared rambled animatedly.

We. That single word warmed Fenix's heart.

CHAPTER EIGHT

Fenix

It was past five o'clock when they got back to Jared's flat. He called the contractors he had in mind for the renovations, and in the meantime, Fenix started collecting his stuff and putting it back in the duffel. His phone vibrated in his front pocket and he fished it out.

"Hello?" he picked up without looking at the screen as he headed for the bathroom to get his tooth brush.

"Hey, doll. Wanna go out tonight?" Ned's melodic voice sounded on the other end.

"Sorry, I promised Joy I'd have dinner with her. I owe her one after bailing on her the last time."

"You two are like an old married couple. It's disgusting."

Fenix rolled his eyes but decided against biting the bait.

"Where are you by the way? I swung by last night and you weren't home. That's incredibly strange, considering what a bore you are," Ned said. Now, if it were someone else, Fenix might have gotten mad or offended. But that was just how Ned was. He had no brain-to-mouth filter.

"We went out two days ago, Ned," Fenix reminded him. "And next time, maybe it's a good idea to call first. Why were you even at my place?"

Ned huffed, his voice sounding incredibly bored when he spoke again.

"I went to this comedy club in Greenwich and wanted to crash at your place. It was closer and I didn't feel like waiting for the night bus. The comedy was torture enough."

"You went to a comedy club?" Fenix laughed disbelievingly.

"Yeah, that guy I'm kinda dating wanted to go, so I agreed against my better judgement."

"You're dating someone?" Ned's idea of dating consisted of sex in public places and the occasional dinner. Not a comedy club.

"Not anymore. So anyway, don't deflect the subject. Why weren't you home? I had to crash at Joy's."

"It's none of your business where I was, Ned."

"You stayed with a guy, didn't you?" Fenix didn't reply. Antagonizing Ned was much more enjoyable than indulging him. "Oh my god! You did! Are you with him now?"

"I'm hanging up," Fenix said.

"You are! Fenix that's..."

"Bye, Ned. Talk to you later," Fenix interrupted him and rang off.

That whole conversation had no point besides Ned's desire to learn the latest gossip. Fenix knew it wouldn't be so easy to ward him off next time – Ned was like a blood hound. Once he smelled the juicy gossip he was relentless. Fenix wondered how Jared would like Ned, if they'd get along. They weren't as close as Adam and Jared were, and they definitely had never had sex, but still – Ned was Fenix's friend and co-star. He loved him with all his quirks and wished Jared would like him too.

"Hey," Jared said from behind, making Fenix jump. He hadn't even felt Jared walk in the bedroom. "Sorry, didn't mean to startle you," he said, wrapping his arms around Fenix's waist. "So, I have good news. The contractor agreed to start tomorrow. We still need to meet in the morning and discuss the details, but he's been here before and has a rough idea what I want." Jared abruptly stopped talking as Fenix turned in his arms to face him.

"What?" he asked.

"What are you doing?" Jared's glanced at the duffel bag.

"I'm packing. I need to go home tonight, remember?" Fenix smiled and gave Jared a soft peck on the lips.

"Why?"

"What do you mean 'why'? I was supposed to stay last night, not move in," Fenix laughed and wrapped his hands around Jared's neck. Jared didn't laugh. He frowned and eyed the duffel bag as if it had personally offended him. "And besides, I promised Joy we'd hang out tonight. I also need to be at the theatre by noon tomorrow for a staff meeting. I was hoping I'd be able to sneak in a work-out before that. I haven't danced in three days and it's making me antsy."

"Stay," Jared said quietly, leaning in to kiss Fenix. The gentle touch of lips and tongue made Fenix want so much more. "I'll cook you dinner," Jared coaxed between kisses. "And then we'll fuck until neither of us can come anymore." Jared's kiss deepened and Fenix groaned.

He'd lost that battle the moment Jared had whispered 'stay'.

"This is the last night I'll spend here and I want to spend it with you," Jared said when their lips finally parted.

"What do you mean?"

"When the contractors start tomorrow I have to move out until they're finished. This place needs a lot of work, and there's no way I can live here in the meantime."

"Where are you going to stay?"

"Adam," Jared said, shrugging easily, like it was the most natural thing in the world to go stay with his ex-boyfriend. Fenix frowned. He could not control the next thing that came out of his mouth even if he'd wanted to.

"Adam? You're going to stay with your ex?" Fenix hated the edge in his voice almost as much as he hated the idea of Jared staying with Adam.

"We lived together before I moved in here. It's no big deal."

Fuck. That.

Fenix was torn – he didn't want to sound like a jealous boyfriend because he *wasn't* Jared's boyfriend, but the thought of Jared staying at Adam's was killing him. The rational thing to do would be to shut up and get over it. Fenix tapped into years of performance training to rein in his emotions and clear his features of any distress. When he felt confident his voice would not betray his unfounded jealousy, he asked,

"For how long?"

"Three weeks. At least that's what the contractor tells me."

Three fucking weeks!

Fenix pressed his teeth so hard together he thought they might fall through his jaw. They needed a change of subject, fast.

"Look," Fenix began and gently removed Jared's arms from around his waist, taking a small step back. "I'd love to stay, but like I said, I have plans with Joy and…"

Jared cut him off, closing the distance between them once again and stealing his breath with a languid kiss. For a moment Fenix forgot about Joy, about contractors and Adam and irrational jealousy. His world shrank and moulded itself to that kiss. He didn't want to go, he didn't want to be out of touching distance from Jared.

Jared moved his wet lips along Fenix's jaw and down his throat, along his collarbone and the hollow of his throat. He traced his way back to his lips, his arms tightening around Fenix as if he planned to physically restrain him from leaving. That would not be necessary. Every desire to walk out that door had already evaporated from Fenix's brain.

"Call Joy and tell her you won't be coming home tonight. You'll make it up to her some other time," Jared whispered seductively in Fenix's ear, sucking on his earlobe for emphasis.

Fenix nodded on an instinct – he was too far gone in a haze of red, hot lust to think clearly.

Jared made baked salmon and steamed vegetables for dinner while Fenix tried to put his brain cells back together. He lay in Jared's bed, listening to him cook in the kitchen, his body still sensitive and trembling. Jared had sucked his cock, bringing him to the edge and then back down so many times he'd lost count. He'd driven Fenix out of his mind with the desire to burst out of his skin. Just thinking about it now, he felt goosebumps erupt all over his body, every nerve ending still over stimulated and *aware*. He'd needed some time to come down from the high of his orgasm, to convince his body that the pleasure was over. Jared had held him, selflessly, not even trying to make Fenix return the favour.

Fenix heard the extractor fan go quiet and Jared started opening and closing cupboards, clacking plates and silverware together. It was time to get up and have something to eat – Fenix had a suspicion his groggy state was at least partly due to his lack of food since breakfast that morning. Sitting up, he found his phone in his discarded jeans on the floor and typed a quick text to Joy letting her know he wouldn't be coming home tonight. Even though a text was the coward's way out, he had no energy to deal with her right then. Turning off his phone in the very plausible case she'd call him the second she got his message, Fenix put his boxers on and padded to the kitchen.

Jared greeted him with a smirk, giving him a once over, pleased with his handy work. Fenix must have looked as relaxed and sedated as he felt. Conversation flowed easily while they ate and talked and laughed in such comfort with each other, as if they'd been doing this years instead of a couple of days. Fenix tried to push the nagging thought of Jared staying with Adam for almost a month out of his mind, but it didn't work. It poked its ugly head and crawled to his frontal lobe until he couldn't think of anything else.

He helped Jared clean up the table and wash the dishes. The domesticity of the situation should have seemed odd, awkward, but it didn't. Fenix had never felt so calm, so comfortable and *safe* in the company of another guy. After they were done in the kitchen, Fenix took Jared's hand in his and guided him back to the bedroom.

Later, after a whirlwind of tangled limbs, harsh breaths, whispered words, muffled cries and sticky, sweating bodies moving together, they lay on their sides, facing each other in the dark. Jared absently traced uneven circles on Fenix's hip, his eyes shinning in the darkness. Fenix could not look away, could not distance himself from the feeling of Jared's fingertips on his skin.

"ADHD?" Jared asked softly. He hadn't mentioned anything about it ever since Fenix had casually tossed the information at him in the bank lobby.

"Yeah. Not the severe, medicated kind. I just find it really hard to concentrate on one single thing for a long time," Fenix said with a smile, trying to make light of the subject. He hated talking about his ADHD because most people didn't get it. They thought he was hiding behind some made-up condition to justify how easily bored he could get.

Then again, Jared wasn't most people. He didn't return the smile when he said,

"I bet that makes your long rehearsing and dancing sessions very difficult." His fingers continued to make patterns on Fenix's hip and distract him.

"Sometimes," he whispered, closing his eyes and remembering his latest episode. He'd been dancing for over two hours, trying to perfect a move he was working on and still not liking what he saw in the mirror. Realisation that he'd been doing that for so long and not achieving his goal, and even worse – that he had to stay here, in this studio, all alone, doing the same thing over and over again until he was happy with it, hit him like a freight train. Suddenly, he couldn't breathe and the walls started closing in on him. He needed to get out of here. Run. Do something.

"Hey," Jared said softly, running his thumb over Fenix's cheekbone. Fenix opened his eyes and the sight of Jared, who was looking at his with concern and tenderness, grounded him back to the present.

"It's not such a big deal," Fenix said hurriedly. "Red Bull relaxes me and coffee makes me sleepy, and I can never finish watching a movie without either falling asleep or getting distracted half way. I hate repetitive, mechanical noises, waking up early in the morning, being restrained for any reason, and sometimes the world around me becomes too noisy, too constricted, too *much,* and I need to get away. But that's the worst case scenario. I'm pretty normal most of the time..." Fenix had to forcibly close his mouth and clench his jaw to stop himself rambling.

"Nothing about you is normal, Fenix. You're as extraordinary as it gets," Jared said and ran his hand down Fenix's arm, coming to rest on his hip. Fenix raised an eyebrow to express his doubt at Jared's words. Jared smiled crookedly. "You wanna tell me what's been bothering you all evening?" he asked casually.

"Huh?"

"You've been distracted all through dinner and even now. I know something's bothering you so you might just as well tell me," Jared said and resumed his insanely tender pattern tracing on Fenix's hip.

Even though Fenix wanted to tell him, he was reluctant to.

"Fen?" Jared encouraged gently. The use of that particular nickname broke down Fenix's last defences. He sighed.

"I don't want you to move in with Adam while the renovations last," he said finally, his voice level and as devoid of emotion as he could make it. For a second, Jared looked confused, but then it dawned on him, his eyes sparkling mischievously.

"Are you jealous?" he asked, grinning.

"No," Fenix denied on an instinct, making Jared laugh.

"You are!"

Fenix hadn't expected Jared to laugh wholeheartedly at that and pushed his hand away, flopping onto his back. Jared followed him immediately, stretching on top of him and forcing him to meet his eyes.

"You have no reason to be. Adam and I are friends; we've always been friends, even when we fucked," Jared said softly, his gorgeous, pink, wet lips just an inch from Fenix's. His jealousy flared even more.

"You said he was your first. That kinda leaves a lasting memory," he said.

There. Proper jealous boyfriend routine.

"But that's what it is – a memory. If we wanted to be together, we would have been. We just don't want to."

That did nothing to ease Fenix's mind. He felt stupid and irrational and out of line for even mentioning it. He hated that he'd even opened his big mouth, and he was afraid Jared might hate it too.

"Baby? There's more, I can see it in your eyes," Jared said, his voice so calm and gentle. No judgement. No impatience. Fenix decided to let it all out, and if Jared decided it was too much to handle, then so be it. But he could not spend the next three weeks keeping all that inside. He opened his mouth and ranted without even pausing for breath.

"Yes, I'm jealous. Even when you say that you're nothing more than friends, I'm still jealous. He was your first lover and you'll never forget that. He'll always be special to you. But what I hate even more than that is the fact that I feel this way, because we just met two days ago! I have no right to feel this way, we're not in a relationship or anything, we don't know anything about each other. And yet, the thought of not spending a single night with you drives me crazy, let alone three fucking weeks. I want you to stay with me, not with Adam. I want to tell you that I don't want to fuck anybody else and I don't want *you* to fuck anybody else either. I want..." Fenix paused, his voice growing quiet at Jared's expression. He had not expected that. "You. I want you, Jared. How can I want you so much after two days? It scares the hell out of me."

Jared stared at him. He was shocked, but he wasn't angry. He wasn't pulling back as if he thought Fenix was crazy. That was a good sign, right?

"You want me to stay with you?" he asked finally.

"Yes."

Jared's lips pulled back in a stunning, happy grin. His eyes danced as he kept staring at Fenix as if searching for a sign he was leading him on.

"And you want to be exclusive?"

"Yes!" Fenix confirmed, unable to stop the joyful grin appearing on his own lips.

"I don't care how long we've known each other, Fen. This feels right. I want you, too. I want everything with you," Jared said as he kissed him, tangling his hands in Fenix's hair and relaxing his body on top of him. All too soon he pulled back and rested on his side again, tugging Fenix to follow him. When they were facing each other again, Jared moved even closer, leaving just an inch between their lips. "You know how in books and movies at the end, just before the happily ever after, they always say, 'I knew you were the one the moment I saw you', or 'I knew I was going to spend the rest of my life with you when I first met you'?"

"Yeah?"

"I don't wanna waste that time – the time between realising that and actually saying it. I don't wanna bend to society's rules about how long we should be together before I tell you 'I love you' or before I know you're *it*. Because I knew it the moment I lay eyes on you, Fenix. Something inside me woke up and jumped and pointed at you and shouted: 'That's him. That's the guy for you.' You're *it* for me, love. I know it here," he took Fenix's hand and placed it on his chest, right over his heart. "And I don't care what anybody else says."

"You're *it* for me, too, Jared."

CHAPTER NINE

Jared

Riiiing.

Ring. Ring. Ring.

Riiiiiiiing.

Jared jolted awake, disoriented. What the fuck?

Shit!

The contractor. Jared was supposed to set his alarm for 8:00 am to be up and ready when the contractor arrived at nine. And now he was here and Jared was still in bed. Naked. With Fenix.

He swore a few more times and jumped off the bed, hastily putting on his sweat pants and a t-shirt he found on the floor, praying it was clean. He padded barefoot to the door and pressed the intercom button.

"Hello?" he rasped, his voice still heavy with sleep.

"Jared Hartley? It's James Seymour. The contractor? We were supposed to meet today, right?"

Jared closed his eyes and gritted his teeth. How could he have forgotten that?

"Yes, of course. Come on up, I'll buzz you in," Jared said and pressed the button for the main entrance.

Jared estimated he had about two minutes before James was up here, ringing his doorbell. He hurried back to the bedroom.

"Fenix. Fenix! Wake up, baby." He shook Fenix's shoulder and he stirred awake. "You have to get up. The contractor is here."

Fenix grunted so unhappily that Jared was almost tempted to let him sleep. Almost. If he had an actual separate bedroom he might have. But he didn't, and he didn't want James and whoever was with him to gape at Fenix's sleeping form.

"Come on, love," he coaxed as he helped Fenix off the bed and collected his clothes from the chair nearby. Ushering him in the bathroom and thrusting the clothes in his hands, Jared said,

"Here. Take as long as you need. They'll want to take a look at the bathroom, but I'll stall them." Fenix looked so cute and dazed that Jared couldn't resist taking him into his arms and giving him a long, wet kiss. Fenix responded instinctively even though his brain was not entirely awake yet. The front door bell rang and startled Jared out of the kiss. With one last squeeze at Fenix's ass, he shut the bathroom door and went to open the front door.

There were two men staring back at him when Jared swung the door open. He recognised James Seymour from their previous meeting a few weeks ago – he was a tall, lean man, probably in his fifties, with closely cropped black hair and intelligent dark eyes. Jared had never seen the other man before – he was probably in his twenties, with dark blond hair and honey coloured eyes that studied Jared unflinchingly.

"Hi, come on in," Jared said, ushering them in. "Thank you for coming on such a short notice, James."

"No worries. You're in luck – we just finished a project the day before yesterday," James said, smiling and running his hand over his short hair. "That's Phil," James said, pointing at the younger man. Jared shook the extended hand and introduced himself. Phil smiled at him, those unnerving light brown eyes still studying him intently.

They proceeded to discuss what Jared wanted done as he offered them both cups of coffee. Jared took out the architectural plans for the bedroom he wanted done as a mezzanine level where his current 'bedroom' was and James nodded, saying it shouldn't be a problem. They talked some more about re-plastering, rewiring, plumbing, and installing new hardwood floors with heating panels, when Fenix walked out the bathroom in all his glory. Freshly showered, dressed in his jeans and t-shirt, his blond hair still wet and looking darker than usual, Fenix sauntered towards them. Jared could not take his eyes off him. That man – that gorgeous, sweet, talented man – was all his.

Jared cleared his throat and glanced sideways at James and Phil, noticing that while James looked unaffected and unsurprised to see a man walking out of his client's bathroom, Phil was gaping at Fenix with open appreciation.

Hell no.

Jared had never been possessive of anyone in his life. He'd always thought that was the way he was. But the possessiveness that flared through him at that moment burned that notion to ashes. He was ready to punch Phil in the face until he closed his mouth and stopped staring and Fenix. Indefinitely.

"I'm Fenix, nice to meet you, guys," he said easily as he approached the table littered with architectural plans. Fenix shook hands with James who didn't show any particular interest in him and continued to mull over the plans. Phil, however, kept staring at Fenix with such undisguised appreciation that Jared was a second away from pulling Fenix in his arms, kissing him senseless and growling 'mine'.

"Fenix Bergman, right?" Phil said as he shook Fenix's hand, managing to form words.

"Yes," Fenix replied with a smile.

"I'm a fan. I saw your show *Poison* a couple of months ago. Can I just say – you can dance, man! The show was amazing! Can't wait to see it at Queen Victoria," Phil gushed.

Great. A fan.

"Thanks, Phil. Glad you enjoyed it. I'm sure we'll be able to score some tickets for you guys to see it at Queen Victoria, if you're interested."

Did he have to be so damn pleasant? Wasn't he aware that guy was imagining how Fenix's cock would feel in his ass right now?

"Hell yeah, I'm interested! That would be awesome! Thanks, man," Phil said excitedly.

"My wife would love that, thank you, Fenix. Let me cut you a deal – you get us some tickets and I promise we'll finish work here on time," James said, winking at Jared.

"Aren't you *supposed* to finish on time? Isn't that what I'm paying you for?" Jared asked, sounding a bit more annoyed than he intended.

"Things can always go wrong, slow the initial schedule down..." James drawled and chuckled.

"No problem. Since I'm housing Jared for the duration of the renovation, don't worry about finishing on time," Fenix joked. "I'd rather have him for a week or so longer." He fixed his impossibly ice blue eyes on Jared and he felt the irritation melting away as Fenix smiled lazily. Phil huffed next to Jared as his annoyance crept back in full force.

"Jared, let's go take a look at the bathroom. I want to see what I'm working with," James suggested as he pushed his chair back and stood up.

They went to see the bathroom and Jared explained what he wanted – new tiles on the walls, shower enclosure with a power shower, new fittings. James explained that they probably wouldn't need to replace the whole plumbing system but couldn't be sure until he took a better look at the pipes. Jared was only half listening. He was acutely aware of Fenix and Phil talking animatedly in the kitchen – Fenix was leaning back against the counter, sipping from his coffee mug, looking impossibly handsome. Phil, was standing in front of him, making it extremely obvious that he was very interested in helping Fenix get undressed as quickly as possible. To his horror, Jared saw Phil take out a business card and slip it in Fenix's pocket. Fenix didn't show any particular interest but didn't throw it away either.

Jared saw red. He wanted Phil out of his house right now.

"OK, I think we're pretty much done for now. If you leave me a key we can start early tomorrow morning. I'll keep you updated on our progress and I'll be in touch if something comes up."

They arranged the rest of the details quickly and Jared walked them to the door, after Phil miraculously managed to unglue himself from Fenix. Jared rummaged through the drawer he kept his spare keys in, and, to his incredible relief, he saw Fenix discreetly take the business card out of his pocket and throw it in the rubbish bin under the sink. Jared gave James the spare key and couldn't be happier to send them on their way.

He walked to Fenix and wrapped him in his arms, kissing his neck.

"I hate that guy," he murmured against his skin.

"I know. I think they caught your scowl on Google Earth," Fenix laughed and Jared drowned in the sound, allowing it to sink in every cell of his body.

And just like that, all was well in the world again.

Fenix went to the theatre for his staff meeting while Jared stayed behind to pack his stuff. There wasn't much he owned anyway – all his possessions could fit in two duffels. He'd given James permission to throw everything that was left behind away. His phone rang just as he was emptying his wardrobe and folding clothes in neat piles.

Adam.

"Hey, you home?" he asked.

"Yeah. I'm packing. The contractors are starting work tomorrow." Jared hadn't spoken with Adam for a couple of days and was suddenly aware he had no idea Jared had started the renovations. Or gotten the loan. Or that he was going to stay with Fenix.

Shit.

"Um, what?" Adam asked, clearly confused.

"I guess we have to catch up. I need to tell you some stuff."

"Clearly." Adam did not sound happy.

"Where are you? Why don't you come by? You can make me lunch while I pack."

"Your boy toy doesn't cook?" asked Adam, his voice dripping with sarcasm.

"He's not here. And don't call him that," Jared scowled without too much heat. He'd been on the receiving end of numerous offensive nicknames coming from Adam's mouth so he knew he didn't really mean them. Mostly.

"Fine. I'll be there in fifteen," he said and clicked off.

"Are you completely out of your fucking mind?" were Adam's first words when Jared finished relaying the story of the last two days. "You took out a loan to fix this place for *him*? You're going to move in with him after knowing him for three days?"

"First of all, I didn't take out the loan to fix my flat for *him*. I did it for me, because it was time. I'm tired of living in a dump. You know as well as I do that I had plans to do this," Jared spoke as he moved around the flat, gathering the last of his belongings and zipping up the duffel bags. "I had already spoken with James Seymour, the contractor, a couple of weeks after I moved in, and I had an architect do the plans for the bedroom," he continued. "I'm not *moving in* with Fenix. I'm just *staying* at his place until my flat is habitable again," Jared explained as patiently as he could manage. He hated justifying his decisions to anyone and Adam was the only person who got away with it.

"Why don't you stay at my place? You lived there up until a few months ago anyway."

"Because I'll get much less sex if I do that," Jared joked, hoping to lighten the mood.

"So in the end it all comes back to that, doesn't it? What's the matter with you, Jared? Has he discovered some magical way to suck cock? Because it looks like your brain is completely sucked out!" Adam was furious. His dark eyes shone with anger as he banged his fist on the table.

"Adam, you need to shut up and back off," Jared said through gritted teeth. He was starting to get angry himself – it was one thing to be a concerned friend, but completely different to meddle in his business.

"He's an opportunistic whore! How can you not see that!" Adam yelled, standing up abruptly, shoving his hands in his hair.

"How is that even true?" Jared yelled back. "I'm staying at *his* place! He didn't have to offer, he knew perfectly well I could stay with you!"

"You're a well-known name in the business, Jared. You're the star of the theatre, the person that everyone respects..." Adam began.

Jared laughed humourlessly, cutting him off.

"Are you even hearing yourself? Fenix will be a much bigger star than me very soon and he definitely doesn't need my help with that."

Adam shook his head and glared at him, not saying anything.

"What's your problem with Fenix, Adam? I've never seen you react to someone like that!" Jared asked, trying to get to the bottom of the problem.

"I told you what my problem is – the little piece of shit is using you and messing up with your head..."

Jared stood up so abruptly that the chair clattered to the floor with a loud bang, cutting Adam off.

"I'll let that slide because of our friendship. But don't say anything we won't be able to recover from, Adam. Don't make me choose between the two of you because you're not going to like the outcome," Jared said, his voice low and deadly. He was prepared to kick Adam's ass out the door if he so much as pronounced Fenix's name incorrectly.

Fortunately, Adam thought better than to test Jared's patience right now and didn't say anything more. He shook his head in disgust as he walked out, slamming the door behind himself.

CHAPTER TEN

Jared

By the time Jared packed all his stuff and arrived at Queen Victoria, the *Poison* staff meeting had adjourned. He went to the dressing room to look for Fenix, but he was not there. Dumping his bags on the floor, Jared walked out and headed towards the rehearsal room. He had a suspicion that's where he'd find Fenix, since he probably hadn't had time to do any dancing before the meeting.

The rehearsal room was made like a replica of the main stage hall, only much smaller. There were a few rows of seats, a stage, complete with lights, music system and even a curtain. Jared felt the bass of the music before he heard the rest of the melody. When he walked closer, he realised it was 'My Songs Know What You Did in the Dark' by Fall Out Boy. They had discovered early on that they had similar tastes in music and Fall Out Boy was a mutual favourite band. Smiling, he pushed the door open and walked inside to see Fenix dancing on the stage, completely lost in the moment. He was oblivious to Jared's presence as he sneaked inside and sat at the back row, blending with the shadows. Only the stage lights were on, so it would be difficult for Fenix to spot him, even if he wasn't completely absorbed by the dance.

Fenix was beautiful. The way he moved was out of this world. Jared could not take his eyes off him as he jumped and flew across the stage, arched his back in an impossible angle, spread his legs in the most perfect split Jared had ever seen. Clad only in black leggings, shirtless and barefoot, Fenix was a sight that imprinted itself in Jared's brain and, he suspected, would stay there forever. His smooth, hairless skin was slick with sweat as Fenix leapt into the air, spreading his arms wide and bowing his back in one flawless move, his lean, hard muscles flexing as he landed back on the stage effortlessly.

Jared was gaping. He knew Fenix had to be very good if his musical was offered Queen Victoria's main stage, but what he'd just seen was beyond good. It was beyond any scale of appreciation. Fenix was in a league of his own.

The song ended and 'Alone Together' began. It was a slower, more sensual rhythm, and Jared's pulse quickened while Fenix danced as if he was making love to the song. He moved with leisurely, yet perfectly executed strokes, and he was exquisite. Jared could not imagine anyone not falling immediately in love with Fenix. His grace, his charisma and charm drew people in and, judging by himself, when you got to know him better, you loved him even more.

That was why Adam's reaction was so puzzling. He'd encountered Fenix just a couple of times and Fenix had never given him any reason to hate him that much. Jared could not wrap his head around his best friend's reaction. There must be something he was not seeing. Adam was not an irrational person.

Lost in thought and mesmerised by Fenix dancing on stage, Jared did not feel someone sit beside him until their shoulders brushed. Adam was sitting quietly, and somewhat apologetically, next to him, looking at the stage straight ahead. Jared knew his friend well – he was a hot head and often raged and yelled and slammed doors, but his fury deflated as quickly as it had appeared. So he knew Adam would seek him out to clear the air when he eventually calmed down, he just didn't think it would be so soon.

Jared waited.

'Alone Together' ended and 'Miss Missing You' started. Fenix transformed his movements seamlessly to fit the new rhythm.

"I'm sorry," Adam said quietly and Jared barely heard him over the music. He nodded, accepting the apology, certain Adam could see him even if he pretended to watch Fenix. "It's just... it hurts seeing you like this with someone else, and after such a short time. You never looked at me like that even though we were together for so long."

So that was the problem! Jared sighed and turned to face Adam, touching his hand lightly.

"Come on Adam. You and I were always friends before all else. It was never like that for us," he said softly. Adam turned to face him, and Jared had never seen such raw honesty in his eyes.

"It was for me," he whispered, casting his eyes away, unable to meet Jared's astonished stare.

What?

Jared had been certain that they both felt the same way about their relationship. All these years Adam had never given him any indication he'd felt differently. Was he trying to say that... that he'd been *in love* with Jared?

"You've never told me this. Why?" he asked, torn between feelings of guilt and anger.

"Because I knew you didn't feel the same way," Adam replied with an annoyed sigh. "It doesn't matter anymore. I've moved on."

"It doesn't matter?" Jared asked outraged. His best friend, his ex-*lover*, had just admitted he'd been in love with him and had the audacity to say it didn't matter!

"Would it change anything? Would you realise you've loved me all along and come running into my arms?" Adam asked sarcastically. Jared shook his head 'no'. "There's no happily ever after for us, Jared. But we'll always be there for each other, I know that and it's enough for me."

Jared didn't say anything. He needed some time to process this information. Adam patted Jared's knee as if to indicate the conversation was over.

"I still don't like him, but if he's what you want right now, I promise I'll behave," he said before standing up and disappearing as quickly as he'd come.

Jared was so stunned that he didn't even hear the music cutting off and Fenix walking towards him.

"Hey. You alright?" Fenix asked as he sat elegantly in the seat next to him. "I saw you talking to Adam. Everything OK?"

Jared shook his head and summarized everything Adam had said today, not leaving out his harsh words or the admission of his feelings for Jared. Fenix listened, his face expressionless, until Jared stopped talking.

"I understand," he said with an easy shrug.

"You understand?" Jared asked incredulously. "What part?"

"All of it. I can see why he thinks I'm using you," Fenix said raising a shoulder again. "And how could he not fall in love with you? Of course he had. Look at you."

Fenix said all that so easily, without any offense or affliction in his voice and Jared instantly relaxed. Maybe part of his problem had been how Fenix would react to Adam's accusations. But as usual, Fenix had been kind and considerate, and Jared felt the last of his remaining anger and confusion drain out of his body. He cupped the back of Fenix's head, bringing him closer for a quick kiss, then touched their foreheads together and whispered,

"Let's go home."

It turned out there was nothing to eat at Fenix's flat. Literally. All the contents of the fridge could be summed up as half a lemon, a tomato, three cans of Red Bull, and a questionable looking piece of cheese.

"How do you even survive on your own?" Jared asked as he slammed the fridge door shut and looked at Fenix, puzzled.

"I don't cook a lot. Or at all. Joy feeds me most of the time, or I order take out from the Japanese place around the corner," Fenix replied, flopping down on the sofa. Jared rolled his eyes.

"Come on," he beckoned, already headed to the front door.

"What? Where? We just got here!" protested Fenix. He looked so comfortable and delicious sprawled on the sofa, but Jared was determined to get some food before any clothes came off.

"To the supermarket. We need to buy some groceries. I'm not asking Joy to cook for all three of us and we're not ordering take out every single night. Besides, you like my cooking."

Fenix grumbled, but got up. He walked to Jared and wrapped his arms around his neck.

"I do. And I like some other stuff you're very talented at," he said, leaning in for a kiss.

"Later, handsome," Jared said as he pushed Fenix gently away. "You're not going to distract me with kisses. We're going."

He turned on his heel and opened the door, followed closely behind by a pouting Fenix.

Two hours, a dozen shopping bags, and a very unhappy Fenix later, Jared was making a stir fry in the kitchen while Fenix dozed off on the sofa. It was so domestic, so comfortable and *right* that Jared could not believe it had happened so *fast*. He'd never particularly wanted a boyfriend or a happily ever after, but now that he had at least one of those, Jared felt content. He hadn't even realised he'd needed that so much. He missed having a family. He missed his mum.

A knock on the door stopped his bleak thoughts from growing even darker. He glanced at Fenix who was peacefully napping and hadn't even stirred at the knocking. Well, Jared was going to live here for the next three weeks so he might as well start opening the door, right?

He padded barefoot to the front door and swung it open, only to see a petit blonde woman in her early twenties with delicate features and long hair tied in a messy bun at the back of her neck. Her bright green eyes widened as she took him in, clearly not expecting to see anyone but Fenix here.

"Oh, hi. You must be Jared," she said and smiled warmly, extending her hand. "I'm Joy, Fenix's friend. I live in the flat downstairs and thought I heard someone walking..." she trailed off as Jared shook her hand and smiled in amusement. "OK, I'm shutting up now. I just wanted to check on Fenix because he hasn't been home since... since he met you actually." Joy grinned and Jared's own smile widened.

"Nice to meet you, Joy. Fenix has told me a lot about you."

"But he hasn't told me nearly enough about you," she joked.

"Do you want to come in? I'm making dinner and he's sleeping on the sofa. I'm afraid I wore him out in Tesco's."

"You managed to get *him* to Tesco's? Wow, he must really be in love with you," she said as she walked in. Jared was taken aback for a second by her off-handed comment, but he had to admit that he liked the idea. Was Fenix in love with him? It certainly wasn't just fucking, but they hadn't actually said the words yet. He was pretty sure what he was feeling was love – he'd never felt such tenderness, such affection, and such fierce protectiveness for another guy, so what else could it be but love? It was all new to him, so he guessed it must be new to Fenix too. The idea of Fenix being in love with someone else before him was nauseating.

Joy was wonderful. They talked quietly in the kitchen as Jared chopped and fried the vegetables and steamed some rice. He invited her to stay for dinner and she happily accepted. He could see why she was Fenix's best friend – she was as easy-going and lovely as him.

Dinner was ready and Jared turned off the hob and the extractor fan, filling three plates with stir fry and rice. Just then it occurred to him that Fenix didn't have a dining table.

"Where are we going to eat?" he asked Joy.

"Oh, usually we just throw some cushions on the floor around the coffee table. Neither of us is a big eater anyway," she said, taking some cutlery and napkins out of a drawer.

Yeah, they all had to watch what they ate and work out regularly. After all, they had to sing and dance without catching their breaths at least four times a week. Jared imagined it must be even harder for Fenix and Joy since their show was much more energetic than *Of Kids and Monsters*.

Fenix stirred and opened an eye as Joy moved around him, pulling cushions from under him to set them around the small coffee table.

"Stop that," he groaned. "What are you doing here?"

"I'm helping Jared with dinner. Unlike you," she scorned, hitting him playfully on the head with one of the cushions.

Jared laughed and brought the full plates to the table, giving Fenix a soft kiss and sitting next to him. They ate and talked, all of them completely at ease, as if they'd known each other for years. It felt good. Jared had a sudden thought that he wanted Adam here as well. It saddened him that it may never happen. Adam had promised to behave around Fenix, but that didn't mean they'd ever get along.

After dinner, they watched a little bit of CSI:Miami before Joy excused herself to leave. Fenix walked her to the door and Jared saw them whispering before she gave him a hug and with one last wave at Jared, left.

"What were you two whispering about?" Jared asked when Fenix cuddled back to him on the sofa.

"Nothing."

"Yeah? You seemed pretty happy to be whispering about nothing."

Fenix turned his head slightly to look at Jared with huge, blue eyes. His hair was sticking out, and Jared couldn't hold the impulse to rake his fingers through it. God, Fenix was so beautiful! It would never stop to amaze him.

"She said she liked you, and that you were good for me," Fenix said, lowering his eyelids as Jared stroked his hair. It looked like he was a moment away from purring like a big cat.

Jared didn't comment on what Joy had said. He was glad Fenix's friend liked him and somewhat approved of their relationship. He wished he could say the same.

Bending down to kiss those gorgeous lips, Jared whispered against them,

"I want you to fuck me tonight, baby."

Fenix's eyes widened and he inhaled sharply.

"Are you sure?"

Jared nodded, pushing Fenix up slowly and taking his hand to lead him to the bedroom.

CHAPTER ELEVEN

Fenix

"Just go slow, OK? It's been a while..." Jared whispered as Fenix positioned himself on top of him. There hadn't been any hurry or frantic clothes pulling. They'd kissed, long and slow and thorough, and Fenix had undressed them both unhurriedly. It felt so good, so normal to have Jared in his bed, asking to be fucked. It didn't feel like it was the first time; it felt like they'd done it a thousand times before. There was no awkwardness, just desire. God help him, Fenix craved this man. He couldn't imagine his need for Jared ever running out.

"We don't have to do this, baby," Fenix whispered back between kisses. He wanted Jared that way, more than anything, but he wanted it to feel right for him. There was no rush, they had all the time in the world to do all the things they wanted to each other.

"I can't stop thinking about it ever since I saw you on that stage, Fen," Jared said, running his hands over Fenix's back. Fenix shivered on top of him, his erection pulsing and dripping on Jared's belly. "I want you. All of you."

Fenix moaned and flexed his hips against Jared's, running his tongue along his jaw, loving the feel of rough stubble against it. He bit Jared's chin lightly and kissed him again, seeking out his tongue and sucking it into his mouth.

"Fenix..." Jared groaned wantonly, weaving his fingers in Fenix's hair and tugging him even closer, mashing their mouths in a desperate kiss.

As much as Fenix wanted to kiss and fondle and grind against Jared's already slick with sweat skin, he needed to progress things faster or it would all be over before he'd even put the condom on. Nobody had ever turned him on so much with just a few kisses that he was ready to come without even touching himself.

Fenix fumbled in the bedside drawer, taking out the condoms and the lube. Jared moaned eagerly and palmed Fenix's ass, crushing their groins together.

"Jesus, you need to stop that or I'll come all over you right now," Fenix grunted and felt Jared smile against his lips, his hold on his ass loosening.

Sliding down Jared's body, Fenix hooked his hands behind Jared's knees and pushed them back against his chest. Jared made a surprised sound but didn't resist.

"Hold your legs, baby. I'll need my hands back," said Fenix and Jared obeyed.

Taking a moment to admire how gorgeous Jared was, all flushed and aroused and readily displayed for the taking, Fenix locked eyes with him, smirking wickedly. He didn't waste any more time, suddenly impatient to make Jared squirm and beg for release. With one swift movement, Fenix took all of Jared's length in his mouth, feeling the tip of his cock at the back of his throat.

"Fuuuck," Jared moaned as Fenix swirled his tongue around his cock and swallowed around the head. "Fenix!" he yelled, a needy, helpless sound.

Fenix wrapped his fingers at the base of Jared's cock, jerking him off while sucking on the head. He knew he was pushing Jared's self-control, but he couldn't stop himself. Seeing, *hearing* Jared like that was a huge turn on, and Fenix was on the brink himself.

He reached for the condom and put it on, slicking his fingers and his sheathed cock with the lube. Deciding against torturing Jared further, Fenix climbed up his body, hooking one arm behind Jared's knee while Jared still held his other leg up. Fenix kissed him as his lubed finger circled Jared's hole, sliding easily inside. Jared moaned deep in his throat, pushing his ass against Fenix's finger, wordlessly asking for more. Fenix added another finger, thrusting in and out, making sure Jared was ready. He felt Jared's gland and rubbed it gently, feeling Jared's whole body growing taunt in his arms.

"Please, baby... I need you," Jared said, so far gone in his pleasure that his words came out as a slurred whisper.

Fenix withdrew his fingers and leaned back on his knees. Jared put his feet on the mattress, and palmed his cock, stroking leisurely a few times as Fenix positioned himself. He saw Jared taking a sharp breath as Fenix breached that first, tight ring of muscle and leaned on top of him, catching Jared's lips in a kiss to distract him. A moment later, Jared exhaled loudly and urged Fenix on, arching his back to take him in further. Once Fenix was all the way in, he gave Jared a moment to adjust. He desperately needed to move, to thrust into this wonderful tight heat, to overwhelm and conquer this man. His whole body was shaking with the barely contained desire to do all that, the only thing stopping him being the thought of hurting Jared if he went too hard too fast.

"Move, Fen. Don't hold back," Jared grunted in Fenix's ear, shattering his last thread of control.

"I don't want to hurt you," Fenix managed to say, his hips already starting to move.

"I like it rough," Jared said, quoting what Fenix had said that first night they were together, and smiled against Fenix's skin.

Fenix really started moving then, pounding in and out of Jared's body, unable to stop himself even if he tried. He knew that the initial sting of penetration only added to the pleasure, at least for him, and he hoped that was what Jared had wanted. Jared moaned, loud and uninhibited, meeting Fenix's thrusts half way, silently begging for more. Fenix leaned back on his knees, grabbing Jared's hips for leverage and ramming into him with everything he had.

"Oh, God, yes!" Jared moaned loudly, palming his cock and locking eyes with Fenix. "Don't stop. I'm so close."

Fenix was on the edge as well, already feeling his orgasm building into his every cell. His body was humming like a charged electric wire. Jared's hand sped up on his cock and it was all too much for Fenix – the sight of Jared's wild eyes, his squirming body, his skin wet with sweat, Fenix's name on his swollen lips... Fenix fell on top of Jared, his movements fast and erratic, and he felt Jared spill between their bodies, shouting Fenix's name as his body shook and his muscles spasmed. He felt Jared's other hand grabbing his ass, squeezing and pulling him closer, urging him on.

Fenix was right there. One more thrust and he'd...

"I love you," Jared whispered just as Fenix's vision blurred with the force of his orgasm. His ears started ringing and all he could hear was the blood rushing in his ears. His arms gave out and he flopped on top of Jared, feeling his arms coming around him, wrapping him in a warm, secure embrace. Fenix's body trembled as he breathed hard, trying to catch his breath.

Fenix hadn't known it was possible for such exquisite pleasure to exist.

When his brain rebooted and he came back into his own body, Fenix heard Jared was still whispering sweet nothings against his skin, still clutching him tightly and still pulsing around his cock.

"That was..." he began but his voice was hoarse and broke off.

"Yeah," Jared agreed.

Fenix pulled out slowly and collapsed on his back. He was spent. Literally. He could not move a muscle if his life depended on it. He felt Jared get up and a moment later he was back, wiping Fenix's stomach clean and disposing of the condom. Fenix tried to mumble 'thanks' but his mouth didn't work. The mattress dipped and Jared lay down again, pulling the covers over them and wrapping Fenix in his arms again.

Fenix was too far gone, too exhausted and too peaceful to react in any way, so he let Jared manoeuvre him until their bodies entwined comfortably. Just before he fell asleep, he thought he heard Jared whisper 'I love you so much' against his hair, but he couldn't be sure.

The piercing sound of the alarm and the frantic vibration of his phone on the nightstand woke Fenix. He jumped upright in bed, his heart pounding, unaware of where he was or what was going on. It took him a few seconds to realise he was home and the ungodly sound was coming from his mobile phone.

"Jesus!" he exclaimed as he fumbled with the phone, trying to stop the alarm. "You fucking piece of shit, I hate you!" he yelled at it, finally switching the wailing off and tossing the phone back on the nightstand. He flopped back on the bed, draping an arm over his eyes with a loud sigh. The mattress shook a little bit and Fenix thought he heard snickering from under the covers. Frowning, he pulled the duvet down to reveal Jared's head and see his poor attempts to hide his chuckle.

"Are you laughing at me?" Fenix asked incredulously.

"I kinda am. You're adorable," he said and hooked his arm around Fenix's waist, tugging him close. Fenix didn't comment, he just glared at Jared. God, he hated waking up with the damn alarm! "Don't glare at me, love. It turns me on," Jared said with a huge smile. Fenix had to bite his lip to stop his own smile from making an appearance. Maybe the alarm going off at 8:00 am wouldn't be so bad as long as he had Jared to wake up to every day. And he did have him, at least for the next three weeks. The thought cheered him up and he felt the corners of his mouth turning up.

Jared cupped Fenix's cheek and kissed him gently.

"Good morning," he whispered, nipping at Fenix's jaw. "Why are we getting up so early?"

"I have this radio interview today and wanted to prepare for it," Fenix said with a heavy sigh. "I also wanted to go to the theatre. I could use a work-out and I wanted to talk to Elijah Goodwin, the executive producer, in private," Fenix huffed, not happy that he had to wake up this early at all. At least when the show started he could sleep in as much as he wanted.

"Oh? Why? Is something wrong?" Jared asked, his brows furrowing.

"No, but he has all these interviews and TV appearances and photo shoots scheduled for me and we couldn't discuss it at the staff meeting. I need to know what he wants me to say, how he wants me to present the show. I've never done this before on such a large scale, and I'm afraid that I might say or do something stupid and damage the show's image," Fenix rambled nervously.

"I doubt that. The media is going to love you, trust me," Jared assured him before he kissed him again.

That statement brought back memories of last night. Fenix could remember Jared saying he loved him, but what if it was a heat of the moment thing? What if he didn't really mean it?

"Jared," he began, running his hands through Jared's hair. He leaned into the touch like a puppy and closed his eyes in bliss. "What you said last night..." Suddenly Fenix felt nervous to ask and blushed. But it was too late to go back now. "That... that you love me," he finished, meeting Jared's eyes. He was looking down at him with such adoration in his dark blue eyes that Fenix had his answer even before Jared said anything. "Did you really mean it?"

Jared traced Fenix's jaw line with his finger and cupped his cheek again.

"Yes. I mean it. I'm crazy in love with you, Fen."

Fenix beamed. He couldn't help it. His chest expanded with happiness and his gut tightened nervously. He knew Jared didn't need to hear it back right now, and that wasn't why he'd said it, but Fenix felt he might burst if he didn't say it because he felt it, bone deep.

"I love you, too," he whispered.

Jared's smile was gorgeous. He leaned down and took Fenix's mouth in a deep, wet kiss, and Fenix thought that if this was all it took to make Jared this happy, he'd say it every day.

CHAPTER TWELVE

Fenix

Fenix's interview was scheduled for 8:00 pm and he'd asked Jared to go with him for moral support. They were lucky the Capital FM headquarters was a ten minute walk from the theatre and they arrived with fifteen minutes to spare. Jared had hurried after his show was over, taking a quick shower and hastily putting on jeans and a t-shirt, running his hands through his hair and not bothering to dry or style it. Despite that, he still managed to look like an Abercrombie and Fitch model, and Fenix had to suppress the urge to jump him before they left the dressing room.

After their talk that morning and the amazing sex last night, Fenix felt calmer, more secure in their relationship, knowing that his feelings for Jared weren't one sided.

Walking into the Capital FM building, they were greeted by a smiling receptionist who informed them to go up to the fourth floor where the studio was.

"Hey, Fenix, nice to meet you, man. So glad you could make it," Dan Hoyt, the evening talk show host, greeted them as they walked into the studio. "And you brought Jared Hartley himself! That's a nice bonus," he grinned at Jared and extended his hand. "My wife and I are huge fans of your show, Jared. We've seen it twice already."

"Thank you, glad to hear it," Jared said politely and shook Dan's hand.

"So, are you guys doing the interview together?" Dan asked, going back behind his desk and sitting in his chair.

"No, Jared is here for moral support. I'm not used to this yet and I thought I could use a friend here with me," Fenix said, glancing at Jared nervously. They hadn't talked about what they would say if people asked if they were just friends. Now it was too late to discuss it ten minutes before the interview started. Dan met Fenix's eyes and smirked.

"That's cool," he said and put on his headphones, clicking something on the computer in front of him. "OK, let's get started. Fenix, you sit here in front of me. Put those headphones on and adjust the microphone so that it's close to you, but not too close," Dan directed and Fenix did as he was told. He felt nervous butterflies fluttering in his belly and his palms began to sweat.

That was ridiculous! He'd been performing on stage in front of big, demanding audiences. A simple, friendly radio interview where nobody could even see him shouldn't be a big deal. He needed to calm down. Dan seemed like a cool guy, he'd guide him through it. Right?

Fenix looked up after he was done adjusting the equipment and met Jared's eyes who had taken the chair next to Dan. He was watching him calmly and smiled when Fenix looked at him. 'You're gonna be fine' that smile said. Fenix knew it because he'd seen it a lot this afternoon when Jared tried to convince him that it would be OK and Fenix would do great. Right now, he sure as hell hoped that was true.

"We start in about forty seconds, right after the ad segment is over. I'm gonna ask you some questions and we're going to take some calls from listeners. Are you OK with that?" Dan asked.

"Yes," Fenix said, his voice shaking.

"Just be yourself, Fenix. People like that," Dan advised with an encouraging nod, and turned his attention back to the laptop screen.

The show started and Dan introduced Fenix as his guest for the next hour. He started asking Fenix questions about *Poison* and Fenix instantly relaxed, feeling competent and comfortable when he talked about his show.

"*Poison* is about a rock band called 'City of Shadows' – it follows them from the beginning, when the idea was born and they used to practise in a garage, through their early days, playing in clubs and small venues, all the way to making it big. It focuses on the relationship between the band members, their ups and downs, and offers a glimpse behind the scenes of what is really going on in a rock band," Fenix said when Dan asked what the musical was about.

"Sex, drugs, and rock and roll?" Dan offered playfully.

"Pretty much, yes," Fenix replied with a chuckle.

"I was told the show is getting a huge makeover to make it suitable for Queen Victoria's stage. Is that true?"

"Yes. The story will stay the same, but we'll be adding a couple of new songs and lots of special effects. We start rehearsals tomorrow."

"That's just three weeks before opening night. Will you be able to perfect it in time?" Dan asked curiously.

"I'm confident that we will. The team working on the show is amazing, there's nothing those guys can't do. The cast has been doing the show for almost a year now so we pretty much know it in our sleep, we just need to rehearse the new songs and dance routines. Oh, and learn how to avoid the pyro-effects," Fenix said, grinning.

"Pyro-effects?" Dan echoed.

"Yeah. There will be fire on stage. Lots of it," Fenix winked as Dan's lips turned up. He knew he had to catch the listeners interest without revealing too much, and he could see Dan appreciated that.

The next song and ad break was on and Fenix exhaled loudly.

"See? That wasn't so bad," Dan laughed.

Fenix nodded and met Jared's eyes for confirmation. He was staring at him with such open pride and adoration that Fenix wanted to throw the damn headphones off and jump into his arms. Jared must have read that on his face because he smirked and winked at him, taking a sip of his herbal tea.

Fenix caught Dan's gaze travelling between them just before he asked,

"Jared, would you mind if I introduced you, too? You're here anyway and we have a lot of time. Besides, you perform in the same theatre..." Dan trailed off.

Jared shook his head.

"I don't want to shift the focus away from *Poison*. I'm here to support Fenix, not advertise my own show," Jared said.

"We don't have to talk about *Of Kids and Monsters*. We can still talk about *Poison*. People would pay attention if Jared Hartley told them to go see a show," Dan coaxed. "It would be in everyone's interest if you took part in this conversation, Jared."

"Including yours," Jared said and smiled sweetly.

"Including mine," Dan confirmed without shame.

Jared met Fenix's eyes across the table, silently asking if he was OK with that. Fenix nodded. Why wouldn't he be? He wouldn't even care if Jared wanted to plug his own show, he'd be happy to do it himself. But the fact that Jared wanted to remain in the sidelines and let Fenix take the whole limelight meant a lot to him. Fenix knew how cut throat this business was. He personally knew people who would sell their friends, families and lovers to get ahead. Jared wasn't like that at all, and that was one of the many reasons Fenix's heart expanded with love for this man.

"Good news, people," Dan began when the break was over and they were back on air. "Fenix brought a little friend with him today, and I managed to convince him to crawl out of the shadows and talk to us." Dan paused for dramatic effect. "It's Jared Hartley, everybody!" he pronounced and the sound engineer played the applause effect.

Jared laughed and said hello, and Dan's eyes sparkled with satisfaction. He was very pleased with the way the show was going and it showed.

"So, Jared, tell us the inside scoop on *Poison* since Fenix here is so tight lipped," Dan began and winked at Fenix.

"There's nothing to tell. It's all top secret. Even I don't know anything yet. But I'm very excited to see the show myself. I've seen Fenix dance and I'd pay to watch just that. The whole production is going to be mind-blowing."

They chatted a bit more about the show – Dan tried to coax Fenix into revealing more about it, but he resisted. It was made very clear by the producers that, as much as they wanted to generate interest, they didn't want anything specific being revealed. Fenix had to use quite a lot of charm and witty responses so that he didn't seem rude. It must have worked, because both Dan and Jared were smiling and in a very good mood. They took some calls from listeners and the reaction to the musical was very positive. Before he knew it, Fenix felt relaxed and at ease as if he'd done that a million times before.

"You guys seem like good friends," Dan said after the last caller disconnected. Fenix didn't like the mischief in his eyes and momentarily stiffened again. "Is that all? Are you just friends?"

Jared looked at Fenix, calm and collected, and Fenix knew what the next thing that came out of his mouth would be.

"You're very perceptive, Dan," Jared drawled as he held Fenix's eyes. "We're not just friends. I'm in love with Fenix, and I'm pretty sure he loves me too." Jared couldn't help the slight blush and the smile that spread across his mouth, even though he bit his lip and tried to contain it. Fenix beamed back at him and suddenly wished they were alone.

"Why are you so sure?" Dan teased.

"Because he told me this morning," Jared replied without missing a beat. Fenix's heart was pounding. It was one thing to say that to each other in private, in *bed*, and completely another to declare it on the radio. He wanted to jump off the chair, throw his fist in the air and *celebrate*. Jared had just announced publicly he loved him and that made him incredibly proud and happy.

"Wow, I knew by the looks you guys were giving each other that there was something there, but I never thought you were in love! Didn't you meet last week?" Dan asked.

"Yeah, we did. And we haven't spent a night apart ever since," Jared replied easily, leaning back in his chair.

"OK, we're going to talk more about this in the last part of the show. Stay tuned," Dan said and cut to an ad break.

Dan grinned, looking between Jared and Fenix who were still staring at each other, processing what had just happened. His smile faded a bit.

"I hope I didn't cause any trouble for you... You could have denied it, I didn't mean..." Dan began.

"No, it's fine. We're not hiding or anything. We just hadn't discussed when and how we were going to go public. But the cat's out of the bag now so..." Jared said. Fenix still hadn't spoken. He didn't know what to say. He wanted to talk to Jared in private, but that was not possible right now. "Fen? Are you OK with this?" Jared asked with concern.

Fenix's heart skipped a beat and he flushed all over whenever Jared called him Fen. He'd only done that when they were alone, usually in the middle of fucking. Using that nickname now made Fenix's gut clench as visions of last night pulsed in his brain.

"Yeah. Of course I am," he said, trying to get his body's reaction under control. "I'm hoping Elijah Goodwin won't have a hissy fit over it. He was very specific how it was all about the show for the next few months and we should be on our best behaviour, not filling the gossip columns with our antics. That was a direct quote. He was looking at Ned when he said it, but I guess it goes for all of us."

Fenix's phone vibrated in his pocket and he fished it out.

"Shit," he muttered. "Speak of the devil. I have to take this, I won't be long," he said and threw an apologetic look at Dan, who waved him off. Fenix stalked out of the room to take the executive producer's call.

"Hello?" he said cautiously, putting the phone to his ear.

"Fenix. What the hell is going on?" Elijah Goodwin began in his booming voice. Fenix took a breath to prepare himself for the inevitable fight. He was not going to act remorseful for something he was definitely not sorry for. "We didn't discuss this today when we talked about the promotional campaign! Did you come up with it on the spot?"

"Um, what?" Fenix asked in confusion.

"The 'I'm in love with Jared Hartley' plot! I must say I'm impressed. That will attract the media's attention in all the right ways. Jared is a very respected part of the community, they're eating from his hand as it is. If he says people should see *Poison* then they will," the producer rambled with glee.

"This is not some kind of a publicity stunt, Mr Goodwin. We're in fact dating. For real." Fenix had to raise his voice to be able to interrupt the producer's rant.

"Oh. Really?" he asked doubtfully.

"Yeah, really. Why are you so surprised all of a sudden?"

"Well, because you met for the first time last week, didn't you?"

"Yes, we did," Fenix said with a sigh. He was so tired of having to explain his relationship with Jared to everyone.

"Oh. Well, it's none of my business. But, I have to say, that's even better! You don't even have to pretend..."

"Mr Goodwin, with all due respect, my relationship with Jared is not going to turn into some media circus. It has nothing to do with the show or with the promotional tour we discussed. Announcing it live on air was an impulsive decision, but I'm not sorry we did it. It would have come out sooner or later anyway."

"Of course. I agree. I'm just saying that it could affect the show's publicity in a positive light, Fenix. You should be happy about that. A lot of people's careers depend on *Poison*'s success, including yours," said Goodwin flatly.

Fenix understood what the producer was saying, and he knew he was right, but he was not in the mood for arguing right now. Fenix would never use his relationship with Jared to promote *Poison* no matter what anyone thought the benefits would be.

"I have to go, Mr Goodwin. The ad break is over and they're waiting for me," Fenix said, his voice becoming flat.

If the producer had caught the change in Fenix's voice he didn't comment on it. They said their goodbyes and Fenix returned to the studio to find Dan and Jared chatting with a caller.

"No, Jenny from Kingston, I don't have any tattoos," Jared said playfully, obviously answering Jenny's question. She giggled and fired back,

"How about Fenix? Does he have any?"

"No. And I've checked. Thoroughly," Jared said with a smirk as Fenix took his chair and put on his headphones giving the thumbs up to Dan.

Jenny giggled again and Fenix found the sound extremely annoying through the headphones.

"I haven't seen it myself yet, but I bet if you come to see the show Fenix will treat you to a few shirtless scenes and you can check for yourself. Right, Fenix?"

"Oh, yeah. There are shirtless scenes involved," Fenix replied without hesitation. He might have reservations about using his personal relationship to promote the show, but he had no such qualms regarding his own body.

"Alright, Jenny, that was a lot of personal questions even though I warned you about those," Dan interrupted Jenny's annoying giggle and disconnected the line. "I'm afraid that's all for tonight, folks. Thank you so much to our special guests Jared Hartley and Fenix Bergman." The sound engineer cued in the applause again. "Don't forget to go see *Poison* when it opens at Queen Victoria on the twenty second of September."

The ad break signalling the end of the show started and Dan stood up taking off his headphones. He shook hands with both Fenix and Jared, and thanked them for the great guest appearance. He wished them good luck with their shows and invited them to come back any time.

Out on the street, it was already dark and a bit chilly. Fenix shivered in his t-shirt and wrapped his arms around himself. Jared hugged him around the shoulders and pulled him close as they walked.

"Steven Hamilton texted me when you went out to take your call. He says he's happy, and I quote, with the development. He thought I was using the opportunity to promote my own musical while you are promoting yours," Jared said and shook his head disbelievingly.

"Yeah, I guessed," Fenix replied, and summarised his conversation with his own producer. "I refuse to use *us* to promote anything, Jared. I'm ready to whore myself out to the media – give them their interviews, pose shirtless for their photo shoots, smile while we discuss the same thing over and over again. But I refuse to use our relationship as a promotional stunt."

"I know, love, me too. I'll set my team straight tomorrow in person. While we're not going to hide, we're definitely not going to do a reality show either," Jared said and hugged the shivering Fenix closer. "Let's go home. I want to warm you up properly," he said with a cheeky grin.

"By taking off my clothes?" Fenix asked, raising an eyebrow in amusement.

"Exactly."

CHAPTER THIRTEEN

Jared

The following two weeks flew by in a blur. Fenix was busy promoting the show, doing interviews and chat shows, photo shoots, and guest appearances. Jared had been right – the media absolutely adored him. He managed to charm every single journalist, photographer and talk show host, and there wasn't a day when he wasn't in the papers. Fenix was quickly becoming one of London's promising new stars and they haven't even seen him in action.

Jared accompanied him whenever he could, and while everyone was quite curious about their relationship, Fenix let it be known he wouldn't discuss it publicly. Most people respected that, and those who didn't were stonewalled with charismatic smiles and clever conversation until they either gave up asking or the interview was over before they knew what had hit them.

Fenix was born to be in the spotlight. He was getting better and better every day and Jared couldn't have been more proud of him. He was quite happy to step aside and let Fenix do his thing, offering support when he needed it, but otherwise not meddling. Fenix was capable of fighting his own battles and paving his own future.

Jared was falling deeper in love with him with every single day that passed.

They were both busy with Jared performing four days a week and supervising the renovations on his home, and with Fenix running around London on promo gigs. There were days when they could barely see each other and Jared couldn't wait to get home to Fenix at night.

It was perfect. Fenix was perfect. And Jared was so happy.

Everyone seemed to notice the positive change and complimented him all the time. Even Adam admitted Jared looked good and 'maybe his relationship with Fenix wasn't a hoax'. Jared took his friend out for a beer that evening after the show. Fenix was filming a chat show so Jared had a couple of hours to kill before he got back, and Adam seemed... lonely. For the first time since he'd known Adam, Jared realised his best friend was in desperate need of having someone not just for the night. And it wasn't his pink new relationship glasses talking. The loneliness was rolling off Adam in waves, even though he'd never admit it. He'd never been a relationship guy – the more, the better was his motto. Had he finally had enough? Was Adam finally ready for a relationship? Jared wasn't about to ask. He knew Adam would only get defensive and they'd get nowhere. But he made a mental note to keep a closer eye on his friend and be there for him if needed.

Before they left the pub, Adam suggested they go to a club the following weekend. There would be live music at Lono's and they all needed a night out. Jared agreed, promising to let everyone know before he hugged Adam goodbye and headed home to Fenix.

Lono's was crowded. *Nix* – the band that was playing that night – obviously had a lot of local fans, even though Jared had never heard of them before. Adam seemed in a better mood than earlier that week when they'd gone to the pub. He led their group to a private table with a crescent shaped sofa big enough for all of them.

Fenix had readily jumped at the idea for a night out when Jared mentioned it. He'd invited Joy and Ned along, as well as some of his other co-stars. Both Jared and Fenix needed a night off to relax, have some fun, and not think about work. Fenix's big opening night was only two weeks away, making him more and more anxious. Jared offered his quiet support all the time, reassuring him that he'd be great, that people would love the show. When that didn't work, he'd proceed to make love to Fenix until he let go of all the worry and anxiety, his body and his mind consumed by pleasure.

Jared could not get enough of his lover. The more he fucked him, the more he wanted to fuck him. He craved their nights together like air after he'd been underwater for too long. The feel of Fenix's willing, pliable body underneath him was addicting, and Jared had long ago decided to give in to his addiction.

"Hey," Fenix whispered in his ear, snapping Jared out of his increasingly erotic thoughts. "I'm going to get us a drink," he said and squeezed past Jared, dragging his palm along his stomach as he did so. Jared watched him saunter away, admiring his grace and beauty, his perfect ass in those tight jeans, his long legs and lean muscled arms...

"I know, it's nauseating," Jared heard Adam say and unwillingly dragged his eyes away from Fenix, trying to pay at least some attention to the conversation going on around the table.

"What is?" he asked absentmindedly.

Joy giggled and Adam rolled his eyes, throwing an arm around her shoulders and whispering something in her ear. The rest of their party was engaged in an animated conversation – Ned was trying to be the centre of attention as usual, waving his arms as he told some story that had everyone staring at him with amusement.

Fenix returned to the table with a tray full of drinks and passed them around. He squeezed to sit next to Jared as everyone picked their drinks and raised their glasses in salute. Jared clicked his Cuba Libre to Fenix's, took a long sip and, after leaving his glass back on the table, cupped Fenix's neck and brought his mouth to his. There was no slow introduction to the kiss. Jared thrust his tongue inside Fenix's mouth and felt him yelp in surprise, but it quickly turned into a moan of pleasure. Jared tasted the alcohol on Fenix's tongue and for some reason that urged him to explore deeper. Harder. Fenix responded equally, gripping the front of Jared's shirt and tugging him even closer, licking the inside of Jared's mouth and tangling their tongues together.

"Hey! Hey!" Adam shouted over the music, and amazingly Jared heard him over the lust filled haze of his brain. His hold on Fenix loosened, and with one last nip at his lower lip, Jared released him. Fenix's eyes were dark and he looked dazed, as if he didn't know where he was or what was happening. Jared pulled him into a hug and as Fenix buried his face in the crook of Jared's neck, he could feel the short, frantic breaths Fenix was taking against his skin. "What the fuck, man? Nobody is nearly drunk enough to witness your necking," Adam said, trying to sound as if he was joking, but watching them with a carefully blank expression.

Jared took a look around the table – nobody was paying them any interest. Ned was still being an attention whore, having drawn Joy into his circle of admirers as he continued to talk and gesticulate, and the club was dark and loud enough that nobody at the neighbouring tables would mind their kissing either.

"Get on with it, then," Jared nodded towards Adam's drink. "Because there's a lot more where that came from." He smiled sweetly at Adam and tangled his hand in Fenix's hair, tugging him off his shoulder and bringing his mouth to his again. This time he went slow and gentle, and Fenix didn't resist.

It turned out *Nix* were great. Their sound was an interesting mix of alternative rock, techno beat, and classic rock solos. The lead singer was something else – the guy's voice was strong and smooth, with a unique tilt at the end of the high notes. He was no taller than five nine, slim, with wild black hair with blue streaks. Even from afar, Jared could tell he was an arrogant motherfucker.

Jared was dancing with Joy, who had complained that he only had eyes for Fenix and she wanted 'a piece of that too'. Fenix had laughed and pushed Jared her way as Ned appeared out of nowhere and snagged Fenix around the waist, taking him away.

Jared spun Joy in his arms, enjoying her skilful dancing when she didn't skip a step or lose her balance. She twirled gracefully a few times before Jared pulled her back into his arms as she giggled. His eyes scanned the overcrowded club in search of Fenix and Ned. He spotted them a few feet away, dancing and laughing about something. Jared's gaze fell on Adam next, who wasn't dancing, but was sitting at the table, nursing his beer and staring at the singer. Jared knew that stare. He didn't even know if the guy was gay, but he would bet he was going to end up in Adam's bed tonight. Sparing a glance in the direction of the stage, Jared noticed that the singer was also staring at Adam, and quite challengingly at that. His eyes were an unnerving deep grey, their intensity brought out even more by the dark eye liner he was wearing.

Adam must have felt Jared watching him because he dragged his eyes away from the stage and looked straight at him, raising his drink in silent cheers and smirking. Jared shook his head and laughed, giving his friend the thumbs up. Singer boy looked like he could provide a decent night of fucking, and Adam seemed like he needed that.

Jared could barely contain his desire for Fenix on the cab ride home. The air between them had crackled with sexual energy all night long, and being confined in a car with Fenix, not able to touch him, was excruciating. The moment the front door closed behind them, Jared pounced, taking Fenix's mouth in a rough, demanding kiss. Fenix responded by completely submitting to Jared's need, pressing his body to Jared's and weaving his arms around his neck. Jared growled, grabbing the back of Fenix's thighs as he picked him up, without interrupting their frantic kissing. Fenix wrapped his legs around Jared's waist, grunting as Jared slammed his back against the door. Jared kissed along his jaw, nipped at his chin, bit his earlobe, all the while trying to hold Fenix and undo his jeans at the same time.

"Baby..." Fenix moaned when Jared put him back down and managed to undo the zipper, pulling down his jeans and boxers. He fisted Fenix's erection, jerking it roughly a few times, inciting a slow, needy groan from Fenix. Jared snapped his hips against Fenix's, but the friction wasn't enough through the denim. He wanted skin on skin contact and he wanted it now. Abruptly, Jared stepped away from Fenix and unzipped his jeans with shaking hands. He took out the pre-lubricated condom he had stashed in his back pocket, and kicked the jeans off, followed closely by his underwear. He noticed Fenix had gotten rid of his own clothes and pawed at his t-shirt, discarding it on the floor.

Jared backed Fenix against the door again, kissing him, touching him everywhere he could. Fenix's skin was so smooth and warm, and Jared couldn't get enough.

"Jared... Stop fucking around and fuck me," Fenix hissed when Jared took his cock into his hand again. Jared snickered and let go of Fenix long enough to put the condom over his erection. When he looked back at Fenix, he was watching him with a mischievous grin. Jared didn't have time to ask what Fenix had in mind before Fenix raised his leg gracefully and propped it on Jared's shoulder with ease.

"God, I love how bendy you are," Jared rasped, wrapping his arms around Fenix's waist and tugging him closer.

"I know," Fenix whispered, nipping at Jared's neck and clutching his shoulders for support. "Now, fuck me," he said, barely a huff against Jared's skin.

Thankfully, they were the same height, or that arrangement would have been extremely uncomfortable. Jared fumbled a little before he managed to position his cock at Fenix's entrance and push in slowly, groaning at the feeling of tight heat enveloping him. Fenix whimpered and shivered in Jared's arms, bending his other leg so that he took all of Jared's length inside.

"You OK?" Jared asked, managing to control himself enough to keep from thrusting immediately after penetration. Fenix nodded and made a desperate sound, wiggling his hips in encouragement.

Jared started moving in long, snapping thrusts, resting his forehead against Fenix's shoulder to watch his cock as it glided in and out of his lover. He wasn't going to last long. This was all too erotic – Fenix's leg hitched up on his shoulder, his needy, unashamed moans, his sleek body trembling with pleasure and glistening with sweat, Jared's dick sinking inside him...

Jared palmed Fenix's cock and started jerking him off in the same rhythm as he pounded into him. Fenix gasped loudly and shouted Jared's name as he came, his body shaking and his ass clenching around Jared. Suddenly it was too much to bear. Jared's orgasm hit him like a tornado and swept him off his feet. He sagged against Fenix who managed to keep them both upright even though he had only one leg for leverage.

Jared felt Fenix's leg slide down his arm but couldn't move to help. He heard Fenix whispering something in his ear but was still too dazed to understand or move. It took him a few moments to catch his breath and clear his mind, but eventually, Jared relaxed his grip on Fenix and moved away, meeting his eyes. Fenix was smiling and his eyes were alight with satisfaction.

"That was..." he began and his smile spread into a full blown grin. "I wanna do it again."

Jared laughed and kissed him slowly.

"Any time," he said against his lips and kissed him deeper, swallowing Fenix's moan of approval.

CHAPTER FOURTEEN

Jared

The following Tuesday, James Seymour called Jared to tell him his flat was ready. Jared was caught by surprise – he knew the work was going well, but he still had expected it to run past the arranged deadline. Somehow it hadn't seemed like it had been three weeks since he'd come to stay with Fenix. Time had flown so fast that Jared hadn't had any time to think about moving back in his flat and how it would feel.

Fenix had two magazine interviews scheduled for the day and couldn't accompany Jared to see the renovations, so Jared all but raced back to his place, eager to see it fully done.

James met him there and walked him through everything they'd done.

It was amazing! The bedroom he'd wanted was perfect – an elegant staircase led to a half-level big enough for a bed, a wardrobe and bedside tables. The bed had arrived two days ago and they had assembled it for him. All the other stuff he'd ordered – the sofa, the coffee table, even the sheets and towels, were neatly arranged in their places. The kitchen and the bathroom were both brand new with polished appliances and fittings. The floor heating worked well and sent pleasant warmth through Jared's feet.

The space under the bedroom was a bit awkward and small, and Jared had requested a few bookshelves to be fitted on the walls. He'd thought it would make a cosy book nook where he could put an armchair, and relax with a good book from time to time. Seeing it done, Jared realised the space was not as small as he'd initially anticipated. He could even fit a desk as well. The shelves on the walls would be able to hold lots of books and Jared could already imagine filling them with his favourite paperbacks.

There was a lot more Jared needed to buy like a TV, some more furniture, plates, cutlery and kitchen equipment, curtains, some paintings, wall art... But the place was habitable and Jared couldn't wait to move back in here.

The thought sent a pang of regret to his chest. He had to leave Fenix's place. As much as he loved his flat, he'd much rather spend his nights in a bed with Fenix than in a luxury accommodation that lacked... well, Fenix.

They hadn't spent a night apart since they'd met. Jared's heart physically ached to even think of a time when he'd have to spend the whole night alone. He knew it was ridiculous – he was a grown man! He'd managed to sleep twenty five years without Fenix, so he was definitely capable of doing that again. Right?

And besides, they'd still spend the night together. Fenix was welcome here any time he wanted and Jared was certain the same was true for him. So why was his chest still so tight with pain? And why did it feel like his stomach was turning up side down?

It was still early when Jared got back to Fenix's flat and hastily packed his stuff. It would be at least a few hours until Fenix got back, so there was no point in waiting. Jared decided he could take advantage of his day off, move his stuff back in, and go shopping for the necessities. Otherwise he'd have to wait until next week when he had a free day again.

He went back to his place to leave his bags and called Adam.

"Hello?" Adam's gruff voice sounded on the other end of the line. Jared blinked in confusion – was he asleep? At 2:00 pm?

"Hey. Did I wake you?"

"Um... yeah," Adam said, sounding distracted. "I was taking a nap."

"A nap?" Jared asked flatly.

"Yes." Adam's voice suggested he wouldn't appreciate discussing the matter any further, so Jared rolled his eyes and decided to drop it. Pick your battles and all.

"Anyway, do you wanna come to Zone with me? I need to buy some stuff. I just moved back in," Jared said excitedly.

"Yeah? They finished on time?"

"Yep. It's amazing! You should come see it. Pick me up in about fifteen minutes and we can go shopping afterwards."

They walked around Zone for a while, Jared rambling about nothing in particular and picking up stuff along the way. Adam seemed out of it. He talked and joked, even helped Jared choose what to get, but something was off.

"Are you alright? You seem a bit... distracted," Jared asked as they sat in the store's coffee shop for a break. Adam didn't answer immediately as if he was wondering how much to say. That in itself raised Jared's warning bells – Adam rarely had any mouth filter.

"You remember that guy, Charlie Shields, Nix's lead singer?" Adam asked, unwilling to meet Jared's eyes.

"Yeah..." Jared drawled. He hadn't actually seen Adam go home with him, but he was pretty sure that was what had happened.

"We fucked," he announced flatly.

"OK. Figured that might be the case judging by the looks you were giving each other during his set." Jared paused, giving

Adam an opportunity to elaborate, and when he didn't, Jared probed, "So what's the problem? Is that why you're mopping around like that? He wasn't a good lay?"

"No. He was a phenomenal lay. We kinda went out again after that," Adam said quietly, finally meeting Jared's eyes. Jared would have laughed if it wasn't for the misery he saw in them. Adam rarely followed sex with a date – it was usually the other way around, and a date wasn't always mandatory.

"I don't get why are you so bummed over this."

"Because I really like him, " Adam said in exasperation, rubbing his face with the palm of his hands.

"And that's a problem? Adam, there's nothing wrong with wanting to sleep with someone more than once and actually liking their company out of the bedroom."

"It's not that. He doesn't feel the same way," Adam said and bit his lip.

Wow. Jared was stunned into silence. His friend had finally developed some feelings for another guy and it wasn't mutual? That was cruel.

"How do you know?" Jared asked carefully.

"I can feel it. He likes it when we're together, and we have a great connection in bed. But then he never stays the night. He always sneaks out the moment I fall asleep," Adam said and sighed heavily. "But what's even more pathetic is that won't stop me from seeing him again."

"Are you in love with him?" Jared asked cautiously, trying to keep his voice as normal as possible.

"No! How could I be! I've known him for three days."

Jared raised an eyebrow at that, biting his tongue against a comment. He could have said something about karma and how Adam gave him so much grief over Fenix, and right now he was in a similar position. Only, Jared had lucked out that Fenix had felt the same way. He didn't even want to imagine how crushed he'd have been if Fenix had rejected him like that.

"I don't know what to tell you, man," Jared said with a sigh. "I mean, I'm happy that you finally found someone you want more than just a one night stand with, and it sucks that he might not feel that way. But you're right, it's been just three days. Maybe things will change, maybe he needs more time. Ride it out, see what happens."

Adam nodded and took a long sip of his coffee. Jared tried to lighten the mood and cheer him up, so they chatted some more before he walked Adam home, declining the invitation for dinner. All he wanted was to go home, unpack all the things he'd bought, and call Fenix.

"Hey," Fenix greeted him when he picked up on the third ring. "Your things are gone," he stated, not too pleased.

"Yeah. The flat was really ready, I couldn't believe it when I saw it. So I went back to your place and packed my stuff. I'm officially not homeless anymore," Jared said and laughed. Fenix didn't comment. "And besides," he went on, "you're probably glad to get rid of me. Have the place to yourself again," he finished, only half joking. He knew Fenix didn't mind him staying at his place, but he felt like the situation forced them into living together. Jared wasn't sure Fenix would have made that choice willingly.

"No, I'm not," Fenix said coldly. "How could you sneak around like that, Jared? Just pack up your stuff and go without even saying goodbye?"

"What? Goodbye?" Jared chuckled. "We're still going to see each other every day, Fen. It's not like I moved to Australia."

"Whatever. I have to go. I have chicken teriyaki for two to eat all by myself," Fenix said, disconnecting before Jared could say another word.

What the fuck? Jared hadn't really thought that leaving would be such a big deal. He'd miss Fenix, he'd realised that the moment he'd set foot in his flat, but he hadn't thought Fenix would react that badly.

In hindsight, it did seem a bit ungrateful of him. Fenix had opened his home so readily for Jared, and what had he done? Packed and left without even telling him.

Jesus, Jared was bad at this relationship stuff. He'd never had to think how his actions would affect the other person because he'd never been in a real relationship before.

He had to apologise and make this right. Fenix loved him, he'd miss him just as much. He could have at least stayed the night.

Jared tried calling but Fenix didn't pick up. A cold chill ran down his spine at the very thought of hurting Fenix, even unintentionally. He called again and again, until he heard Fenix's voice on the other end of the line.

"Jared, stop calling."

"Please, love, don't hang up. I'm sorry, OK? I didn't think of it like that. I really thought you'd be glad to have the place to yourself again. As for not waiting for you to get back – I wanted to take advantage of my day off and move all my stuff back here. I knew I was gonna call you later and see you tomorrow anyway so I didn't think it was such a big deal," Jared rattled off without even pausing for breath.

Fenix sighed loudly.

"It's OK. I overreacted, I'm sorry. I just... when I got back and every trace of you was gone..." he paused as his voice wavered. "I panicked. I knew you'd move back to your place eventually, I was just shocked when it happened so fast and so abruptly."

"I miss you, too, Fen," Jared said quietly. He'd had such a busy day that he hadn't had time to *be* in his apartment, all alone. It suddenly felt very lonely and cold.

"Maybe it'll be good for us to spend some nights apart?" Fenix said doubtfully.

"Maybe..."

Jared felt like there was an invisible string connecting him to Fenix and right now it was so taut that it might snap any minute.

"OK... Well, goodnight then. I'll see you tomorrow," Fenix said.

"Goodnight, Fenix."

Jared disconnected the call and felt empty. Fenix's quiet 'goodnight' had sent a sharp pang of pain straight to his heart. Jared wanted to say 'I love you' but he hadn't. What was wrong with him? He also didn't want to say goodnight over the phone. He wanted to whisper it to Fenix as he lay curled in his arms every single night for the rest of his life.

The thought hit him like a slap with a wet rag.

That was it. He didn't want to be here in this big, empty space. He didn't want to sleep alone. He didn't think it would be good for them to spend some nights apart. All he wanted right now was Fenix, right here with him, and he'd sell his soul to the devil to get that if he had to.

Jared grabbed his wallet and his keys and ran down the stairs. He thought about getting a cab but didn't see any around, so he jogged to the tube station, jumping on the first train and hoping like hell Fenix would agree to what Jared was about to ask.

Jared knocked on Fenix's door loudly. It was past 10:00 pm, but Jared knew Fenix never went to bed early. He was sure Fenix was still up. Why wasn't he opening the door? Maybe he should have called. Knocking on the door again, Jared took out his phone and dialled Fenix's number. He heard the phone ringing inside and hurried steps coming closer to the door.

"Jesus! What's going on?" Fenix swung the door open, holding his ringing phone in one hand. He had his bathrobe on and his hair was still dripping from the shower. Jared drank him in, flushed and wet, and could not for the life of him resist kissing him. Without saying a word, Jared grabbed the front of the robe and pulled Fenix close. He took his mouth in a possessive, nearly violent kiss, pushing them both inside the apartment and kicking the door closed.

"Jared?" he said questioningly between kisses. Jared slowed the kiss down and wrapped his arms around Fenix affectionately.

"*How can I call the lone night good, though thy sweet wishes wing its flight? Be it not said, thought, understood – then it will be – good night,*" Jared quoted Shelley quietly, still clutching to Fenix. He felt Fenix nod, but he was silent. Jared was afraid to pull back and look into his eyes. "I never want to say goodnight to you over the phone ever again, Fen. I don't think spending some nights apart is good. I want you in my bed every night," he said, finally leaning back to meet Fenix's eyes. They were shiny with unshed tears, making the pale blue appear almost translucent. "I love you so much, baby. I want you to move in with me."

"Are you sure?" Fenix asked, smiling hopefully.

"I've never been more sure of anything," Jared said and caressed Fenix's cheek. He leaned into the touch and closed his eyes for a moment.

"OK."

Jared laughed with relief. He hadn't realised how tense he'd been until now. His shoulders sagged and he felt twenty pounds lighter.

He picked Fenix up who yelped in surprise that immediately turned into laughter, carrying him to the bedroom to get that damn robe off him and celebrate.

CHAPTER FIFTEEN

Jared

Jared took his place next to Adam in Queen Victoria's Dress Circle. It was *Poison*'s opening night and Fenix had insisted they watch it from the seats instead of backstage. He wanted Jared to experience the show as it was meant to be, and not to be distracted by the madness behind the scenes. Jared had agreed – he'd have plenty of opportunities to watch it from backstage later.

Fenix had been a nervous wreck all day. Jared could sympathise – he knew how it felt to open the show you've worked so hard on in front of a huge audience.

"You OK?" Adam asked him, noticing that Jared wouldn't stop bouncing his knee and looking around anxiously.

"Yeah. I'm just nervous for him. I can practically feel him standing behind the curtain over there."

Adam patted Jared's knee and gave him an encouraging smile.

Soon, the lights dimmed, and the music signalling the show was about to begin started playing. The audience quieted down, an air of excitement and expectation falling like an invisible cloak over the hall.

That's it. That's Fenix's big night. Nothing is going to be the same after tonight, Jared thought, mentally crossing his fingers, wishing with his whole being that everything would be fine. He knew how many things could go wrong in a live show, and he prayed that nothing would spoil Fenix's big night.

Abruptly, the hall went absolutely dark. The audience stilled to a point where they were barely breathing. A moment later, a bass line sounded, loud and clear in the darkness. People gasped in surprise. A drum beat joined the bass line, followed by an electric guitar.

> *I knew what I was getting into was reckless.*
> *I knew I might end up dead in a ditch instead of at the top*
> *of the charts*
> *I knew I should have known better*
> *And yet I jumped head on*
> *And God knows I enjoyed the free fall*

Fenix's voice sounded over the music. It was smooth and seductive, with a hint of danger. Jared had never heard him talk like that before.

Hit it, Fenix shouted, and in the next moment the curtain fell down and the music really started. The song was fast and pure, old school rock and roll. Jared's cheeks hurt, but he couldn't stop smiling.

Fenix appeared on stage through a gust of fog, the lights playing tricks on the eyes and making him seem sinister. Dangerous. His blond hair was styled messily with his bangs hanging over his face. He wore heavy black eye make-up around his icy blue eyes that made them seem almost menacing. The tight leather pants, cut off black vest with a phoenix rising from the ashes at the front, solid biker boots and various leather cuffs on his wrists, completed the rock star look.

He was striking.

Jared could not look away. His voice, his movements, his whole attitude on stage was mesmerising. It was a far cry from the happy, easy-going Fenix Jared knew and loved, and yet he pulled it off effortlessly.

Fenix danced, sang, and acted his heart out on the stage tonight. The musical was nothing like Jared had ever seen – it was edgy, loud, controversial. There were sex scenes and drug use, and at one point, just like Fenix had said on the radio, there were pyro-effects that made the people in the first few rows yelp in surprise, cringing away. Joy played Fenix's love interest and the woman that led him to his eventual doom. She drove him crazy with lust and jealousy until he overdosed and almost died. That seemed to shake Fenix's character – Ben Amery – out of his obsession and he cleaned up his act, leading his band to the top of the charts once again.

It was breathtaking to watch. The script, the dance routines, the songs, the special effects, the performance – Jared could not find a single fault in anything. He loved every second of it, and he was so proud of his boyfriend that he felt ten feet tall. He was glad that he'd listened to Fenix and hadn't tried to sneak in on one of the rehearsals. *Poison* was something that needed to be experienced in its full glory.

When it was over, the cast were treated to a standing ovation. They came out three times to bow and thank the audience. Fenix's eyes found Jared's in the crowd and he grinned so widely that Jared almost ran on stage and kissed the hell out of him. Ever since he'd first seen him Jared had known Fenix was a natural born star. Now the whole world knew it too.

Jared waited for Fenix in their dressing room. He'd snuck out as the curtain fell and knew Fenix wouldn't be long. God, he couldn't wait to see him! Jared was so turned on that even thinking of Fenix on that stage sent painful waves of arousal through his body and straight to his cock. It took all the willpower he possessed not to go into the bathroom and relief the pressure.

He sprawled on the sofa and ran his hand along the length of his erection through his jeans. Just then, the dressing room door opened and Fenix walked in, talking to someone and stopping mid stride as he saw Jared. His eyes flashed with something dark and primal, and he spun around, hastily getting rid of whoever was with him. Jared was too far gone in the haze of his desire to care.

Fenix slammed the door closed, turned the lock, and took the distance between them in three long strides. He was still wearing his stage clothes and make-up, and Jared whimpered at the sight of him. Fenix climbed on the sofa between Jared's legs, pushing his thighs apart with his knees. He fell ungracefully on top of Jared, crashing their lips together in an open mouthed, urgent kiss. Fenix caught Jared's lower lip between his teeth and pulled, soothing the pain with a couple of licks, then nipping all along his jaw and neck. He panted, moaned, and growled all at the same time, dry humping Jared until he thought he was going to explode.

Jared had never been so aroused, ever. All he could hear, all he could feel and think about was Fenix on top of him, kissing him, touching him, biting him...

"Jesus, Fen!" Jared managed to grind out. "Please, please, baby. I want you to fuck me. I need you. I can't..." his voice completely cut off when Fenix nipped below his ear, hard. Jared yelled his name again and started begging, writhing underneath Fenix, making desperate sounds and way past caring. His whole body was trembling, alive under Fenix's touch.

Fenix leaned back long enough to discard his t-shirt and unzip his pants, pawing at Jared's clothes at the same time. Jared sat up and made a quick job of undressing. He lay back on the sofa, naked, his cock swollen, pulsing and erect on top of his belly.

Fenix stood up, took his pants and underwear off, and leaned down to kiss Jared messily.

"Stay," he commanded and headed to the wardrobe. He came back a moment later, holding a condom and already opening the bottle of lube, slicking his fingers. Laying back on top of Jared, Fenix pushed his tongue inside his mouth, licking and probing and conquering. Jared felt a cool lubricated finger slide inside him and made a sound of protest.

"No, don't. I don't want that."

Fenix pulled back and looked at him questioningly. They always prepared each other before they fucked, just in case. Pain wasn't in their list of kinks. But Jared was too aroused, and if Fenix started stretching him with his fingers, he'd come on the spot. "Please, no prep. And..." Jared bit his lip, not sure if that was the right moment to discuss this, but he desperately wanted Fenix's bare cock inside him. "Skip the condom, too." Fenix's eyes widened in surprise.

"Are you sure?" he asked.

"Yes. I'm clean, and I trust you."

Jared was sure Fenix wasn't fucking around. He trusted him completely when he said he loved him. They were living together, were committed to each other, and Jared saw no reason to keep using condoms.

Fenix nodded, his fingers trembling as he palmed the bottle of lube again. He slicked his bare cock liberally and positioned himself on top of Jared, their chests so close that their hearts beat together. Fenix pushed the head of his cock inside Jared. He tensed, breathing heavily through the initial sting. Jared wanted this, so fucking much, it hurt more not to have Fenix inside him. Running his hand along Fenix's ribs, Jared grabbed his ass and pushed it down while thrusting his hips up at the same time. Fenix groaned when his cock was balls deep inside Jared and his body stilled.

"Come on, baby. Move," Jared whispered. Fenix buried his face in the crook of Jared's neck and he could feel his wet, gasping breaths.

"I need a second," he rasped. "Fuck, Jared. You feel so good I'm afraid if I move I'll come. I'm close, baby. So close."

"Me too," Jared replied and rolled his hips.

Fenix pulled back, kissed Jared frantically, and then leaned back on his knees. He grabbed Jared's hips and started moving, his face taut with concentration. Jared's cock twitched at the sight of his lover – dark eyeliner around pale blue eyes, high Scandinavian cheekbones flushed with heat, tousled blond hair falling over his face, plump, wet lips...

"Fuck, yes," Jared yelled, fisting his cock and starting to jerk himself off. He stole a look down Fenix's body, and the sight of his cock disappearing in and out of Jared did him in. His earth-shattering orgasm swept him away and for a few long moments Jared couldn't see or hear or feel anything else but the blissful pleasure spreading through his whole body.

He felt Fenix shudder as he pulsed inside him, emptying himself as he rode out his own orgasm. Jared managed to get himself together just in time to open his eyes and witness his gorgeous boyfriend arching his back, and coming, his head thrown back and his muscles flexing.

Fenix flopped back on top of Jared and he could feel his heart beating frantically against his own. He pulled out gingerly, and Jared felt a trail of slick come drip down his thigh. He wrapped his arms around Fenix and buried his face in his neck. They stayed like this for what seemed like hours, neither of them capable to move or speak.

"You were incredible," Jared murmured when he felt like he could trust his vocal cords again. He weaved his fingers in Fenix's hair and tugged him towards his lips for a gentle kiss.

"You weren't so bad yourself," Fenix said, smirking.

"On stage, you idiot," Jared laughed.

"Thanks," Fenix said, almost shyly, and he kissed Jared again.

"And, it turns out, I have a rock star fetish," Jared added, unable to keep the smile off his face.

"Does that mean you're going to pounce on me every night after the show?" Fenix asked, arching an eyebrow in a challenge.

"Yeah."

"Then this job is worth it even if they weren't paying me."

"Baby, you know I'd pounce on you no matter what you did for a living," Jared said and caressed Fenix's cheek.

"Yeah, but this was incredible," Fenix said seriously. "I've never done it bare before."

"I can't wait to feel you without anything between us, too," Jared whispered against Fenix's skin, kissing it. Fenix shuddered, obviously liking the idea himself.

Someone pounded on the door and said something, but they didn't hear what. They kissed and touched, caressing warm, sensitive skin, and whispered tender words to each other. The banging stopped eventually and Fenix stood up, helping Jared off the sofa and heading to the bathroom to clean up.

CHAPTER SIXTEEN

Jared

The next eight months passed so quickly that Jared felt as if his life had suddenly been fast forwarded. There weren't enough hours in the day, enough days in a month to do everything he and Fenix wanted to do. They spent every moment together – in the theatre, at home, out with friends, at night. Jared got anxious if Fenix had to be away for longer than a few hours. He watched *Poison* every night backstage, accompanied Fenix to interviews and photo shoots, even watched him rehearse and dance, sometimes for hours. Jared would sit in the rehearsal room, work on his laptop, play a game on his phone or even read a novel, but more often than not, he'd just watch Fenix move on stage. He needed to be close to him even if each of them did their own thing. Fenix would sometimes indulge Jared by singing a song for him, serenading him from the stage, and Jared would be completely mesmerised by his boyfriend's talent.

Every morning when Jared opened his eyes and saw Fenix sleeping quietly next to him, a powerful wave of emotion slammed into his chest, momentarily suffocating him. He couldn't contemplate that he was physically able to feel so much for another person. The more time they spent together, the more Jared couldn't get enough of him, of *them*. He wanted this for the rest of his life, and he knew Fenix felt the same. Because he'd told him one night, as he buried his face in Jared's neck, trying to calm down after particularly intense love making.

"I want you, Jared. Only you. For the rest of my life. I want you to be the last person I'll ever kiss, the last person I'll let see all of me. Please tell me you want that, too," Fenix had whispered, and Jared had to swallow hard a few times before he confirmed that yes, he wanted all of that too.

Jared managed to cure Fenix of his aversion to supermarkets, and even taught him how to cook. They both had to watch what they ate, especially Fenix, and Jared was glad he could teach Fenix something valuable, like how to prepare fresh, healthy meals himself.

That new skill, and the fact that Fenix wanted to practice his newly found cooking obsession, came in handy when the media started taking more than a healthy dose of interest in them. Because of *Poison*'s growing popularity, and Jared and Fenix's relationship, the photographers started jumping out of nowhere every time they set foot outside their flat. Neither Jared nor Fenix minded the ever growing throng of fans waiting for them at Queen Victoria's back exit, asking for pictures and autographs – it was very inspiring. Their hard work and dedication was touching other people so deeply that they were willing to stand in all weather conditions, waiting for a glimpse of them. They both spent close to an hour every night signing theatre tickets, musical programmes, and taking photos with their fans.

But the paparazzi were something else. They'd intrude on their down time, following them as they walked down the street or went out for dinner. It was ridiculous – who would care about that? Who would pay money to see a photo of Jared and Fenix eating at Flagrante? Jared was pretty good at ignoring them, nodding politely when they called his name, but other than that he kept his head down and pretended they were not there. But Fenix... he had a very hard time overlooking some of the things they shouted at them in order to squeeze out a reaction, or crowded them, disregarding any personal space as their cameras flashed in their faces.

Logically, Fenix knew none of that mattered, and sooner rather than later they would leave them alone. But Jared had seen how stressed Fenix would get after ploughing through a mob of people to get inside their building. He'd seen the way his hands shook and his eyes flashed angrily when he closed the door behind him.

Jared knew one day a stupid paparazzo would cross the already thin line and Fenix would flip out. He just hoped he'd be able to prevent it.

That day came when they tried to sneak out through the back exit of Stage Academy after watching a new musical. They were invited to the previews because the producer was a friend of Jared's from college and he wanted his feedback. It was very low key – the previews were by invitation only and were not advertised in the media. Nobody followed Jared and Fenix on their way to the theatre, but when the show was over one of the ushers advised them to leave through the back exit because some photographers were obviously waiting for them outside. How they knew about that was a mystery to Jared.

Unfortunately, some of the paparazzi were lurking at the back, too. Fenix had been feeling off all day, worried that he was coming down with a cold, but Jared knew he was stressed over a bad review of *Poison* in ART. The theatre critic that had written it, Arlen Nicholson, was very well known and respected in their world, but he was also a narrow minded, old fashioned, bitter, old asshole. Jared hated that bastard long before he'd pegged Fenix as an 'attention seeking, average dancer who does not belong on a West End stage'. He'd described *Poison* as an over-praised rock concert relying on controversy to gather audience and media attention, but lacking severely in any artistic value.

Both Fenix and Jared knew that wasn't true. They both also knew Arlen Nicholson should have been stripped of his critic status a long time ago. He might have been a greatly respected art journalist back in the day, but it was clear his knowledge or taste didn't evolve as quickly as the musical theatre world.

Despite that, his words hurt. Fenix was moody for days, but when he'd woken up this morning and felt his throat getting uncomfortably scratchy, his mood had plummeted even more. Jared had hoped a night out to see a new show would do them both good, especially if they managed to fly under the radar.

No such luck.

One asshole photographer started shouting quotes from Nicholson's review and actually had the nerve to ask Fenix to comment. Jared felt Fenix's whole body buzzing with anger beside him as they tried to walk past the photographers. Fenix slowed his pace, glared at the photographer and stiffened, preparing for an attack. Jared wasn't sure if it was going to be physical or verbal, but he had only a second or two to do something. He put his arm in front of Fenix and pushed him behind himself, shielding him from the flashes. Jared was so angry he saw red, and he wanted nothing more than to beat the bastard to a pulp.

"Back off and shut up before I kick your teeth in!" Jared snarled right in the man's face. His eyes widened as he paled, obviously realising Jared was not kidding. The other cameras continued to click and flash around them, but Jared didn't even attempt to give a fuck. All he wanted was to shield Fenix from all this.

Thankfully, they got the message, and Jared and Fenix managed to walk alone the rest of the way to their apartment. Fenix didn't say anything, but he didn't pull his hand away when Jared grabbed it either. They walked in silence until they reached their street. It was quiet and deserted this late in the evening. There were a few street lamps, but it was still very dark and eerie.

"You shouldn't have done that," Fenix said quietly as they walked towards their building. "They're going to print all kinds of shit about you tomorrow, blowing this out of proportion..."

"Better me than you," Jared replied. Fenix suddenly stopped and tugged on their clasped hands. It was starting to drizzle lightly, and when Jared turned to face him, his hair was a damp mess, falling into his face. His eyes were colourless in the dim light, but they were blazing with emotion.

"Don't say that. You can't do that, Jared. You can't stick out your neck for me like that. You know they're vultures looking for the next sensational photo..." Fenix's skin was wet from the light rain and flushed as he spoke passionately. Jared could not resist taking the small distance between them and kissing him.

He tasted of rain and love.

Jared took his time, kissing Fenix until he felt the anger and frustration leaking out of him. He separated their lips, but didn't pull back, resting their foreheads together.

"I still had some control left. You would have hit him," Jared stated, his voice carrying no question. "That would have caused all kinds of trouble for you, and I'm not having that."

Fenix sighed and nodded, silently agreeing with Jared. He did not lose his temper easily, if ever, but when he did, it got really bad. Jared had witnessed an epic fight between Fenix, Ned and Joy when, after rehearsing the same song and routine for over an hour, Joy still couldn't do the move Fenix wanted of her, and Ned still couldn't sing the note Fenix wanted him to. The director had left the rehearsal room, resigned that he wouldn't convince Fenix that everything was fine the way it was. Fenix's obsession over perfection knew no boundaries, however. He continued to torture Joy and Ned for another half hour before Ned finally had enough and attempted to leave. Joy tried to follow, and Fenix had the biggest meltdown Jared had ever witnessed. Tired, overworked, and unsatisfied with the results, let alone his ADHD kicking in at least forty minutes ago, Fenix imploded before Jared's eyes. He screamed at his friends, his hands balling into fists, his whole body shaking with anger, his eyes blazing with fury.

Joy and Ned were having none of it, screaming back at Fenix and giving as good as they got. Jared did not want to think what would have happened if he hadn't been there to push them out the door and calm Fenix down.

He also didn't want to think what tomorrow's headlines would have been if Fenix had gotten hold of that photographer. Or how good the man's bloody face would have looked on the front page of The Sun.

Jared tugged on Fenix's hand, leading him towards the entrance of their building. The rain was starting to fall faster and the last thing Fenix needed right now was to catch pneumonia.

Fenix had been right. The next morning the press and the internet exploded with pictures of Jared snarling in the photographer's face while shielding Fenix behind him. Jared really tried to care, especially when he talked to the producers, his agent, Adam... He tried to inject some remorse in his voice, but the truth was he'd do it all over again tomorrow.

By the time the two week summer break came, both Jared and Fenix desperately needed a holiday. They needed to get out of London, out of the West End, out of the public eye. Fenix suggested they go visit his family in New York, and Jared readily accepted.

The two weeks that followed were some of the best of Jared's life. They warned everyone who might want to get in touch that they didn't want to be disturbed unless it was a matter of life or death. Most people respected that, but they both got texts from their agents and their friends occasionally. Still, it was more than they had hoped for when they'd made their request.

Fenix's parents were amazing. His dad was kind and patient, full of quiet charisma and charm. He watched them with affection and pride when he thought Jared wasn't looking, and even though he never said the actual words, Jared knew he was happy for his son. Fenix had shared that his dad was a bit disappointed when Fenix decided to plunge into a career of musical theatre because he knew all the struggles his son was going to face. But it seemed like Eric Bergman had made his peace with it and was proud of everything his son had achieved.

And his mum... God! Jared had been awe struck the first time he'd seen the great ballerina Evelyn Bergman in person. She was still the striking woman she'd been on stage, regardless of the wheelchair she now sat in. Evelyn was talkative and smiling and so genuinely *nice*. Fenix looked exactly like his Scandinavian mother – tall and slim and blond haired. Sometimes, without realising it, Evelyn would slip into speaking Swedish and both Fenix and his dad would reply in her native tongue as if it was the most natural thing in the world, until they realised they'd excluded Jared from the conversation and switched back to English.

Fenix's parents tried to insist on them staying in their apartment, but Fenix knew Jared would feel more comfortable in a hotel, and kindly declined. Despite that, they went to dinner at Evelyn and Eric's place almost every night.

Sitting around the Bergman's table, watching them talk and laugh, and share such close-knit family connection, Jared wished he could offer Fenix the same. He wished he could take Fenix back home to his mum now and then, have dinner and... be a family. But he knew he could never do that – he wasn't welcome in his own childhood home anymore.

He wasn't welcome in his mother's heart anymore.

Fenix must have sensed Jared's sadness that enveloped him when he thought of his mother, because he always found his hand under the table and squeezed. Jared had told Fenix about his mum and he'd told him he was over that, that he'd made peace with her decision, but Fenix could see right through him. He knew the dull ache of his own mother's rejection was still buried deep in Jared's heart and probably would always be.

After dinner that first night, Fenix had taken Jared to see his childhood room. His parents still kept it intact as if Fenix still lived there. They didn't need the extra space of a spare room and saw no reason to destroy his childhood memories, Fenix explained.

The room's walls were covered floor to ceiling with Broadways posters, musical programmes, tickets, drawings, printed out quotes... It was a shrine to Fenix's dream.

Fenix talked about Broadway often, and Jared accepted that as a part of him, of his interests. He'd never thought of his obsession with Broadway as Fenix's dream, even though he'd mentioned multiple times how he'd love to star in a Broadway musical someday.

Now though, Jared got it. He got a glimpse at Fenix's childhood, at the way he'd been raised watching his mother perform, going to musicals, learning all there was to know about Broadway.

He also realised, for the first time, that London's West End was Fenix's stepping stone. It wasn't where he really wanted to be. How could he have not seen that sooner? Fenix had *told* him multiple times that he dreamed of performing on Broadway. Why had Jared blocked it out?

What would happen if, no – *when*, Broadway came knocking on their door?

The sudden fear that overtook Jared's mind was too much to bear. He didn't want to spoil their holiday and wonder about the what ifs. They'd cross that bridge when they came to it. If there was one thing Jared was confident about, it was that their bond was stronger than anything life could throw at them.

They went to see as many shows as they could cram into two weeks. Fenix was like an overexcited child – he smiled so broadly that his cheeks must have sustained permanent damage.

His eyes were full of so much joy, so much awe and enthusiasm that Jared couldn't help but catch some of that Broadway bug too.

The end of their holiday came faster than they expected. Between sightseeing in New York, Broadway shows, and dinners with Fenix's family, time flew incredibly fast. The night before they had to go back home, Jared's phone rang and vibrated on the coffee table in their hotel room. It caused quite the racket, but Jared was too busy sinking his cock into Fenix's warm, pliable body to pay it any attention. It started going off again later that night and Jared groaned, unwillingly leaving Fenix's sleeping form in bed as he padded across the room to get it. Just as he picked up, he heard Fenix's phone ringing from somewhere inside the pile of clothes next to the bed. Fenix stirred and growled deep in his throat.

Jared smiled and looked at the display – it was his agent Samantha Durell. She had been his agent ever since he'd graduated from LAMDA. She'd chased him mercilessly until he agreed to sign with her, because she definitely didn't look like someone Jared wanted to represent him. Samantha was tall, thin as a stick, with dark hair cut into an elegant bob every three weeks, and the most piercing, intelligent grey eyes Jared had ever seen. Add all that to her posh upbringing, her Oxford University education, and her rich family and Jared didn't want to touch her with a bargepole. He'd always imagined his agent as more of an old school, hippy, in-love-with-the-theatre-and-the-arts kind of person.

"Hey, Sam. What's up?" Jared said after he slid his finger along the display to accept the call. If she hadn't left a message and continued to call, even though she knew they were on holiday, then it must be something important.

Jared watched Fenix as he flopped on his belly and stretched his arm down towards his clothes, looking for his own ringing phone.

"Sorry to bother you so late, Jared. But I have great news," she practically squealed which was really weird coming from his posh, always collected agent. "*Of Kids and Monsters* has been nominated for a Laurence Olivier award – Best Entertainment and Family!" Samantha declared proudly.

"What?" Jared rasped, his voice suddenly refusing to work properly. The Laurence Olivier awards were the UK's answer to the Tonys and Jared had never even dreamt of being nominated for one. They weren't known for their sympathy for musical theatre aimed at younger audiences.

"You heard me!"

"Wow, I don't know what to say, Sam. That's amazing!" Jared's head was still spinning. After all the hard work he'd put into this show, the critics finally started to appreciate it.

"It is. But it gets better," Sam said, her voice dripping with satisfaction.

"It does?" How can it get better than this?

"Yes. Your boy Fenix and his show have been nominated too! Best Actor in a Musical as well as Best New Musical."

Jared's head snapped in Fenix's direction and he saw that his boyfriend had just gotten the same news from whoever was calling him. Fenix grinned at him from where he was sitting in the messy bed and raised his fist in a gesture of victory.

"I gotta go, Sam. Thank you so much for calling. We'll be back tomorrow and I'll come to see you next week, OK?"

Jared hung up the phone just when Fenix hung up his and raced to the bed, falling on top of Fenix.

"Congratulations," he murmured before he took Fenix's mouth in a deep, hungry kiss. He wasn't sure what he was happier about, his or Fenix's nomination. But both together – Jared was ecstatic!

"You too," Fenix managed to say before Jared overpowered him with his body, pinned him to the mattress, and didn't give him a chance to say another word.

CHAPTER SEVENTEEN

Fenix

Fenix could not look away from Jared's eyes as he moved on top of him. The intensity in them, the love and desire and hope and faith that shone in them in the dim early morning light coming from their bedroom window, sent shivers all over his body. Fenix's skin prickled with goosebumps as Jared moaned under him and flexed his hips upwards, getting impatient with Fenix's slow, sensual movements.

"For fuck's sake, Fen! Ride me faster or I swear to God I'll flip you over and fuck you through the bed and you won't be able to perform for a week."

Fenix smiled evilly and leaned down to kiss his boyfriend. Jared grabbed his face and attacked his mouth with barely-contained ferocity. Man, Fenix loved when Jared got all hot and bothered, unable to control himself. He loved that *he* was the one to make Jared snap and overreact, and get a little rough – just as Fenix liked it.

"We wouldn't want that now, would we? I think we should keep it slow and gentle to make sure my ass will be up for tonight's show," Fenix murmured against Jared's lips, and rolled his hips agonizingly slow to get his point across.

"Is that so?"

"That is so," Fenix whispered in Jared's ear and bit on his soft earlobe, while he continued to move leisurely on top of him.

The growl that escaped Jared's throat made Fenix's cock twitch and achingly hard. With one swift, graceful movement Jared flipped them around, pinning Fenix underneath him.

"You like to provoke me, don't you, love?" Jared said, a wicked smile pulling at the corners of his full lips. Fenix was just about to reply with a witty come back when Jared thrust his cock so deep inside him that he saw stars.

There was no more talking. All that could be heard in the early Saturday morning were their harsh breaths, pleasure filled moans, and sweat covered bodies grinding together.

"I love you," murmured Fenix as he reached his climax. He knew that would bring Jared over the edge too, because as dirty and rough their sex usually was, underneath it all the love they shared always showed.

Later, after they'd cleaned up as much as they could with a damp towel, Fenix listened to Jared's calming heartbeat as he rested his head over his chest. It was the morning after the Laurence Olivier awards when they had both won, in a way. Fenix had won the award he had been nominated for – Best Actor in a Musical and *Poison* had won Best New Musical. *Of Kids and Monsters* had won Best Entertainment and Family and since it was Jared's creation, he had proudly walked on stage and accepted the award. Jared was graceful enough not to shove his way to the front and grab the award. He let the director and the producers take all the limelight as he hung back with the rest of the cast. But they had made him go forward and say a few words, acknowledging that, without Jared, they'd never be here. He had pulled Adam along with him – after all it had been both of them who had originally created, produced and directed the musical.

Fenix yawned and felt the familiar post-sex relaxed daze settle over his mind. He inhaled Jared's scent through his nose, kissed the warm skin on his chest, and closed his eyes. His half-conscious mind drifted off and his last thought before he fell asleep was how perfect his life was – he was an award winning star in London's West End; he was healthy and happy and strong enough to perform every night for weeks on end; and he had the most loving, gorgeous, amazingly talented fellow performer for a boyfriend.

Life could not get any better than this.

Only it did.

Fenix's phone rang just as he was following Jared into the bathroom for a well-deserved shower and, hopefully, round two of Saturday sex.

"Go ahead, baby, it's Cathleen. I'm right behind you," Fenix said as he slid his finger over the screen to take his agent's call.

"I hope so, it's your turn," said Jared and winked, heading into the bathroom. Fenix stared after him, appreciating the hard muscles on his back and his perfect, round ass.

"Talk fast, Cat, because the hottest man on the planet is waiting for me naked, wet, and turned on," Fenix groaned into the phone.

"Hello to you too," said his agent, and Fenix could hear the smile in her voice.

"What do you want, Cat?"

"Can't I just check in with my favourite client?" Cathleen purred on the other side of the line, obviously enjoying herself.

"Get to the point or I'm hanging up. Man, Jared's probably already started without me!"

"Alright, alright! Geez. You're shameless. Do you have to shove your hot boyfriend in everyone's face?" Fenix took a breath to reply to the obvious pun, but Cathleen beat him to it. "I swear to

God if you make a joke about shoving things in people's faces I'm hanging up and you'll never hear the amazing news I have for you."

"Amazing news?" Fenix asked, grinning.

"Yes. Just make sure you're sitting down because this is huge, Fenix."

"How huge?"

"Broadway huge."

"Cat, you know I love you, but if you're kidding right now, I'm gonna buy the first ticket to New York and strangle you."

"No joke. *Poison* received an offer for Broadway two weeks ago. I couldn't tell you because I signed the fucking confidentiality agreement everyone's so fond of these days. It was all hush hush until this morning when they signed the papers. They were waiting for the results from the Laurence Olivier awards, I can bet my BMW on it," Cathleen said and huffed, voicing her distaste. "Anyway, I wanted to be the first to tell you, but you should expect calls from the producers, the press, and a shitload of other people any time." Cathleen stopped talking, probably expecting some reaction from Fenix, but he couldn't make his brain work or his tongue form words.

Broadway.

His dream.

It was coming true right this second and Fenix didn't know how to react. Cathleen's voice brought him back to the present.

"You're going to Broadway, baby!" she said with a squeal of delight.

I'm going to Broadway.

Fenix managed to register that Cathleen said something else about mailing him all the documents and expecting him in her office in two days, but he couldn't respond. He mumbled a 'mhmmm' before he hung up.

Broadway.

He was going to Broadway.

In two days.

"What's going on, love? What did Cat say?" Jared's voice startled him and as he looked at the man he loved – naked and dripping wet, skin flushed from the shower, Fenix felt his whole perfect world starting to collapse around him.

Jared.

Jared had his own musical, his own starring role. Broadway had never been his dream – the man lived and breathed London.

Fenix cleared his throat before he spoke, unable to meet Jared's eyes.

"She said *Poison* is moving to Broadway. The papers have been signed this morning. I have to be in her office the day after tomorrow."

His voice was flat and emotionless. Jared didn't speak, and Fenix couldn't even hear him breathe. He managed to gather enough courage to look at his boyfriend who was standing in the middle of the room, still dripping wet, holding a towel in his hand as if he'd completely forgotten about it. And he was white as a ghost.

Fenix jumped up and went to him, afraid he might topple over any second.

"What did you say?" Jared asked finally.

"I don't have too much of a choice, do I? I have signed a three year contract, of which I have two years left. Wherever *Poison* goes, I go too."

"Don't do that, Fenix!" Jared snarled, the colour coming back to his face, his cheeks reddening with anger. "Don't blame it on the contract. We both know Broadway has always been your dream, that you were biding your time here until you got your chance over there!"

"Yes! You're right! We *both* knew that! Then why are you so angry? This shouldn't come as a surprise for you if you think you know me so well!" Fenix shouted back, stepping away from Jared and creating the space he needed to unleash his rage.

"I'm angry because all this," Jared spread his arms wide, gesturing around them, "has apparently been temporary for you. Every time you fucked me and whispered in my ear how much you loved me, how you wanted to spend the rest of your life with me, it has been a *lie*."

Fenix closed his eyes, his chest tightening so much he thought his heart might jump out.

"Don't say that, Jared. You know it's not true! I do love you, and I do want you for the rest of my life, but I can't say no to Broadway."

"You *won't* say no to Broadway, there's a big difference," Jared growled and strode past him toward the bedroom. Fenix followed him.

"No, I *won't* say no. Are you asking me to give up my dream and put my career on hold for you?"

Jared's shoulders sagged and he ran a hand over his face in frustration. But when he spoke his voice was calmer. Even. Flat.

"No, I'd never ask you that, Fen," he turned around and headed for the dresser to get some clothes. "I knew it would come to this eventually. I just... I never thought you'd throw away everything we have so easily, without even stopping for a second to think about it."

"But it's not like that, Jared. My going to Broadway doesn't mean we are going to break up. You can come with me," Fenix said quietly as he went closer to Jared, just a breath away from his bare back. He felt the heat and scent of his skin assaulting all his senses and wanted nothing more than to touch him. Reassure him that everything was going to be OK. Breaking up hadn't even crossed his mind.

"Yeah? So I'm supposed to throw away *my* dream for you? I'm supposed to pack and go, abandoning what I have worked all my adult life for?" Jared turned to face him and Fenix was thrown back by the hostility in his eyes. "Unlike you, this here, the show, our home, you – it wasn't a stepping stone towards a bigger, brighter goal. It's everything I've ever wanted. Everything I have worked so hard for. Everything I love with all my heart." His voice broke and his eyes filled with tears.

Fenix's heart shattered.

He had never seen Jared so distraught. The thought that he was the reason Jared was hurting so bad was killing him.

"We're stronger than the distance that's going to separate us, Jared. We can make this work. We can visit each other, talk on the phone, video chat..." Fenix began, but Jared's bitter laugh cut him off.

"When exactly are we going to visit each other, Fenix? You know very well how gruelling the Broadway schedule is. We'd be lucky if we get a week off per year at the same time." Jared put on his sweat pants and t-shirt and padded down the stairs, brushing past Fenix without sparing him a second glance. "Skyping and talking on the phone might be enough for you, but it's nowhere near what I want for us."

Fenix followed him down the stairs to the living room and almost collided with Jared when he stopped and abruptly turned.

"I want you in my life, in my home, in my bed every single night, Fen. But I can't just drop everything off and follow you across the world. I have obligations too, I have a contract, people who are counting on me..." Jared trailed off, looking up at the ceiling, probably trying to hold his emotions at bay. "I'm not going to ask you to stay, because if I do, you'd hate me for it."

Fenix didn't confirm it. But he didn't deny it either. They both knew it was true.

"But I also can't forgive you for leaving." Jared's lower lips trembled as a tear slid down his cheek. Fenix realised his vision was also blurring which meant his tears would spill over soon enough too.

"And I can't forgive you for staying," Fenix said.

There was no happy ending to this situation. Fenix needed to go and pursue his dream or he'd always wonder what if. True, he wanted Jared to drop everything and follow him, support him, love him every step of the way. However, he knew Jared was not that kind of a man. He'd never leave everything he'd worked so hard for and let everyone around him down, even if it broke his heart and shattered his own personal happiness.

Fenix grabbed his keys, phone, and wallet from the coffee table, heading for the door.

"I need some time to think about all this. I'll be back soon," he said without turning around. He walked out, closing the door quietly behind him.

CHAPTER EIGHTEEN

Jared

Jared could not believe this was happening. Deep down, he'd known the invitation from Broadway would come sooner or later. But he never imagined it developing so fast. They were perfectly happy one moment, and the next, Fenix was leaving. Literally. He'd be gone in two fucking days.

Fatigue slammed into Jared, and suddenly all he wanted to do was crawl back into bed and forget about all this. But he couldn't. He had a show tonight.

Sighing heavily, Jared got dressed and headed for the theatre. At least work would keep his mind off the mess his life was turning out to be.

Jared didn't see Fenix all day in the theatre. He didn't wait for Jared in the dressing room like he usually did. Jared decided not to dwell on that. Instead, he went home. After a long, hot shower, he fixed himself a drink and his mind wandered.

Fenix had made up his mind long before the call had even come. Broadway was his ultimate goal, and nothing, not even Jared and what they had, could stand between him and his dream.

Was Jared right to judge him when he was doing exactly the same? He could go with Fenix and find a job in a musical without a problem. It wouldn't be a lead, but at least they'd be together. Instead, he was choosing to stay behind to continue building his own career.

Jared didn't wait for Fenix to come back home after his show. He wasn't even sure he *would* come back home. The hot shower and the drink relaxed him to a point where he couldn't keep his eyes open anymore. He dragged his exhausted body into bed and fell asleep almost immediately.

Jared woke up when Fenix's warm body slid behind him and curled around his back. He held him so tight Jared thought he might break his ribs. Fenix was shaking all over, but Jared didn't turn to face him. He knew what was coming, and, like a coward, didn't want to look Fenix in the eyes when he said it.

"I'm sorry," Fenix whispered, barely audible as he continued to tremble and clutch at Jared.

Jared knew what this was – it was Fenix saying goodbye.

"Me, too," he replied. Closing his eyes, he felt the hot tears streaming down his face and soaking the pillow.

When Jared woke up in the morning Fenix was gone.

CHAPTER NINETEEN

Jared

Three months after Fenix left, Jared still wasn't used to the fact that he wouldn't be there when he got home. That Fenix wouldn't be sleeping quietly next to him when he woke up. At night, Jared unconsciously tried to reach for him, to wrap his arms around him and pull him close, only to wake up in panic that Fenix was not there. It always took him a few seconds before he remembered.

Fenix was gone and he was not coming back.

Jared tried to erase Fenix's presence in his home, but it was impossible. He took down all the vintage Broadway posters Fenix had picked out and put them in the back of the closet, still unable to throw them away.

It didn't help.

Fenix was everywhere. Jared had contemplated selling the flat because it drove him insane to live there without Fenix. Of course he couldn't do it – it would drive him equally insane not having anything of Fenix left.

So the torture continued every single day. Jared had never felt so miserable, so close to depression and complete despair.

The show and Adam were the only things that kept him from drowning in his grief. Jared worked harder on the show than he ever had. He rehearsed every day and demanded the very best of his colleagues, blaming the show's newly found popularity. Ever since *Of Kids and Monsters* had won the Laurence Olivier award, it was sold out for months in advance. The theatre offered the show's producers an extra night to perform and they readily accepted. Jared walked around the theatre, moody and irritable, quoting the extra stress the show's new schedule caused for his ill temper, but everyone knew better.

Jared knew Adam must have had a talk with all the staff, warning them against ever mentioning Fenix's name in front of Jared. There was no other explanation why three months on, Jared had never heard anyone even whisper a single word about Fenix, while at the same time people walked around Adam on egg shells. His friend's mood had suffered a great deal because of Jared, too.

Enough!

Jared rubbed his tired eyes and got up, bracing himself to face another day. He was so sick and tired of feeling this way, like he had a lead ball at the bottom of his stomach. Like his chest was squeezed in a vice. Like his heart didn't even beat anymore.

Fenix was gone. Life went on.

Fenix had gone to chase his dream, to further his career, to claim his place in the world. Jared wasn't blaming him for it, not really. He was angry and he was sad, but more at the situation, not at Fenix.

Jared wanted to get over him, wanted to feel happy again. Wanted to be able to go out with friends and lead a normal conversation. Wanted to *enjoy* something again.

But he couldn't. Everyone annoyed him or bored him to death. He wasn't interested in talking to anyone or *doing* anything.

God, he was pathetic.

Padding to the bathroom, Jared took a long, hot shower, before he got dressed and headed to Queen Victoria. He'd much rather spend the day there than at home.

Walking down the street, Jared passed by the same newsagents, pubs, and bakeries as he did every day, but something on the window of a small souvenir shop caught his eye. He stopped and neared the window, taking a closer look – it was a wall clock, plain and round with a white dial and black letters. It wasn't anything special, but Jared couldn't look away. He walked inside and asked to take a closer look at the clock. The girl behind the counter took it down and brought it to Jared, making a surprised face when Jared leaned in and listened. Tick-tock, tick-tock. The sound was loud and clear. Jared smiled and paid for the clock, walking out of the shop with a plain blue plastic bag, the clock wrapped safely inside.

He couldn't wait to go home later today and hang it in the living room. Fenix hated repetitive sounds like clock ticking. As long as that clock tick-tocked on Jared's wall, every second that passed by would remind him that Fenix was not here and was never coming back.

Jared walked in the rehearsal room to find everyone piled around one of the support actors, Aiden, looking at something in his hands and so deep in conversation that they didn't even see him coming in.

"I told you he was a little slut, even before he dropped Jared like a hot potato the moment a better opportunity arose. Look at him! Sneaking out of the back entrance like that, smug and well-fucked," Aiden was saying, provoking a few nods and huffs from the rest of the cast.

Jared's vision blurred and the sound of his pulse roared in his ears. He instinctively knew who they were talking about. Taking the distance between the small group and himself in a few long strides, Jared pushed everyone out of the way until he stood face to face with Aiden. He raised his head and looked at Jared, his face going pale and the hand that held a magazine going behind his back in a rush.

"Jared, I..." he began, taking a step back. "We were just..."

"You don't talk about him like that, do you hear me?" Jared snarled, his voice low and dangerous. He must have looked like a rabid dog because everyone else stepped away from him too. Aiden seemed to collect himself and Jared saw him squaring his shoulders and raising his chin.

"Fenix Bergman is a bastard, Jared. He used you and then he dumped you. And now he's in the gossip columns all the time, sneaking out of hotels' back entrances with a different guy in tow every time," Aiden said, his voice rising with every word. Jared was a breath away from losing all his control and beating the shit out of him. "He's a whore and you deserve better..."

Aiden couldn't finish his sentence – Jared snapped and pounced on him, punching him square in the jaw. He stumbled backwards, clearly surprised by Jared's violent outburst, falling ungraciously on the floor, his eyes widening as he saw Jared advancing on him, determined to do much more damage.

Strong arms wrapped around Jared's waist and pulled him back, lifting him off his feet. Jared thrashed and fought, his mind blank and his vision blurred. He screamed and kicked, trying to get away, trying to make the pain stop. Trying to breathe. Trying to erase every single word he'd just heard.

"Shh, it's OK, Jared. It's OK. You're OK..." Jared could hear Adam's voice whispering in his ear as he dragged him away, but it was coming from too far away. The thick fog around Jared was consuming him and he thrashed, screamed, and cried, trying to make it go away so that he could see clearly again.

After what seemed like hours, Jared was unceremoniously dumped into a bath, and he felt cold water all over his body. His clothes were soaked within seconds and his teeth started to chatter. The fog dissipated and Jared realised he was in his dressing room's bathroom and Adam was standing outside the bath, looking at him with a mixture of anger and concern.

Jared brought his knees to his chest and started shivering violently under the cold water. He didn't turn off the tab, though. It helped him concentrate on something other than what had just happened.

Adam reached and turned off the water, folding his arms over his chest.

"Are you done?" he asked in a flat voice. All Jared could manage was a nod. Adam walked out of the bathroom and came back a minute later with a towel. He helped Jared out of his wet clothes and wrapped the towel around him. Jared was still shivering as Adam led him to the sofa and sat him down.

They didn't speak. Jared wasn't even sure he *could* speak. Suddenly, he felt so tired, so lost and directionless. Adam wrapped and arm around his shoulders, and pulled him closer.

"I think you should let the stand-in take over for today," he said quietly.

Jared nodded.

CHAPTER TWENTY

Fenix

"For fuck's sake! Are we going to make a decision any time soon? Preferably before I die a slow, painful death?" Fenix groaned. He'd been stuck in that staff meeting for over an hour, going on and on about a cast member being caught with drugs in a nightclub and his arrest. The producers felt the whole thing reflected badly on the show and wanted the man gone, but didn't have a suitable long-term replacement. "I've been stuck here for hours, listening to something that has nothing to do with me. I don't fucking care if you fire his ass or if you pretend nothing has happened. I don't give a flying fuck either way," Fenix said, enunciating the last words slowly. He rose from his chair and headed for the door, completely disregarding the protests from both producers and several cast members. He was their star, his opinion mattered. Whatever. Fenix could not spend another second confined in this room. He opened the door, suppressing the urge to slam it behind him, and walked out.

Seven months had passed since he'd left London. Seven months since he'd abandoned the only person that had ever made him happy.

Poison was a hit on Broadway. It sold out every night, got rave reviews from fans and critics alike, and Fenix was allowed to do whatever he wanted. Everyone closed their eyes and didn't comment on his outbursts. The darkness inside him helped develop his character – a temperamental, unstable, arrogant rock star. Fenix didn't even have to pretend to be all those things anymore.

His ADHD was out of control. He could barely concentrate enough to perform for two hours every night. By the time the show was over he felt drained – physically, emotionally, mentally. But his mind wouldn't relax, wouldn't let him fall asleep and forget about everything.

Fenix couldn't sleep for more than four or five hours a night. And even then, he woke up several times without any reason. It would take him ages to calm down enough to get back to sleep, and sometimes he didn't even bother. He had dark circles under his eyes and he'd lost weight. His body was on the verge of collapsing – Fenix barely ate, and combined with the gruelling work-outs, dance rehearsals, and the demanding performance ever night, he was lucky he still hadn't fainted on stage.

If the producers, director, choreographer, or his fellow cast members had noticed something was wrong, they never said anything. Who would care anyway? As long as Fenix went on stage every night and gave the audience the show they eagerly expected, who cared if Fenix had lost the will to live?

Even Joy and Ned, the only people among the cast he counted as friends, stopped trying to get through to him. In their defence, they did try. At first. Fenix pushed them away as hard as he could. He didn't need anyone fussing over him. He didn't want to talk about his feelings. He didn't need anybody to care.

What he needed was a long, hard fuck every now and again. That was the only way to lose himself, forget about the mess his life had turned into and not think about Jared.

The only time Jared's name fled his mind was when he had a guy's cock so deep inside his ass that his brain turned into mush and his thoughts became white noise.

Broadway was his dream come true, so why the fuck wasn't he enjoying it? Why wasn't he *happy*? He loved going on stage, and that was probably the only part of his day when he felt something close to happiness. When he got that standing ovation or when he saw the pride in his parents' eyes he felt accomplished. He felt like he'd made it.

That was it. He was on Broadway, making huge waves.

So why did Fenix curl into the foetal position every night in his bed, trying to hold on to the memories of Jared while desperately wishing them away at the same time?

"Harder!" Fenix yelled, turning his head over his shoulder to look at the man who was fucking him. "Fuck me harder or get lost!" he snarled. Mike, or John, or whatever his name was, smiled evilly and grabbed Fenix's shoulders for leverage.

"As you wish," he growled and started snapping his hips in a brutal, punishing rhythm while squeezing Fenix's shoulders painfully.

Fenix welcomed the pain. He needed the pain. It was that or cut himself, and Fenix had enough sense left to pick a hard fuck over bodily harm with a cold weapon.

The guy drove his cock inside Fenix's willing body over and over again, letting go of his shoulders and pushing him face first on the mattress. Fenix moaned in appreciation, fisting the sheets and biting the pillow to stop himself from screaming.

He craved the emotional release these sessions brought him.

Fenix felt the wave of anger, despair, sorrow, and misery rise inside him, building and growing larger with every thrust. His balls tightened and his orgasm crashed into him, exploding in a white light behind his closed eyes.

He didn't even feel it when the guy behind him came, or when he pulled out, took the money from the bedside table, and left. Fenix was incapable of feeling anything else but his own agony spreading throughout his whole being, rising and falling, expanding and shrinking back until it burst into millions of sharp little shards.

Fenix's sobs shook his body. Those shards pierced his soul for what seemed like ages before his body gave out and he fell into an exhausted, miserable sleep.

CHAPTER TWENTY ONE

Jared

On the last day before the summer break, Jared fucked up his performance for the first time in his life. He forgot his lines, messed up the dance moves, lacked stage presence and charm. Most of the audience probably didn't notice his mistakes. Instinct took over and he managed to perform around them. The cast worked as a well-oiled machine by now and covered for him as well, so nobody asked for their money back in the end of the show. Still, Jared felt like a failure.

This time last year he and Fenix had been so excited to go on their trip to New York. They had made plans and booked theatre tickets and argued whose fault the excess baggage was. What was Jared going to do with himself for two weeks? Work was the only thing keeping him half sane, what would he do when that rug was pulled from under him, too?

He couldn't stop thinking about it. That was why his performance had suffered. He was stressed, overworked, sleep deprived and... sad. Mostly sad.

Jared walked to his dressing room straight after the final curtain call, ignoring anyone who tried to talk to him. He'd just closed the door behind him when there was a firm knock. Jared didn't bother replying. He knew that knock and he also knew that no matter what he said, Adam would still walk in.

"We're going away tomorrow," Adam stated as he flopped on the sofa next to Jared.

"Excuse me?" Jared looked at him incredulously.

"You heard me. You and me. Away."

"Where the hell would we go? Why?"

"We'll go to my house in Margate," Adam said without missing a beat. This wasn't a spur of the moment decision. Apparently he'd thought about it beforehand, which surprised Jared. Adam's grandparents had left him the house in Margate but he hardly ever went there. Jared wasn't even sure it was habitable. "As for why... Do I really need to answer that?"

"Adam... I appreciate what you're trying to do. I really do. But it's not necessary. I'm fine..."

"You're so far away from 'fine' that you don't even remember how to spell it!" Adam snapped. "We're going. I wasn't asking you. I was telling you so that you can pack a bag. I'll be at your place at 8:00 am tomorrow and I'll drag your ass if I have to," Adam said, his eyes flashing dangerously. Jared knew that face, and he knew not to argue. Adam would definitely drag him out of his flat kicking and screaming, Jared had no doubt about that.

Jared nodded and Adam stood up, heading for the door. Pausing with his hand on the knob, he turned his head slightly and said,

"It's not just for you, you know. It's for me too. I haven't been doing so good myself, ever since Charlie left. I need to get away from everything for a while. I need my best friend." Without waiting for a reply, Adam pulled the door open and walked out.

God, Jared was such a useless, selfish motherfucker. He knew Charlie had left for L.A. when his band got offered a record deal about a month ago. Jared wasn't sure what their relationship had been like – for the past year all he'd been thinking about was himself. But he knew Adam cared for Charlie even if Charlie hadn't fully returned the sentiment. Just because Adam hadn't fallen apart like Jared didn't mean he wasn't feeling like shit, too.

Adam's house was a two-bedroom bungalow overlooking the English Channel. It was in much better shape than Jared had anticipated. Adam had probably paid someone to fix it up, clean, and stock up the fridge so that they wouldn't have to do any of those things.

They unpacked and started on dinner, neither of them speaking much. It wasn't uncomfortable at all, though. It was probably the first time in a year that Jared felt somehow normal. Peaceful.

They ate, drank a couple of beers, and decided to take a walk on the beach. It was a beautiful evening, a bit windy and chilly, but they put their hoodies on to keep warm. The sky was several shades of orange as the sun started to set.

"What happened with Charlie?" Jared asked, stealing a look at his friend. Adam's jaw muscles clenched and it took a while before he answered.

"He left," was all he said.

"I know that. I mean the whole story. I know I haven't been much of a friend lately, and I'm sorry, Adam. I'd like to take a step towards changing that."

Adam looked at him sharply, as if to argue, to blame, to deny. But he didn't. What he saw in Jared's eyes must have changed his mind, and he sighed loudly before he spoke.

"You were the only person I'd ever had any feelings for, before Charlie. And I was so confused at first, because what I felt for him was so different from what I used to feel for you. How can both those feelings be love if they were so different? So I convinced myself I wasn't in love with him. I cared for him and I loved his body. Sex with Charlie was something I've never experienced before, even with you."

Adam paused and Jared didn't push him to continue. He'd already shared so much. Jared wasn't even sure Adam had ever shared this much with anyone, even him. He was not the kind of person to dwell on things, or talk about his feelings. Adam lived in the moment – if he wanted something, he took it; if he felt something, he said it loud and clear.

"In time, something changed. I started caring if he called or stopped by, if he was alright, if he was happy. I knew I was falling in love, but I could also see he wasn't. He was affectionate and attentive, and must have cared for me on some level, but he was not in love with me. Anyway, long story short, his band got offered a record deal and he moved to L.A."

"I'm sorry," Jared said quietly, lacing his fingers with Adam's.

"It's OK. I'm happy for him," Adam said with a shrug, not letting go of Jared's hand. "I just... I don't know how many more chances I'm going to get, Jared. First you, and now Charlie..."

Jared tried not to show his surprise at Adam's words. He'd always thought Adam was alone because that's how he wanted it. He liked his freedom. Was he waiting for the right person all this time? Hoping?

"You'll get as many chances as you need. It'll be OK," Jared said, squeezing Adam's hand.

"Yeah, right. Looks who's talking," Adam said with a huff. "You've turned into a zombie over the last year, and now you're suddenly Mr Positivity."

"It's different," Jared said, stiffening.

"How is it different? You've lost all hope, Jared."

Jared didn't reply. He *had* lost all hope. He knew there would be no one else for him but Fenix. He knew that he had nothing left to give to anyone else because he loved Fenix with everything he was.

"I don't want to talk about this. Please," Jared whispered.

Adam didn't push him. They walked in silence for a while. Jared stared at the water which looked black now that the sun had set. Black and angry. It roared, fought and moved dangerously.

Jared wondered if the blackness in the bottom of the sea was much different than the blackness at the bottom of his soul.

After the walk, sprawled on the big L-shaped sofa that took up most of the living room, they watched a DVD called 'Free Fall' that Adam had brought among a dozen others. He didn't have Sky installed in the house, and the Freeview channels sucked, so DVDs were their only option of evening entertainment. At first Jared grumbled that it was a German film and he had to read subtitles, but he grew to like it. It was quite sexy and Jared found he got a hard on before the first half hour was over.

Jared hadn't been with anyone since Fenix. He rarely got an erection anymore, and if he did, he took care of it hastily, not looking for pleasure but wanting to get rid of the uncomfortable situation. The reason Jared hadn't even thought of being with anyone, not even a one night stand, was that he couldn't bear the thought of a stranger touching him. After the closeness he and Fenix had shared, Jared felt vulnerable. Exposed. He didn't want someone he didn't even know seeing that part of him.

Jared stole a look at Adam and noticed his friend's visible erection under his sweat pants. A need to be touched, held, kissed overwhelmed Jared. Adam was no stranger. Adam was the person who knew everything about him. Adam was safe.

Jared scooted closer to Adam on the sofa, wrapping an arm around his waist and resting his head on Adam's chest. If Adam was surprised, he didn't show it. Instead, he draped his arm around Jared's shoulders and pulled him even closer.

The film became particularly heated at one point, and Jared could not resist flexing his hips towards Adam's thigh to release some of the pressure of his cock. The movie and Adam's warm, familiar body turned him on so much that he craved an intimate touch.

"What are you doing?" Adam rasped. Jared turned his head to look at him and saw desire written all over it. Adam's hooded black eyes were intense and focused on him.

"I'm humping your thigh," Jared said, giving Adam an option to turn all this into a joke.

"Why?" Adam asked, his voice low and husky, the word barely more than a growl. No, he didn't turn it into a joke. He wanted Jared just as much as Jared wanted him.

"Because I have a massive hard on," Jared replied. Propping his body on his elbow, he lifted off Adam and leaned so close to his face that he could feel Adam's breath on his lips. Adam didn't pull away. Jared swallowed difficultly before saying, "And I want you to fuck me."

Jared pressed his lips to Adam's, praying that he wouldn't push him away. Adam did exactly the opposite. He opened his mouth immediately, letting Jared in. Jared explored Adam's mouth with his tongue, nipping at his lips, sucking on them, until kissing was no longer enough. Adam dragged his body fully on top of him, enveloping him in his arms. He pulled Jared's t-shirt off and dropped it on the floor, closely followed by his own. Adam's hands roamed Jared's body, touching, caressing, squeezing, as if he knew exactly what Jared needed.

They kissed and touched for what seemed like hours, bringing each other so close to the end so many times, but always pulling back, not wanting it to end yet. Jared lost himself in the sensation of another human being touching him, of *Adam*, his closest friend, touching him, and for the first time in twelve months, he felt real, undiluted pleasure building inside him.

Their clothes were gone a long time ago and they thrust and ground against each other, both lost in the sensation of skin against skin, lips against lips, tongue sliding over tongue.

Adam pushed off Jared suddenly and Jared cried out at the loss of his warm, heavy body on top of him.

"Don't move," Adam said and disappeared. He came back a moment later, his cock already sheathed in a condom. He poured lube on it liberally and positioned himself between Jared's thighs.

"How long?" Adam asked breathlessly.

Jared just shook his head and his vision blurred. He blinked a few times to clear the tears away – he'd be damned if he cried during sex like a virgin!

Adam seemed to understand what that meant because he withdrew slightly and carefully prepared Jared with his fingers, slicking his hole generously, stretching and probing until he was satisfied it was enough. It still hurt when he pushed inside, but Jared breathed through it, and the pain passed quickly, leaving only pleasure behind.

Neither of them lasted long. They were both so turned on by now that a few thrusts of Adam's hips and a few strokes on Jared's shaft and they were both coming. For several blissful seconds, Jared lost himself in the sensation. His mind was completely blank and he relished the feeling.

Later that night, Jared lay almost on top of Adam in his bed. He didn't want to be alone after this and neither did Adam. Silently, they had walked to Adam's room and gone into his bed together, curling against each other, limbs entwining and breaths synchronizing. Jared knew Adam wasn't asleep, even though his breathing was slow and even.

"I know you're not in love with me anymore," Jared said against Adam's skin. Adam hummed questioningly. "I'd never have allowed this to happen if I had even the slightest suspicion you still had feelings for me. What you told me about Charlie... I thought about it. I think you were in love with him, but you never were with me. You cared for me, still do, and you wouldn't mind having me in your bed, but you're not in love." Jared turned to meet Adam's eyes. "I know this doesn't mean anything. I'm not stupid. We're not getting back together... We're just..." Jared struggled finding words to explain the situation.

"We're alone together," Adam suggested.

"Did you just quote Fall Out Boy on me?"

"Sometimes quoting your favourite bands is the only way to get through to you," Adam said and smiled widely.

Jared laughed and it felt like a foreign feeling. He couldn't remember the last time he'd laughed in the past year.

"I haven't been with anyone since Fenix," Jared said quietly after a while. "I didn't even want to. But it's different with you. I..." Jared paused and tried to swallow the giant lump in his throat. Adam's arms tightened around him.

"I know, Jared," he said. "I'm under no illusion we're ever going work as a couple. But right now I need you just as much as you need me," Adam said, summarising exactly how Jared felt in a single sentence. He buried his fingers in Jared's hair and massaged his scalp until Jared relaxed again.

They didn't speak after that. Jared thought about what Adam had said and wondered if Fenix had someone to do this for him. The image of Fenix alone and sad like Jared, but with no one to take away the pain even for a little while, was too much to bear, and Jared didn't want to think about it anymore.

Soon, fatigue took over, and he fell asleep.

CHAPTER TWENTY TWO

Jared

The time Jared spent with Adam in Margate helped. He felt somewhat calmer. More... himself. Sadness was still wedged so deep in his heart that sometimes he had difficulty breathing, and he was not fine, not yet. Probably never would be. But at least desperation didn't drive him so close to the edge that he didn't see any point of existing anymore.

Eight months on and Jared could safely say he hadn't fucked up any more performances, nor had he tried to beat someone into a pulp. He even went out with his friends a few times – not enjoying it, but the effort it took to leave his flat still counted.

Next week was the anniversary of his father's death. He always went to his grave around that time, not on the exact date because he was afraid he might meet someone he used to know. He was afraid he might see his mother.

Jared hadn't spoken to her in almost nine years. She hadn't tried to get in touch either. If the woman who gave birth to him and raised him didn't love her child anymore because of his choice of lovers, Jared didn't want anything to do with her either.

It didn't mean it didn't hurt, though.

So, two days before the anniversary, on a crisp Monday morning, Jared headed to Liverpool street station and caught the train to Colchester, where his mother still lived and his father was buried. The cemetery was deserted when he arrived two hours later. He found his father's grave and stood next to it awkwardly. Jared's mother had told him his dad would have been ashamed if he had lived to see Jared 'turn out to be gay'. But Jared knew that wasn't true. Whether it was wishful thinking or the truth, he would never know.

Jared squatted next to the tombstone and brushed his fingers over his father's engraved name. Just like every time he'd come here, he tried to remember some nice things about him. As the years passed those memories were slowly fading and Jared found he had to think harder and harder every time he came here. But it didn't matter. That was not why he was coming here.

Jared wondered what the reason was for his rare visits, but he couldn't put a name to it. The simple truth was that he missed his dad and he was the only parent Jared had who hadn't rejected him, even if he was dead.

Jared stayed for a bit longer, and then stood up to leave, patting the stone with the palm of his hand in a silent goodbye. He turned and his eyes fell on a woman about ten feet away. His mother. She stood frozen in place, her face set in a cold mask, clutching a bouquet of colourful daisies. Jared gasped involuntarily – he couldn't believe his mother was standing in front of him after such a long time. She'd changed a lot – her hair had more grey in it than black; she'd lost weight; her skin was an odd greyish colour and she had huge bags under her eyes. Her eyes, so much like Jared's, looked at him with a mixture of disgust, astonishment, and anger. No child should see that look in their mother's eyes, ever. Jared felt like someone punched him in the gut, torn between saying something to her and just walking away without a word.

She made the choice for him. Silently, she turned away as if he'd offended her merely with his presence, and walked away.

Jared's encounter with his mother brought the sleepless nights back, until one day he overheard his fellow cast members whispering that Fenix had been nominated for a Tony. Jared didn't lash out on them. He just pretended he hadn't heard anything but inside he was rejoicing.

Fenix would finally get the recognition he deserved. Jared had no doubt he would win the award.

That night when he got home, he switched his computer and browsed through the Tony Awards page. He hadn't googled Fenix since he'd left, hadn't bought any magazines that might have a publication about him, and since Adam had scared everyone into silence, Jared had no news about Fenix. Apart from that photo Aiden had been waving around that almost cost him a broken jaw.

The nomination listing stated that *Poison* has been nominated for Best Musical, and Fenix himself has been nominated for Best Performance in a Leading Role in a Musical. That was amazing! Jared smiled widely, mentally congratulating his... Jared stumbled to find a proper title for Fenix. Putting an ex in front of anything would seem wrong since Fenix was not an ex and never would be. Deciding against pondering that any longer, Jared checked his email and read the news, before logging off and heading to the kitchen to make dinner.

The night of the Tonys, Jared came home early, prepared a quick meal, and went to bed, setting his alarm for 3:00 am when the show would start in New York. When his phone woke him, Jared stretched to get his laptop from the bedside table where he'd left it, switched it on, and loaded the website with the live stream. The show was just about to start.

Jared's heart beat frantically inside his chest. He was going to get a glimpse of Fenix for the first time in almost two years. For a second he wondered if that was a good idea, but nothing would stop him from being with Fenix, even virtually, during his big moment.

The show started, and a few awards were given before it was time for the big one. Best Supporting actor and actress went first, as well as Best Director and Best Original Score. Fenix's category was next.

Thud. Thud. THUD.

Jared could barely hear anything besides his own heartbeat. Any moment now the cameras would zoom in on Fenix.

"And the nominations for Best Actor in a Leading Role in a Musical are," Leon Rolf, a two-time Tony winner announced, and Fenix's face filled the entire screen of Jared's laptop. "Fenix Bergman for *Poison*."

Jared didn't hear anything after that. Fenix was on screen for no longer than five seconds, but to Jared it seemed like hours. Time slowed as he drank in Fenix's features – his cheekbones were even more pronounced than he remembered, but what made Jared take a sharp breath were his eyes. Fenix's usually warm, calm, playful blue eyes had grown hard and cold. They made him look older, like he had been through a lot. Jared hadn't allowed himself to think about what Fenix could be going through, how he was coping with their separation, and with the gruelling Broadway world.

Maybe he should have. Maybe he should have made more of an effort, called to check on him, done something, anything. But Jared had drowned in his own pain and let Fenix down along the way.

"And the winner is," Leon Rolf said cheerfully, catching Jared's attention again. "Fenix Bergman for *Poison*."

The audience erupted in applause. Jared grinned. The camera followed Fenix as he walked towards the stage to accept his award. Jared touched the screen with the pads of his fingers, his emotions spilling out of him. He was crying a mixture of sad and happy tears and he was entirely unashamed of it.

Fenix shook Rolf's hand and accepted the award. He rested his palms on the pedestal, bowed his head as if concentrating until the applause died down. He looked up and the camera zoomed in on his face.

Jared could not breathe.

"I've sacrificed so much for this award," he began, his face set in an emotionless mask. He was not smiling, and he didn't look happy or grateful. "I lie awake at night wondering if it was all worth it." He looked at the statuette as if it had offended him. Fenix closed his eyes briefly before he continued. "I still don't know. But what I do know is this: *How can I call the lone night good, though thy sweet wishes wing its flight?*" Jared's heart stopped. Fenix had just quoted his favourite poem. The one *he* had quoted to *Fenix* when he asked him to move in. What did that mean? "I want to dedicate this award to my mother, Evelyn Bergman, who deserves it much more than me, but never got a chance to win it. I'd never be standing here if it weren't for my parents who are my lifeline when I feel like I'm drowning. Thank you," Fenix finished and walked off stage, the music signalling his exit playing in the background.

Jared pushed the laptop off his legs and got up. He needed to walk, to move, to *do* something. That was the most depressing acceptance speech he'd ever heard. Why had Fenix quoted Shelley? And why hadn't he even pretended to look cheerful for the millions of people who watched?

Something was terribly wrong, Jared could feel it in his gut. It was much worse than he imagined if Fenix couldn't summon his acting skills for two minutes and pretend to be happy that he'd won a fucking Tony!

Jared had to suppress the urge to jump on a plane and run to him. His whole body was trembling with desire to be near Fenix, to tell him that everything would work out.

To tell him how stupid they'd been for ever letting their job come between them.

"And now, for the award everyone's been waiting for. The nominations for Best Musical," a man announced dramatically and Jared had no idea who he was. He'd missed the introduction lost in his thoughts.

The nominations rolled and *Poison* was the last name to be announced, the camera zooming on the table where the cast, the director and producers sat. Fenix was not there.

"And the winner is," dramatic pause, "*A Moment Towards the End.*"

The audience erupted in applause again and Jared's heart plummeted. He had hoped *Poison* would win and prove all the critics who called it 'a glorified rock concert' wrong.

Jared couldn't bother with feeling disappointed about this. His thoughts were with Fenix. Where the hell was he? It had been at least fifteen minutes since he'd accepted his award. He had plenty of time to go back to the table.

It would be idiotic of Jared if he just dropped everything and flew to New York right now. He'd sacrificed his relationship with the only man he'd ever loved for his career and almost destroyed them both with that decision. How stupid would it be to let all that go to waste and do it anyway? After two years? What if Fenix didn't want him anymore? What if what Jared had seen tonight had been a lapse in judgement, nothing more? A momentary bad mood that had nothing to do with them?

But his eyes....

Fenix's eyes had said it all. He'd been crushed and chewed raw and spit out and left to rot by Jared's decision, by his own choices, by the meat grinder called Broadway.

What if it was too late?

Jared's phone rang loudly in the quiet room. He'd fallen asleep across the bed without even realising it, images of Fenix haunting his dreams. His laptop lay to his right, screen open and black. The show was over.

"Hello?" Jared mumbled into the phone. Nobody spoke on the other end, even though Jared could hear some background noise. He looked at the display to see it was 10:00 am and the number was withheld. "Hello?" Jared said again, more clearly.

Nothing. Jared's brain kicked into gear despite the abrupt awakening. His heart lurched in his chest and he instinctively knew who was calling.

"Fenix?" he whispered. A strangled sound came from the other end of the line. "Fenix!" Jared said, his voice rising alarmingly. All blood rushed away from his head and he felt dizzy, like he might faint or throw up or both. It was 5:00 am in New York, what was Fenix doing calling him?

"Yeah, it's me," Fenix said, his voice hoarse and small.

Oh God. Oh God. Oh God.

A thousand reasons for this call rushed through Jared's mind in a second and none of them good.

"Fenix? Are you alright? Are you hurt?" Jared asked, unable to hide the panic in his voice.

Fenix made a sound that must have been a humourless laugh but came out as if he was choking.

"I'm OK. Just wanted to hear your voice," he said, sniffling.

Was he crying?

"Fenix, talk to me. What's wrong?" Jared asked gently, even though he clutched his phone so tightly it dug into his fingers painfully.

"I..." Fenix began, but huffed and paused. "It doesn't matter. I'm sorry, I shouldn't have called."

The line went dead.

Jared threw the phone on the bed in anger. What was that all about? Two years without any contact, and now Fenix had called out of nowhere? Without any reason? Jared couldn't believe that. He knew if Fenix had called after all this time, he must have had a good enough reason.

There was something in Fenix's voice that scared the hell out of Jared. He sounded like he'd reached the end of his rope... But how was that possible? The man had won a fucking Tony a few hours ago. Wasn't that his ultimate life goal, his dream come true?

Jared wanted to get him back on the phone, but he realised he didn't have Fenix's number. Jared did the first thing that came to mind – dialled his agent. Samantha would be able to find Fenix's number, Jared was sure of it.

He was right. An hour later Jared stared at the text he'd just gotten from Samantha containing Fenix phone number. A few simple digits that would connect him to Fenix.

Without hesitation, Jared dialled the number. It rang for several long moments before voicemail picked up.

"Dammit, Fenix!" Jared yelled and disconnected.

He tried again, and again until Fenix's phone switched directly to voicemail without even ringing.

"Fucking stubborn bastard!" Jared growled and started pacing around the living room, wondering what to do. He couldn't just forget about it and move on with his life as if nothing had happened. He knew, *knew*, that something was wrong and he'd be damned if he just stood around and pretended otherwise.

He dialled again.

"Sam, it's me," Jared said into his phone when his agent picked up. "Do you have Cathleen O'Riley's number?"

"Jared, calm down," Cathleen said after Jared launched into a rapid interrogation about Fenix.

"I won't calm down until you tell me what going on, Cathleen. Why is he suddenly calling me in the middle of the night? Why isn't he picking up when I call? Why isn't he *happy*?"

Cathleen sighed heavily before responding.

"He's been in a bad shape lately, I won't lie to you about that."

"Shit," Jared muttered and covered his eyes with his hand. *What have you done, love?*

"He called me about an hour ago and said he needed to talk with me and that it was urgent. We have a meeting this evening. I don't know what this is all about, but he sounded good, better than I've seen him in a long time. That's why I'm surprised at what you're telling me about his phone call to you."

That calmed Jared down a bit, knowing that Fenix hadn't done something, like slitting his wrists or overdosing on sleeping pills, because frankly, that's how he'd sounded on the phone.

"OK. I'm glad to hear that. Just promise me something, Cathleen. Call me after you talk to him."

"Jared, you know I can't discuss my client's private meetings with you..."

"I know, that's not what I'm asking. Just call me to tell me he's alright. That's all I need to know. Please?"

Reluctantly, Cathleen agreed before Jared ended the call.

Thankfully, it was Monday and Jared didn't have a show that day – he wouldn't have been able to concentrate on anything until Cathleen called him back. Grabbing his gym bag, Jared walked out of his flat, hoping like hell Fenix would figure out whatever was wrong in his life and be able to fix it.

CHAPTER TWENTY THREE

Fenix

"Are you sure about this, Fenix?" Cathleen asked for a hundredth time since their talk on Monday. They were sitting in her office three days later when her PA informed her that the people they were expecting had arrived.

"I'm sure," Fenix said.

"Invite them in, Andy," Cathleen said to her assistant. A few moments later the door opened and three men in expensive suits walked in.

Elijah Goodwin, Bernard Morton, and Cayden Anderson – the producers of *Poison*.

After everyone had shaken hands and settled around the table in Cathleen's office, coffee cups in front of them, Goodwin took a thick folder out of his leather briefcase and passed it to Fenix across the table.

"I'm sorry it took us so long to organise this meeting, Fenix. We should have offered you the new contract a while ago, but..." Goodwin began with an apologetic smile that was not entirely sincere.

"But you had to wait and see if I'd win the Tony because the Osbert theatre wouldn't sign the new contract without it, right?" Fenix interrupted. There was no point in beating around the bush. All of them had been in this business long enough to know how it worked. The Osbert theatre wanted to write 'A Tony Award winner' on the posters advertising their main feature, and if it wasn't *Poison* it would have been some other show. *Poison* had missed out on the Tony for Best Musical, but Fenix winning must have been enough for the Osbert theatre if the producers had waltzed in here, offering Fenix a new contract.

"You know how it works, Fenix," Anderson shrugged unapologetically. "Broadway requires excellence."

Fenix rolled his eyes. He was sick of this shit. He pushed the folder back across the table towards Goodwin and leaned back in his chair.

"I'm not signing this," he stated blankly.

All three producers raised their eyebrows in unison. It was comical. Fenix could see their world crashing and burning behind their eyes. Everyone in this room knew *Poison* would not be as successful without Fenix. They also knew the Osbert theatre would never sign them on for another season without Fenix.

"What do you mean? You haven't even read it! We've increased your pay and we've amended the terms like you wanted..." Morton began, but Fenix interrupted him.

"I don't care about that," he said, leaning forward, resting his forearms on the table. He looked each of the men straight in their eyes before he spoke, focusing on Goodwin. "I want *Poison* to move back to the West End."

All three producers gaped at him in shock. Goodwin spoke after he managed his bearings.

"London? You want us to quit Broadway and go back to *London*? Are you insane?"

"No, I'm not insane. And yes, this is exactly what I want in order to sign that contract."

Goodwin laughed humourlessly, and said,

"You can't do that!"

"Watch me!" Fenix replied, getting tired of the whole thing. He was getting restless and wanted out of the room as soon as possible. "Without me, the Osbert theatre will not sign *Poison* for another season. I won the fucking Tony, not the musical. I'm your star. I'm the one who's pulling the audience in every night. I'm the one who rehearses and dances and has sacrificed everything for this fucking show!" Fenix hadn't even realised he'd pushed his chair back and was standing up, leaning over the table and yelling. The three men in front of him stared at him in shock.

"Fenix, please sit down. Let me take care of this," Cathleen said, walking closer to him and helping him back into his chair. She'd been quiet during the meeting so far, but Fenix knew it wasn't because she'd changed her mind about supporting him in this. It was because she wanted him to try and handle the situation himself like he'd wanted. Obviously, he'd failed.

Fenix nodded and fell back in his chair gracelessly. The producers continued to stare at him before Cathleen spoke and attracted their attention.

"Gentlemen, what Fenix said is true, even though his delivery wasn't very polite. I have spoken with Queen Victoria in London, and they assured me they would welcome *Poison* back with open arms. Their current main musical is going on tour overseas in a month and they have not yet signed a new contract, even though they have had preliminary talks with the producers of another show. However, I have to let them know by the end of the day if we're serious about this, and then we can move on to discussing the details and contract terms," Cathleen finished smoothly, unflinching under the producers' bewildered stare.

"You can't be serious about this," Bernard Morton said, more in astonishment than anger. The three men were still in a state of shock, and Fenix wondered if it was going to take them a long time to recover because he really wanted to leave.

"OK, look," Fenix began, calmer this time. "If you don't want to accept this offer, then don't. I'll walk right now and you'll be free to find your next big star and stay on Broadway. If you're willing to go knocking on theatre doors, explaining to everyone why the Tony Award winner Fenix Bergman has been scratched from your poster, then fine. Take that risk. I don't care either way. I'll find another job in London easily enough, but I'm going back there with or without *Poison*."

Goodwin, Morton, and Anderson exchanged looks, seeming to communicate silently between them, before Goodwin spoke.

"We need to discuss this in private before we make a decision," he said as he stood up. "We'll be in touch by the end of the day."

"That went well," Cathleen said, shortly after the door closed behind them. Fenix rolled his eyes and leaned his head over the chair's back, looking at the ceiling and not giving a damn if it went well or not. "I want to make sure you're prepared for the outcome, Fenix. Are you ready to hear them say 'no'?" Cathleen asked.

"They won't say 'no'," Fenix huffed in distaste. "All they care about is making money. *Poison* is going to attract huge crowds if it returns to London and they know it."

"Fenix..." Cathleen began with a sigh, but he interrupted her.

"I can't go on like this anymore, Cat," he said quietly. "I thought Broadway was all I ever needed to be happy," he continued and laughed sardonically. "I was such a fool! What I need is someone to hold me during the night when I wake up screaming in pain because my muscles are seizing with exhaustion. What I need is someone to share the fucking Tony award with because it doesn't mean anything just gathering dust on the shelf."

"Don't say that. That award is a testament of your hard work. You deserve it."

"I know I deserve it. But I also know it's not worth it." Fenix stood up – this was getting all too intense for his taste. He wanted the conversation done with so that he could go to his empty apartment and start packing his few belongings into a suitcase.

"You know you could have had anybody to take Jared's place, right? You didn't have to do this alone..."

"But that's exactly it, Cat – it's *his* place. I don't want anybody in *his place*. I want *him*. I haven't felt anything remotely resembling happiness ever since I walked out of our home and left him alone and broken. I don't even know if he had someone to pick up the pieces I left behind." Fenix started pacing, itching to get out of this office, this city, this *life*. "It's time for *Poison* to go back home, Cat. It's time for *me* to go back home and pray that he'd take me back."

"What if he doesn't? You haven't exchanged as much as a birthday card during the last two years. What if he's moved on, Fenix? What if you risk everything you've worked so hard for just to get your heart broken again?"

"I have to try," Fenix said with finality before he walked out of his agent's office.

CHAPTER TWENTY FOUR

Jared

It was too fucking early to be summoned to the theatre on a Sunday morning. Jared flopped on the seat next to Adam and sighed dramatically. His best friend didn't look bothered by Jared's lack of greeting or his apparent bad mood. Glancing to his right at Jared, Adam mumbled something that might have been 'hello' or 'fuck off' – Jared couldn't be sure – and continued to play Candy Crush on his phone.

Great.

Jared looked around the hall and saw that most of the staff, including actors, dancers, tech support, even the cleaners and ticket sellers, were already present. He couldn't see anybody from *Underground* but he supposed they were all still sleeping after last night's show. No self-respecting late night performer woke up before noon on a week day, let alone on a Sunday.

The stage was lit up and empty, as if waiting for something to happen any minute.

"What's going on?" he asked Adam.

"Fuck if I know," his friend replied without glancing away from his phone.

Jared shrugged and took out his own phone. He had a strict rule not to check his email or reply to work related messages on a Sunday, but he didn't have anything better to do right now. He might as well check if anything needed his immediate attention.

An email from Fenix Bergman titled 'Don't delete. Read it. It's important' made all the air rush out of his lungs with an audible gasp.

Fenix.

Jared hadn't been able to get him to pick up the phone ever since that weird conversation a week ago, but true to her word, Cathleen had called him back and assured him Fenix was fine. She had hinted at some huge development in his life but hadn't wanted to say more.

Jared had been satisfied with the little information she had managed to give him. He was happy Fenix was doing fine and that phone call had been an exception, not the rule.

Jared's finger hovered over the email and he pressed 'open' just as Simon McAllister, the infamous chief executive of Queen Victoria, walked on the stage and grabbed everyone's attention.

"Good afternoon, everyone. Thank you for coming on such a short notice. I do apologise for disrupting your weekend, but what I have to say is time sensitive."

The hall went so still and quiet that Jared was certain people were collectively holding their breaths. Simon McAllister had that effect on people – when he talked, you listened.

"As you all know, *Underground* is going on tour overseas in three weeks. We've been in talks with a couple of other shows over the past month, but we haven't been able to reach a satisfactory, for both sides, agreement."

There was suddenly a buzz like a live current through the entire hall – what did this mean? Surely, they had something else lined up? People started whispering among themselves, slightly panicked that Queen Victoria had no main feature signed up yet.

"Please, let me finish," Mr McAllister said. The crowd calmed down. "I'm sorry if I gave you the wrong impression. The news I have is actually very good. None of you are losing your jobs, on the contrary. We might have to hire extra staff because we're expecting a sold out season ahead."

There was a collective gasp and an intake of breath as everyone prepared for the news. Jared rolled his eyes – no wonder that guy's been the chief executive of London's most famous theatre for a decade. He knew how to work a crowd and keep the suspense till the very last second.

"I asked you all here today because tomorrow the papers are going to print what I'm about to tell you, but I wanted to give you the wonderful news personally." He paused for effect and Jared heard Adam groan impatiently beside him. Loudly. Mr McAllister must have heard him too because he gave him a stern look before continuing: "I won't stall any longer, I can see Mr Fischer is getting impatient, and as we all know that is very hard to achieve." Everyone laughed and Adam flipped them off, frowning. "Ladies and gentlemen, I'm happy to officially announce that *Poison* is coming back to Queen Victoria in three weeks."

The crowd erupted in claps, whistles, and cheers all at the same time. Jared's ears started ringing.

Poison *is coming back to Queen Victoria.*

Fenix was coming back.

Wait! Maybe that was what the email was about? Maybe Fenix knew Jared would find out today and wanted to tell him that he wasn't coming back? Surely he'd never leave Broadway, especially after winning a Tony? He could pick and choose any show he wanted – maybe he signed with another musical, and that was why *Poison* was being thrown back to London?

Jared needed to read that email.

He picked up his phone again, glancing around to make sure everyone was busy talking and congratulating Simon McAllister to care about what Jared was doing. He slid his finger down the screen and unlocked the phone. It took him straight to the already opened email.

"I can't fucking believe this," Adam grumbled beside him, startling him.

Jared needed to find a quiet corner and read this damn email before he strangled someone, even if it was his best friend. "Aren't you gonna say something?" Adam asked, moving to stand up. Jared jumped out of his seat and hurried towards his dressing room. "Jared! What the hell, man?" Adam called after him, but he didn't stop.

Quiet place. Alone. Now.

Jared swung the dressing room door so hard it banged on the wall behind it. Not caring, he slammed it shut and turned the lock. Sitting on the sofa, Jared unlocked his phone again with trembling fingers and started reading.

Jared,

I hope you'll read this. And I hope you haven't already heard.

Poison is coming back to Queen Victoria. And I'm coming back with it.

I didn't call you on the phone because I want to talk to you in person. I don't know if you'd want to talk to me after all this time, but I hope you would.

Give me a chance, please.

Love,

Fen

Jared started shaking. His breath was coming out in uneven gasps. Sweat popped out on his forehead, and he felt like he was going to pass out. The walls seemed to start moving towards him and were going to crush him any second now.

"Jared!" Adam's voice boomed outside the door, followed by loud banging a second later. "What the hell is the matter with you?"

"Get lost, Adam. I need a minute."

"The fuck I will! Unlock the door or I'm taking it down and dragging you out. Your choice."

He totally would.

Jared sighed and opened the door, letting in a very furious Adam. He left his phone on the coffee table and went into the bathroom, splashing his face with cold water. The man staring back from his reflexion in the mirror looked scary. His usually wild, shiny, dark hair was limp and dripping wet at the front; his eyes were frantic, and his skin was flushed, as if he'd run five miles.

"*Love, Fen*? You've got to be kidding me! What a useless, arrogant, stupid piece of shit!" Adam raged when Jared walked out of the bathroom. His fingers were clutching Jared's phone so hard he thought it'd snap in half. Thank God he'd backed up all his contacts and information after the last 'accident'. "We have to go, mate. Right now. Go pack your stuff and we're leaving this evening."

"What? Are you mental? I'm not going anywhere!" And for a second Jared thought *he* was the crazy one.

"You can't be here when he comes back!" Adam yelled, spreading his hands and still holding Jared's phone. Jared grabbed it and put it in his pocket. The hassle of getting another phone seemed like too much work right now.

"I can and I will. This is my city, my theatre, and my career. I'm not going to run away like some coward just because Fenix is coming back."

"You're going to forgive him, aren't you? Take him back." It wasn't a question. Adam was looking at Jared with burning fury, like he was ready to throw Jared over his shoulder and spirit him away, somewhere the evil sorcerer would never find them.

"There's nothing to forgive, Adam. What happened was as much my fault as it was his," Jared said and watched Adam's face twist into an ugly, angry scowl.

"What?" he growled. "Are you even serious right now? He dumped you, walked out of your life without a moment's hesitation! And for what? Fame? Money? His *dream*?"

"And I stayed here! I could have gone with him. But I didn't. I chose my career, my life here over him. I was hurt and angry when he left, but I can't deny that we both could have made different choices."

Some of Adam's rage leaked out of his body when he absorbed what Jared said. They had never talked about this before, and Adam, being fiercely protective of Jared, had assumed it had been all Fenix's fault. Jared knew that, and he hadn't tried to talk to him about it to change his mind simply because it had hurt too much to even say the words. And it hadn't really mattered until now, had it? Jared hadn't imagined that Fenix would ever come back.

Adam started pacing around, mulling over his next words. Jared sighed and dropped on the sofa.

"So you are taking him back? Just like that?" Adam finally said, his tone calmer.

"No. I..." Jared began but didn't know what to say. Up until fifteen minutes ago he didn't even know Fenix was coming back. He needed some time to think what he was actually going to do when he did come back. They were going to see each other every day, it was inevitable. Jared's body ran cold with the thought that he'd see Fenix every day without being able to touch him, hold him, feel his skin...

"Yes, you are," Adam stated and sat down next to Jared. "He has this hold on you, this *pull* that you haven't been able to shake even when you've been apart for two years. When he gets here, he'll get you back," Adam said with certainty. "But before you welcome him in your life again, answer me this: are you going to survive it when he leaves again?"

Jared felt like Adam stabbed him with a knife right through the heart. He put his palm over his chest and rubbed, trying to soothe the pain away so that he can breathe properly.

No, he wasn't going to survive if Fenix left again. That much he knew for sure.

CHAPTER TWENTY FIVE

Jared

The moment Jared walked into the theatre, he knew something was different. Off.

The last few days he'd been agonizing over Fenix's return, going back and forth between fear, joy, and panic. He didn't know exactly when Fenix was going to arrive in London. He'd almost called him a few times because the wait was killing him. Jared knew he was stressed and in a bad mood, snapping at everyone and throwing temper tantrums like a five year old, but he couldn't help it.

Adam had suggested, numerous times, that they cut and run, as fast and as far away from here as possible.

"You'd really do that for me? Drop everything and run away with me?"

"Of course. How can you even ask me that, you bastard! I'd do anything for you and you fucking know it."

Yes, Adam had the incredible ability of making you feel loved while insulting you in the same sentence.

As he walked through the foyer of Queen Victoria, not really seeing anyone, Jared thought for a brief moment how much easier it would have been if he and Adam had managed to fall in love with each other, to develop a romantic relationship that would have been satisfying for both of them.

"You're too much alike," Fenix used to joke. "You both are impulsive, stubborn, hot headed brutes. While the visual of you two having sex is hot, you'd never work as a couple. You need someone you can boss around. Like me."

"Ha! Look who's trying to be funny and not succeeding! I've never managed to make you do anything you didn't want to do!"

"Make me do something I really want to do then," Fenix said as he climbed in Jared's lap and started kissing his neck, sucking at his Adam's apple as he reached it. "Like suck your cock until you scream." Fenix moved his sinful lips over Jared's ear and moaned seductively. "And then maybe, just maybe, I'll let you come." Jared threw his head back on the sofa and licked his lips in anticipation.

"Jared!" Adam's shout right next to his ear brought him back to the present. "The fuck? I called you like five times! What the hell are you doing spacing out in the middle of the foyer?"

"You really need to stop screaming in my face," Jared said and headed for the dressing rooms.

"Stop acting like you have a learning disability and I might," Adam grumbled as he followed him.

Jared laughed despite himself and opened his dressing room's door to find Fenix just as he was peeling off his sweaty t-shirt. Fenix startled as the door jerked open and dropped the t-shirt on the floor, remaining only in his black, tight leggings. The sight of that toned, muscular, *familiar* body displayed in front of him sent Jared in a whirlwind of memories.

Fenix leaning back, riding him, supporting himself with his arms extended behind him, as his erect, leaking cock bounced up and down, and all the strong, lean muscles on his stomach, thighs, and shoulders flexed with the effort.

Fenix in their bed, looking at him under his blond bangs, his sleepy blue eyes barely open, and his lips turned down in a grimace because of the early morning wake up call.

Fenix whispering 'I love you' before he fell asleep on Jared's chest.

Fenix dancing on stage as if his body was boneless. His singing voice filling the hollow theatre and trying to burst out because the hall wasn't big enough to contain it.

Shouting. Tears. Jared's world collapsing. His heart bursting out of his skin.

Silence.

Alone.

"Hi," Fenix said. Jared took an instinctive step back only to find Adam's chest behind him. He could feel the low growling that had started in that same chest. He had two choices – freak out and run, leaving Fenix alone with Adam, or keep calm and politely ask Adam to leave, pretending like he didn't just have the biggest shock of his life.

While Jared knew Fenix could hold his own in a fight and get a pretty good use of his six feet height and strong dancer's muscles, he didn't want to take the chance of Adam hurting him. Because Adam was a mountain of a man who could crush mere mortals between his thumb and forefinger.

He chose option two.

"Hi," he replied, as calmly as possible. He turned to look at Adam over his shoulder. His best friend was looking at Fenix without even blinking, his eyes narrowed to hateful slits and his mouth pursed into a thin, white line. Yep, he was ready to pounce. "Adam, it's OK. Can you maybe give us a minute?"

"No," Adam snarled, not moving an inch.

Jared turned to fully face his friend and placed his hands on his cheeks until Adam's eyes focused on him.

"Please. It's OK. I'll handle this."

Adam must have seen the desperation in Jared's eyes because he slowly nodded, and, casting one last evil glare at Fenix, left the room, slamming the door behind him.

"Wow. I can see he hasn't changed a bit," Fenix said and rolled his eyes.

"What are you doing here?" Jared asked quietly, his eyes following Fenix as he moved around the room.

He was here. Fenix was really here! God, he'd missed him so fucking much.

"I sent you an email. Didn't you read it? It was titled..."

"I read it," Jared interrupted him. "I meant what are you doing *here*, in my dressing room?"

Fenix's lips twitched as if he was trying not to laugh.

"Oh. That. You were sharing a dressing room with Albert Burns, the lead *Underground*, right? So now that he's not performing here anymore I was offered his dressing room and I accepted."

"Why did you accept? A Tony award winner could have demanded his own dressing room I imagine." Jared said, angry that Fenix had just assumed he could take his place back in Jared's dressing room, Jared's *life*, without even asking first. Like he was entitled to it.

"I could have, yes. But I didn't. I'd rather share with you." Fenix's intense blue eyes were burning holes into Jared's heart. He didn't know how to respond to that – should he switch dressing rooms with someone else? He could bet anyone currently working in Queen Victoria would be beyond happy to share with Fenix.

"I can see your wheels turning, Jared. Stop overthinking and let it go. It's not such a big deal – I perform at night, you perform in the afternoon. We'll barely even cross paths."

"We're crossing paths now. What are you even doing here before noon?"

"I wanted to get a feel of the stage again. And sneak in a work-out in the rehearsal room – I'm still jetlagged and can't sleep well, so I needed to exhaust some of my built up energy."

Jared's anger leaked out of him as quick as it had appeared. He could never stay mad at Fenix for too long.

But this was different, damn it! They were not together anymore. Jared had all the right in the world to be angry.

Jared.

The way he said his name still sent goosebumps all over his skin and made his cock twitch in his jeans. He had to get out of this room. Fenix was right – they'd barely even see each other with their schedules being different. Today was an exception. He wasn't going to do anything about this situation and create additional drama. One theatre housing two musicals already had more drama queens than a Mexican soap opera, and he'd be damned if he became one of them.

"Whatever. I have to start getting ready in about an hour, so I'd appreciate it if you're finished by then," said Jared, turning to open the door. He'd barely opened it an inch when it slammed forcefully shut. Turning to look over his shoulder, Jared saw Fenix's face inches away and his hand against the door.

"Wait," Fenix commanded in a low voice. His hair had grown longer and his blond bangs were hanging over his eyes. He looked even more striking as the muscles in his stubble-covered jaw clenched. "I want to talk to you."

"Not now..." Jared whispered and tried to open the door but Fenix kept it firmly shut. He needed to get out of here. His emotions after seeing Fenix were running into overdrive and he needed some space before they could talk.

"Jared..." Fenix said in a low, husky voice, his warm breath brushing Jared's ear.

Jared visibly shivered. He couldn't help it. Fenix was so close that Jared's body acted on its own accord – he'd spent two fucking years trying to convince his body and his brain that Fenix was never coming back, and that he'd never, ever feel the way he was feeling right now. And yet, he kept craving the man like he craved water after the end of the show.

Jared dared to turn just a little to steal a look at Fenix. His pupils were so huge that his light blue eyes were almost entirely dark. He was breathing heavily, buzzing with energy. Jared lowered his eyes to Fenix's crotch and saw that he was fully erect in his tight leggings.

When his gaze returned to Fenix's face, Jared saw the raw hunger in his eyes and instinctively knew what was going to happen. Fenix was on him so fast that he couldn't react. His lips were soft and warm and delicious, and his tongue was pushing inside Jared's mouth, demanding entrance. Jared's brain short circuited. He opened his mouth and let Fenix in, returning the kiss just as ferociously.

He'd missed this.

He'd missed *him*.

Jared would do anything, *anything*, to have this forever.

Fenix pushed him back against the door and caged his body, pressing their cocks together as he grinded against him. In about three seconds Jared was going to come in his pants. But he didn't care. He licked Fenix's lips and explored his mouth with his tongue and nothing else mattered in the world. Jared wanted more. He wanted to touch Fenix everywhere. His palms slid down Fenix's back and cupped his ass through his leggings, provoking a loud moan from Fenix. He unglued his mouth from Jared's long enough to whisper a desperate 'Yes, baby, please...' and buckle his hips even harder against Jared's.

Jared's control snapped. In a single, forceful movement he exchanged their places so that Fenix was crushed against the door, and turned him around. Pulling his leggings down, Jared wet his fingers with saliva and probed at Fenix's hole, pushing a finger inside and making Fenix moan loudly. Jared wet his fingers some more and pushed two inside, placing open mouthed kisses on Fenix's neck.

They both breathed hard, and their whispers and moans of pleasure were desperate pleas for more. Jared had no connection with his brain. All he knew was that he wanted Fenix right now, he wanted to be inside him, claim him, fuck him until Fenix promised he'd never leave again.

"Condom," Jared managed to rasp against Fenix's skin. His brain might be in a fog of lust but he still cared about their safety.

"My bag," Fenix said as he pointed at a duffel on the floor next to Jared. "Front pocket." Jared took the condom out of the pocket, pulled his jeans down along with his boxers, and sheathed his aching cock with the pre-lubricated condom. With trembling hands he guided himself inside Fenix.

"Yes, oh God! Jared!" Fenix moaned, thrusting his hips back so that Jared's cock was fully inside him. He fisted his own erection and started jerking off, moaning incoherently.

Jared had to summon all his control not to come right then. He'd wanted this every single day for the past two years, and now that he finally had it, he was so sensitive and over stimulated that he wasn't sure he'd last longer than a few strokes.

"Fuck me, Jared, please. I need you. Only you..." Fenix trailed off. Jared grabbed his hips and started thrusting, long and hard, seeing the effect he had on Fenix's body. He was shaking all over, whimpering, thrashing, cursing...

"I'm gonna come, Fen. I can't last. Not now," Jared said with difficulty as he pressed his chest on Fenix's back and nipped at his neck.

Fenix yelled and came, spurting ribbons of come all over the door. His ass clenched around Jared and that was all he needed to push him over the edge.

They stood like this, trying to catch their breaths for a long time, until Fenix moved under Jared and prompted him to pull out. Jared padded to the bathroom without a word. He disposed of the condom, washed his face and his hands, and, before his brain could start shouting what an idiot he was, he walked out. Fenix had pulled himself together and even wiped the door clean. Jared couldn't talk with him right now, couldn't even look at him.

"I'm sorry," he said without meeting Fenix's eyes, hurrying to open the door.

"Jared," Fenix called after him, trying to stop him again, but Jared was faster and walked out before Fenix could reach him.

CHAPTER TWENTY SIX

Fenix

Fenix snuck in at the back of the Dress Circle and hoped like hell he was hidden enough and Jared wouldn't notice him. The man was like a hawk. He paid attention to the audience –

he loved performing for kids and young people and the interaction with the audience was crucial. As much as Fenix tried to disregard the audience as he performed because he found it incredibly distracting, Jared craved communicating with his audience. Fenix was certain the huge success *Of Kids and Monsters* had had so far was largely because of Jared and his charisma. Not that the musical itself wasn't amazing – it was an incredible story of courage, finding yourself, and learning to believe in the unbelievable, all wrapped up in a witty, fun, poignant package for kids. Sometimes, however, the parents seemed to enjoy it even more than their children.

Fenix slouched in his seat as much as he could, getting a strange look from the woman sitting next to him who was craning her neck to see the stage. She had two boys aged around eight with her who, judging by the glint in their eyes, were very excited to see the musical. Thankfully he'd chosen a seat next to the aisle and could bolt any time he wanted.

The lights in the theatre went out, the stage lit up, and the music began. Fenix could feel the collective intake of breath as the show started. Jared appeared on stage, dressed casually in blue jeans and a t-shirt. Despite the elaborate stage decor, he still managed to stand out even in his simple clothes. And then he began singing. Fenix closed his eyes and let Jared's soft, melodic voice sink into every cell of his body.

Jared wasn't a singer or a dancer – he could do both pretty well, but what he was born to do was *act*. When Jared talked, people listened. When Jared focused those intensely navy coloured eyes on you, you didn't look away. Yet, Fenix marvelled at his voice. It surrounded him and hugged him tight, and he couldn't help the shiver that ran down his body and woke up his cock.

He let all the emotions from a few hours ago flood him, overwhelm him. Jared had fucked him in their dressing room. Jared still wanted him. The connection they had shared before was still there, Fenix could feel it, and it wasn't only physical. Fenix had been fucked by numerous men during the time he was gone, but he'd never felt this way with someone else. How was that possible? The act was exactly the same. Jared didn't have a magical cock that could melt Fenix's insides with a single thrust of his hips.

And yet, he had.

Every touch, every kiss, every whisper made Fenix's body turn inside out.

Fenix consciously dragged his mind off Jared and what they'd done, and focused on the musical. It was just as good and he remembered, if not better.

All the 'monsters' were on stage now, singing and acting their own stories, letting the children help them find the good inside themselves. It was beautiful, absolutely breathtaking. He could feel the energy buzzing through every single person in the audience. Queen Victoria was alive and it was all thanks to the actors on stage right now.

Fenix left his seat before the show ended. He headed for his and Jared's dressing room and sprawled on the small sofa. He knew Jared wouldn't be happy to see him. The man needed some space to, undoubtedly, agonise over what had happened between them and over think it to a point of no return. Well, Fenix wasn't giving him that chance. He'd come back to London for *Jared* and he'd be damned if he didn't get him back sooner or later.

Fenix grabbed a magazine he saw lying around when he heard voices coming closer to the dressing rooms. He started casually flipping through the pages as if he had nothing better to do.

"Not tonight, mate. I just want to go home and pass out in my own bed. I'll take you up on that offer soon, though," Jared was saying to someone right outside the door. Fenix perked up, trying to hear everything that was being said. What offer?

"No worries. Catch you later," Adam replied.

It was only Adam. Jared's first-lover-turned-best-friend Adam. Fenix had never gotten along with the guy, but they used to have an unspoken agreement to be civil to each other for Jared. Fenix could imagine how much the guy hated him now, because, he supposed, Adam had been the one who'd tried to put Jared back together after Fenix had left.

At least Jared had someone close to him to help.

The door opened and Jared walked in, closing it firmly behind him. The moment he noticed Fenix sitting on the sofa he stopped mid stride and glared at him.

"Why are you here? Your show doesn't even start for two weeks," he said with a scowl.

"I was rehearsing my lines," Fenix said and pointedly turned the page of the magazine he was holding.

"Your lines are printed in *Attitude*?"

"Yep. You know how much they love their musicals," Fenix replied without missing a beat. "The whole issue is dedicated to me and my Tony award."

Jared rolled his eyes and didn't comment any further. He started stripping off his stage costume, throwing the clothes over the chair in front of his dressing table. With all the mirrors in the room Fenix had a perfect three hundred and sixty degree view of Jared's body. They were pretty much the same height – around six feet, but Jared was *built*. He had broad shoulders and defined muscles on his back, stomach, arms and legs. Fenix knew from his own experience that Jared didn't work out simply for vanity. He needed to be fit for performing – there were no breaks in the show for the actors and dancers to catch their breaths. It was all one big, dynamic whirlwind, and if you weren't fit enough to dance and sing and say your lines without looking like you might topple over and die, you had no place performing on stage.

Something clattered on the floor and shook Fenix out of his thoughts. His eyes focused on Jared once again to find him stark naked, walking around the dressing room, and, judging by his annoyed expression and things falling to the floor as he rummaged through them, was looking for something.

Fenix licked his lips unintentionally as he stared at Jared. He wanted nothing more right than to drop on his knees and beg Jared to take him back. That, and suck his cock until he couldn't remember why they'd broken up in the first place.

"What are you looking for?" he asked instead, his voice wavering a little.

"My fucking towel. I'm sure I put it in my bag this morning. Now I can't find it."

"Here," Fenix stood up and went to his side of the wardrobe, opening the door. "Use this. I brought a few in today." He offered Jared a fluffy white towel, but he eyed it suspiciously and didn't immediately reach to take it. Now that Fenix was standing an arm's length away from Jared, he could actually feel the post-show heat radiating from him. He smelled so delicious – sweat mixed with cologne and his fruity shower gel. Fenix could not stand here any longer and be held responsible for his actions – the man was temptation reincarnated.

"It's clean," he said, prompting Jared to take the towel. Jared took another second to consider the offer, but in the end snatched the towel off Fenix's hands and headed for the bathroom.

"You're welcome!" Fenix called after him. The only response he got back was the bathroom door slamming shut.

Jared would probably expect him to be there when he finished his shower, but Fenix decided against it. He'd give him the space he needed. Tonight.

Fenix saw Jared's phone thrown casually on the coffee table and took it, programming his new British number in the contact list. Then, he sent him a text saying, 'call me' and quietly left the dressing room.

Fenix was staying in Hotel 41 on Buckingham Palace Road while he managed to find a more permanent residence. It was a luxury, boutique hotel with direct views of the heart of London. It took him less than twenty minutes to walk from Queen Victoria to the hotel and he welcomed the brisk walk. It was the beginning of August and London was beautiful at that time of the year. Fenix had forgotten how much he missed his adopted city. New York was great – it was where he was born, where he fell in love with musical theatre, where his parents lived. But London was his home.

Beware London, Fenix Bergman is back! Did you miss me?

Fenix smiled as he strolled down The Mall towards Buckingham Palace.

He'd booked the Conservatory Master Suite because he'd fallen in love with it just looking at the photos on the hotel's website. It was a penthouse with a living-room area, two bathrooms – one with a whirlpool bath – and a master bedroom with a glass ceiling. It felt like sleeping under the stars, only surrounded by exquisite goose down duvets, Egyptian cotton sheets, floor heating, and room service.

The hotel was also known for their impeccable customer service and discretion. Fenix had been here a few days and the press hadn't gotten a whiff of where he was staying yet, and he hoped it'd stay that way. The concierge greeted him warmly yet respectfully as he walked into the main reception area. Fenix requested a light dinner to be delivered in about an hour and headed for the elevator. He had a whirlpool bath waiting for him upstairs and intended to take full advantage of it.

This is soooo goooood, Fenix groaned internally. The water was hot and the whirlpool jets were doing wonders for his sore muscles. He'd had a good workout today in the rehearsal room and his whole body felt tired. Add that to the jetlag he still couldn't get over and Fenix was in sharp need of a full body massage, and a few extra-long nights of sleep.

Fenix's phone rang the moment he stepped out of the bathroom. There were a handful of people who knew his new number, so Fenix wasn't surprised to see Joy's name on the display.

"Hey," he said when he picked up. "Are you all packed yet?"

The cast were supposed to arrive next week, but Fenix couldn't wait that long and had hurried ahead.

"Almost. I wanted to check on you, see how you're settling in."

"Yeah, right. You want gossip," Fenix said and laughed.

"That, too," Joy said, her voice full of mischief. "So, how's Jared, the man responsible for relocating a whole Broadway musical across the world?"

After the faithful night of the Tonys when Fenix had made his decision to return to London no matter what, he'd taken both Joy and Ned out to dinner to apologise for the hurtful way he'd been behaving and to ask them if they were OK with what he was about to do. After all, it was their life and their careers, too. Joy was glad they were moving back to the West End – Broadway had been a bit too much for her lately. Ned had been ecstatic! His love for English men was widely known and he couldn't wait to get back to 'a country full of them'.

Not everyone in the cast had taken the news well, and a couple of people had quit. The musical theatre world was unpredictable, and at any given time a show could be moved to another continent or sent on tour for six months. If people weren't ready to sacrifice their personal lives for the show, then they had no place in it. Despite that, Fenix felt guilty about costing people their jobs, and had asked his agent to put a good word out for them, hoping they'd manage to find something else.

"Fenix? Still there?" Joy's voice rang in his ear, dragging Fenix back to the conversation.

"Yeah, I'm here. Sorry," Fenix mumbled. "Um, Jared is good. Really good," he added, inserting the appropriate amount of double meaning into his words.

"Oh my god! Do not tell me you guys kissed and made up already?"

"We didn't make up, yet. But he did fuck me against the dressing room door," Fenix said casually.

"Fenix!" Joy shrieked, followed by a laugh.

Fenix refused to volunteer any more information about Jared and in the end Joy gave up. They chatted a bit more before

Fenix started yawning uncontrollably and wrapped up the conversation. It was good to hear from Joy. He'd missed his friends, and it was his own fault they'd stayed away. But all that was in the past now – Fenix had no intention of falling back into the darkness that had consumed him and push everyone away again.

Fenix lay exhausted in the big, comfortable bed, but sleep wouldn't come. He'd relaxed his muscles in the bath, had some wonderful, fresh sushi for dinner, and read until his eyes got tired and blurry. And yet, he couldn't sleep.

The sky above him was unusually clear and he could see the stars sparkling in the darkness. What was the point of paying extra for this glass roof if even the fucking twinkling stars couldn't get him to sleep?

Sighing, Fenix threw the covers off and rubbed his hands over his face. He was restless, tired, hot, anxious... His mind drifted to evaluating the choices he'd made in his life so far and the choices he was about to make in the future. How long could he dedicate his life to the stage? To the show? He loved to perform, but he was tired of everything else.

This business was so cut-throat that if you were one of the best you had to watch your back all the time. There was always someone who felt they deserved your place and would do anything to get it. The performers were brainwashed since they were kids – they needed to be perfect, beautiful, composed, talented.

Emotionless.

Uncompassionate.

Cruel.

Although, they called it determined.

If it meant wrecking your body with too much practise, or drugging yourself on coke or morphine so that you didn't feel the pain during a performance, so be it. You could go and cry and scream in pain later, when the show was over. If it meant sabotaging someone else, stomping all over them, and never turning back until you've reached the very top, so be it.

What not all of them knew was that the top was a fucking miserable place. Fenix had been there. Fuck, he still was, and he *knew*. It was cold and lonely and so empty. You didn't have friends, you had people who kissed your ass and waited for you to fall; you didn't have a family, you had people who endured your constant absence, bad moods, and injuries until they got sick of it and left.

His mother had been at the top as well and that was why she was stuck in a wheelchair for the rest of her life. She understood. One look into Fenix's eyes the day after the Tonys and Evelyn had known. She'd looked towards Fenix's dad and the man who loved them both so much that had stuck by his wife even when she had returned on stage three months after giving birth; that incredible, strong, generous, loving man had said:

"Son, you're holding everything you've ever wanted in your hands right now and you've never been more unhappy. I can't watch the other person I love most in this world get wrecked by dance."

Fenix had broken down then, his mother had hugged him and whispered gentle words, and his dad had made tea, and they had talked. Fenix told them everything he'd felt and they'd understood. Their support had given him courage to do what he desperately wanted – go back to Queen Victoria, to London, to Jared. Fenix wanted to dance, to perform, but being the best, being a Tony award winner, didn't mean what he'd thought it would. It didn't make him as happy as he'd thought it would.

CHAPTER TWENTY SEVEN

Jared

Jared woke up with his phone ringing loudly somewhere close by. He groaned, rolled over, and sighed heavily. It had not been a good night. He'd tossed and turned until the wee hours until he'd fallen into a fretful sleep. The annoying ringing was still going on, so obviously whoever was calling had no intention of hanging up before Jared picked up. Unfortunately, he had no recollection of where he'd tossed his phone after he'd stared at it for hours, trying not to call Fenix.

"For fuck's sake!" he swore, and patting the covers, tried to locate his damn phone.

"What!" he yelled once he picked up, not bothering to look at the screen.

"Jared, it's Samantha."

Great. If his agent was calling him so early and so insistently, the news was either fantastic or someone had died. Jared put all his chips on the latter.

"Hey, Sam. Sorry I yelled. What's up?"

"Are you OK? You sound terrible," his agent asked in her clipped, posh accent.

"I'm fine. Had a rough night," Jared replied, flopping back on the bed.

"Does Fenix Bergman have anything to do with your rough night?" Samantha asked, her voice conversational.

"So you know." Of course she knew. Samantha knew everything the moment it happened. That was one of the things that made her such a brilliant agent.

"My knowing is not the problem. The press knows."

"Fuck," Jared groaned. He knew they'd find out eventually – the press release for *Poison*'s return to Queen Victoria had been issued after Simon McAllister had talked to them a week ago. They didn't know when the cast was going to arrive, but Jared had hoped to avoid the whole press frenzy as long as possible.

"The paparazzi are camping outside his hotel and you might have some in front of your flat as well," Samantha warned.

"What? Why would I?" Jared huffed as he jumped off the bed, regretting it immediately when he felt dizzy.

"Why wouldn't you? You two were the golden couple of the musical theatre, Jared. Remember how long it took the press to lose interest in your relationship after Fenix left?"

"Over three months," Jared grumbled with a clenched jaw. The damn vultures had been circling him for months, feeding off his misery and selling their pathetic pictures to the tabloids, which, in turn, had bombarded him with requests for interviews. Their relationship had always been somewhat in the spotlight, but when they broke up so suddenly, it became an obsession for all the gossip hungry media.

"Shit!" Jared cursed as he looked through the blinds and saw at least five paparazzi standing on the curb opposite his building.

"I assume that means they're waiting for you?" Samantha asked, unsurprised.

"Yes. Bastards!"

"Please tell me Fenix is not there with you."

"What? Of course he's not! Why would you say that?"

"Sorry I asked," Samantha apologised, clearly not sorry. "Listen, Jared, we need to decide how to play this. It's not going to go away on its own. Think about it and we'll release an official statement. But don't think too long, I've already got five calls from major newspapers and entertainment channels, and my twitter is going crazy. #FenixAndJaredBackTogether is trending," Samantha said dryly, obviously not amused.

"Fuck," Jared swore again. He didn't want to deal with all this again. He hated the press and all the celebrity aspects of his job.

"I suggest you come up with a more eloquent response. We need to address this, Jared. The sooner the better."

They said their goodbyes and Jared stared at the screen long after he hung up. It was just after 9:00 am. He'd slept for about four hours. It wasn't good for his mental state, especially now after all this shit he had to deal with. Fortunately, he didn't need to be in the theatre before 1:00 pm. He had time to take a long, hot shower and at least try to look and feel presentable.

He wanted to talk to Adam, but the guy rarely woke up before noon. Jared didn't want to wake him up because that would be a whole new shit storm he'd have to endure. No, he'd talk to him at the theatre later on.

The phone started ringing again as Jared made his way round the bed and towards the bathroom. He decided to screen the call before he answered, in case it was an unknown number, which almost certainly meant a nosy reporter.

The name Fenix flashed on the screen and Jared froze in place.

"Yes," he said after picking up.

"You're awake so I assume Samantha already called you," Fenix said as a greeting. His voice sounded heavy and tired, like Jared's. A sudden wave of longing spread through Jared so violently that he had to sit down on the edge of the bed before he lost his balance. An image of Fenix still in bed flashed through his mind before he closed his eyes and shook his head.

"She did. They know you're here and they're literally drooling over the prospect of having something to print and talk about for the next few months."

"Months? I was hoping they'd get bored in a week or so," Fenix said. Jared could hear the rustling of sheets as if he was moving on the bed.

"Judging by how it took them over three months last time..." Jared said, trailing off, not really wanting to talk about that.

"Last time?"

"Yeah. When you left," Jared said. He was surprised that his voice came out soft and quiet. He heard a bit more rustling and Fenix's soft breathing, but he didn't say anything.

"So," Jared cleared his throat in an attempt to move the conversation forward – Fenix breathing in his ear was too much to bear right now. "How many do you have camping outside the hotel?"

"A lot. They tried to sneak in and bribe the staff but it didn't work. They were escorted outside the premises and security strongly recommended they stayed at a respectful distance," Fenix chuckled. "Any at your end?"

"Yeah. Some. I'll slip out from the back entrance and call a cab instead of walking today."

Fenix was quiet for a moment, as if deciding what to say next.

"Listen, Jared. I had a very long conversation with Cat this morning and we've come up with a plan. I really don't want to discuss it over the phone. Do you wanna meet me for coffee or something and we can talk?"

Jared was shocked into silence. He didn't want to meet Fenix to discuss this because the guy fucked up all his rational thoughts and sent his emotions into overdrive.

"We have to talk, ba... Jared. About this and about us. I have so much to say to you..."

"OK. You're right," Jared interrupted him. "We do need to talk about everything, and especially about how we're going to handle the press. I'd really hate it if I have to look over my shoulder for the damn photographers all the time," Jared said, summoning all his strength. He could do this. Jared had already fucked the man, so he could talk to him. Like a normal person. It was going to be fine.

Fenix rattled the directions to a coffee shop where he thought they wouldn't be bothered and they arranged to meet in an hour.

Good.

It was all good.

Right?

Jared arrived at the coffee shop about five minutes early. It looked like nothing special from the outside, but when he walked in, a wonderful scent drifted to his nose – freshly ground coffee and freshly baked... something. Jared wasn't sure what they baked here, but it smelled fantastic. And if Fenix frequented the place that meant the food was organic or super healthy or sugar and fat free, or all of the above.

The place was small – barely three tables fit around the counter – but Jared noticed a winding staircase leading to what he assumed was a second floor. He ordered a soy latte and a skinny blueberry muffin, and then headed upstairs. There, sitting at a table next to a huge window overlooking St Paul's cathedral was Fenix, already waiting for him. There was nobody else at the surrounding tables and Jared released the breath he was holding. The coffee shop was nice, but he'd been worried that, because it was so small, everyone would overhear what they were saying. And he definitely didn't want any eavesdroppers around when he had his first civilised conversation with Fenix.

"Hey," Fenix greeted him as Jared put his stuff on the table. He noticed Fenix had ordered exactly the same as him.

"Hi. Alright?" Jared said and sat down opposite him.

Fenix shrugged. "Been better."

Jared nodded and wrapped his fingers around the hot mug, lifting it to his lips and blowing gently. He met Fenix's eyes over the cup and was once again mesmerised by the sheer perfection of the man – high cheekbones, aristocratic nose, full lips, and those amazing crystal clear blue eyes. Fenix Bergman was perfection – a Nordic god in human form.

Fenix turned his head slightly to look out the window. The bright August sun touched his face and his blond hair shone like gold while his eyes practically lost their colour. He looked thoughtful and Jared didn't want to interrupt his thoughts – Fenix had a hard enough time concentrating as it was. After a while Fenix turned back to face Jared and caught him staring. A slight blush appeared on his pale skin and he looked down, grabbing his own coffee cup and bringing it to his lips.

"So," he said. "Cat and I were talking and she came up with this brilliant idea. Or at least, she *thinks* it's brilliant."

"What do *you* think?"

"I think it'll solve our problems, at least for now," Fenix said, but it was obvious there was more to it.

"But?"

"But... I don't think you'll be too happy about it," he finished, meeting Jared's eyes again.

"We'll never know unless you tell me."

"Well... The editor in chief of *Entertain Me* is a very close friend of Cat's. It's a weekly magazine that comes out every Wednesday and Cat managed to arrange a last minute exclusive for us."

"Wait. An exclusive? What does that mean?"

"A photo shoot and an interview," Fenix said, never looking away from Jared.

"Together?" Jared asked raising an eyebrow.

"Yes."

Jared nodded and it was his turn to look out the window and think about all this. What kind of a photo shoot? And an interview? What would they say? Did Fenix actually think it was a good idea to say they were back together? Was that the plan?

"Jared," Fenix said softly, touching his hand over the table. His warm fingers sent an involuntary shiver through Jared's whole body and goosebumps appeared on his arm. Fenix noticed and slowly removed his hand, dragging the tips of his fingers over Jared's own fingers, reaching for his mug. "I know you have questions, I can see it on your face. Just ask everything you need to know and we'll figure it out."

"Are we telling the press we're back together?" Jared blurted out, because, for him, that was the most important question.

"Is that what you want?" Fenix asked, furrowing his eyebrows.

"No."

"Me neither. Cat thought that it would be a good idea to do this magazine spread and tell people that yes, I'm back in town, and yes, we'll be working in close proximity of each other, but no, we're not back together. She thinks that if we come out and say we're friends and we aren't holding any grudges, the press will lose interest much quicker. They want scandal and gossip. If we manage to convince them they're not getting any of that from us and that our lives are actually pretty boring, they'll leave us alone."

"That sounds... good. In theory. But you know how they are – we'll say something and they'll twist and shorten and edit it out until it means something completely different..." Fenix started shaking his head even before Jared finished his sentence.

"No, that won't happen. I told you, this guy, the editor – Michael Jameson, is a very close friend of Cat's and she says she trusts him completely to do a spread that will be entirely in our favour. And besides, you know how Cat gets when she's angry – I wouldn't risk getting my balls ripped out, and I guess he wouldn't either," Fenix said and smirked. Jared couldn't help but laugh – yeah, he knew Fenix's agent was pretty fierce.

"OK then. Let's do it," Jared said, the smile still lingering on his face. It might work or it might not, they'd never be sure until they actually did it, but it was a good plan. It was worth giving it a try if it meant they'd get rid of the paparazzi that followed them everywhere.

"Really? You're game?"

"Yeah."

Fenix's smile transformed his chiselled, perfect features into something prettier. Calmer. Much more approachable. He had a dimple on his left cheek that showed only when he smiled widely, and right now it was showing. Jared wanted nothing more than to pull him into his arms and feel him smiling against his skin.

With that settled, they fell into silence for a while, drinking their coffees and eating their muffins. Jared was surprised to find that the silence was not at all uncomfortable, on the contrary.

"You said you watched the Tony Awards," Fenix said after a while. "Did you like my speech?" He looked at Jared cheekily, trying to make light of the subject.

"No, I didn't." Jared said honestly.

"It was for you," Fenix met Jared's eyes head on.

"You looked so unhappy, Fen," Jared said, not flinching away from Fenix's piercing gaze. "And when you called me after that you sounded so miserable that I honestly thought you were going to do something stupid. I freaked out, found your number, and when you refused to take my calls, I was on the verge of jumping on a plane to come and get you. Thank god I talked to

Cathleen. She said you had called to arrange a meeting and you sounded OK."

Fenix looked away then, but Jared managed to catch the shame that crossed his face.

"Fenix," Jared said gently. Fenix looked at him reluctantly. "I'm sorry about what happened in the dressing room yesterday. I should have controlled myself better. But seeing you..."

"Don't apologise," Fenix interrupted, placing his hand over Jared's again. "I'm not sorry."

Jared shook his head and closed his eyes but didn't remove his hand from the table. He'd lied. He wasn't sorry either.

"I don't know what you want from me, Fenix. From *us*. Why did you come back? I thought Broadway was your dream. Why did you give it up? I know *Poison* missed out on the Tony and was probably kicked out of the Osbert theatre, but I bet you could have found a job anywhere you wanted." Jared stopped talking because Fenix started shaking his head in denial.

"*Poison* wasn't kicked out. All I had to do was sign the contract and we would have had another season on Broadway," Fenix said, and then paused, staring at Jared with conflicted eyes.

"But?" Jared prompted.

"But I wanted to come back home."

Jared was confused – New York was Fenix's home. He'd been born and raised there.

Wait. Did he mean what Jared thought he meant?

The realisation must have shown on his face because Fenix laced their fingers together before speaking.

"Yes. Home. Here, in London. With you. I came back for you."

Jared's head started spinning. He couldn't believe what he was hearing, what that meant.

"How?" was all he managed to say.

"I bullied the producers into moving the musical back to Queen Victoria," Fenix said with a smirk.

"What? How the hell did you manage that?"

"I have my ways," Fenix winked. "But even if they had said 'no', I'd have come back. I couldn't stand to be away from you a day longer, Jared."

That information was too much to take in. Jared kept staring at Fenix as if he'd grown a second head, unable to even begin to understand how Fenix had achieved that. He had no doubt Fenix was telling the truth – one thing they had in common was always being honest with each other. That was one of the reasons they had worked so well as a couple – there were no secrets, no assumptions. They said whatever was on their mind and resolved any issues the moment they arose.

Suddenly, Adam's words sounded loud and clear in Jared's mind:

Are you going to survive it when he leaves again?

They struck him like lightning, flooding his mind with memories of those awful two years when Fenix had been gone. Jared could not go through that again. If Fenix left, this time he was not going to recover. He'd be as good as dead.

Jared pulled his hand back and Fenix frowned.

"I understand that all this is too much for you to find out all at once," Fenix said. "Unlike you, I've had time to think this through. I just wanted you to know that I love you, Jared, and I'm not going anywhere. I'll wait for you," he finished, leaning back in his chair, not attempting to touch Jared again.

"OK," Jared said, thankful that Fenix understood, not pushing him to answer straight away. He did love Fenix, there was no doubt about that, but he also wanted to absorb all this new information.

"OK," Fenix said and smiled.

CHAPTER TWENTY EIGHT

Jared

Jared felt the urge to throw his phone against the wall when his alarm started ringing at 10:00 am. He'd barely managed to fall asleep at all during the night, tossing and turning and unable to stop thinking about what Fenix had said.

He'd forced a whole fucking musical out of Broadway for him.

That was unbelievable. Jared would have said impossible, but apparently it wasn't. But that wasn't what made Jared's heart do a somersault every time his mind wondered back to their conversation.

Even if they had said 'no', I'd have come back. I couldn't stand to be away from you a day longer...

Jared wanted to believe that so badly.

"So let me get this straight," Adam said as he opened the door, holding it for Jared as they both walked into Queen Victoria later that day. "You agreed to go in front of the whole world and announce that you're absolutely unaffected by what Fenix did to you, and now that he's back you're best friends?" He stopped in the middle of the foyer and spread his arms wide, almost spilling his coffee through the small drinking hole of the take-away cup.

"I doubt the whole world reads *Entertain Me*," Jared said as he continued walking, ignoring Adam's outrage.

"This is what you choose to address? *Entertain Me*'s circulation figures?"

"Not really, no," Jared said as he walked through a door, letting it close behind him.

"Jared!" he heard Adam shout after him. "Seriously, wait!" Adam caught up to him easily – the man's leg span was twice a normal person's. "This is bullshit and you know it."

"It's not. It's the best way to deal with this situation," Jared said as he stopped walking to turn and face his very angry friend. "I know you're looking out for me, but it's OK. Fenix and I met for coffee..." Adam's eyes widened and he tried to protest, but Jared raised a hand to stop him. "And we talked. We're good now." Adam started shaking his head even before Jared had finished speaking. It was obvious he had a lot to say, but he pursed his lips until they lost their colour and nodded silently.

"Excuse me," someone said, catching their attention. They both turned in unison to face a young man, standing a few feet away from them, looking lost. "Do you guys know where the costume supervisor's office is? I've been trying to find it for half an hour, but this place is a maze!" He smiled at them and his eyes sparkled.

Both Jared and Adam stared at him with wide, unblinking eyes. He was quite attractive – lean, about five nine, with dark blond hair cut below his jaw line, intense grey eyes and plump lips that spread into a very charming smile.

And he was the spitting image of Charlie Shields – the lead singer of *Nix* who had broken Adam's heart.

Jared glanced at Adam who was gaping at the guy, clutching his coffee cup as if it was a life line. His face was pale and he looked shocked.

"Charlie?" Adam whispered.

The guy frowned instantly and took a step back.

"No," he said, looking at Adam suspiciously. "My name is Penn. Charlie is my brother. By the look on your face I take it you know each other."

Adam swallowed loudly and closed his eyes, shaking his head side to side.

"How is that possible?" he murmured almost to himself.

"Well, when a woman gets pregnant, sometimes she gives birth to two identical twins. It's not a miracle or anything, happens quite often," Penn said sarcastically. Jared couldn't help but smile.

"No," Adam said sharply, fixing his black eyes on Penn menacingly. Most people shied away from that stare, running for cover almost immediately. Penn's eyes flashed and the guy visibly shuddered, but not with fear. He was attracted to Adam, and even Jared could feel it. "I meant, how is it possible that I dated Charlie for almost a year and he never mentioned he had a twin brother!" Adam's voice rose and he looked at Jared incredulously, as if looking for answers. Jared shrugged – he'd never really known Charlie, but from what he'd heard, the guy was a jerk. He wasn't surprised he hadn't shared much about himself with Adam.

"We're not really close," Penn supplied with a humourless laugh. "Look, I'd love to stand here with you and chat about my brother," he continued, clearly not meaning it, "but I have to be in the costume supervisor's office in about ten minutes. Can one of you point me in the right direction or should I find someone else to ask?"

Jared cleared his throat and decided to help the guy out since, obviously, Adam was still pondering the whole Charlie-has-a-twin-brother-he-failed-to-mention situation.

"If you go that way," Jared pointed towards the corridor on their left, "and turn left at the end, it's the second door on the right."

"Thanks," Penn said and smiled politely. He turned to leave but paused and added: "It was great meeting you," he looked at Jared first but his eyes quickly travelled to Adam and stayed there. "I'm a huge fan of yours. It's my dream come true to work here."

Adam remained silent. Jared felt he needed to fix the situation before they ruined Penn's first day at his dream job.

"Thank you. Hope you like it here," he said with a polite smile.

"Oh, I'm sure I will," Penn said, his eyes never leaving Adam. A slow blush crept his cheeks and he quickly added, "Thanks again," and then headed in the direction Jared pointed him in.

Once Penn walked away, Adam rubbed his hand over his face, sighing.

"I can't fucking believe this," he said as he looked at Jared desperately.

"My dressing room. Now," Jared commanded.

Jared let Adam go in first and then closed the door behind them. Adam sat on the sofa, his elbows on his knees and his head in his hands.

"So what are you going to do?" Jared asked, sitting in the chair by the dressing table. Adam's head snapped up and he looked at him in surprise.

"I wasn't aware I had to do anything."

"Come on! Charlie is the only guy that managed to hold your attention for longer than a single night. He broke your heart when he left. Now, fate drops his *twin brother* in your lap. He looks so much like Charlie, but Penn seems *nice*, unlike his brother. Don't tell me you're not attracted to him because he's exactly your type."

Adam shrugged, silently admitting Jared was right, but he didn't seem particularly interested in continuing to discuss that.

"And, what's more," Jared continued, "I noticed how attracted to you he was. When you glared at him I swear I could feel him shudder from where I was standing. I bet he'd be exactly what you need in bed..." Jared rambled, knowing Adam wouldn't be able to take it much longer.

"Alright, alright!" Adam interrupted him, falling back on the sofa. "Just stop talking."

"I will if you *start* talking," Jared teased.

"Of course I'm attracted to him, he's gorgeous," Adam said with a sigh. "But I'm not as big of a bastard as you think I am."

"What do you mean?"

"I can't go after him exactly because he seems like a nice guy. I'm not sure if I'm attracted to *him*, or to the fact that he looks so much like Charlie. I don't want him to feel like a substitute or something," Adam explained, staring at the ceiling.

"Oh," Jared said, genuinely surprised. "Well, maybe, for the first time in your life, you should get to know someone before you fuck their brains out," Jared said conversationally. Adam groaned.

"How is this going to help?"

"I bet Penn is nothing like Charlie, even though they're twins. If you get to know him, you won't think of him as Charlie's brother anymore. He'd create his own profile in your mind, so to speak, and when you eventually get to the fucking his brains out part, you won't feel guilty you're doing it because he reminds you of Charlie. You'll be doing it because you want Penn."

Adam groaned louder and stood up.

"This was deep, man," Adam said mockingly, heading for the door. "I don't have time for that. I'd rather go out this weekend and pick someone for a quickie. Much less effort."

"Adam!" Jared called before he managed to open the door.

"Just drop it, OK?" Adam said before he walked out of Jared's dressing room.

"You're a fucking idiot!" Jared yelled after him through the open door, getting an odd look from someone passing by. He smiled sheepishly and closed the door, shaking his head.

It was Saturday, and the theatre was always crowded on weekends. *Of Kids and Monsters* was a popular show, and it was often sold out, but Jared couldn't remember a single Saturday when there had been an empty seat. Not that it mattered to the performers – everyone, including the children, were professionals to their core. They'd perform the show the same way regardless of whether the theatre was bursting at the seams or half empty.

Jared was in the middle of a song when he thought he saw Fenix's familiar form backstage. Was he watching the show? The idea of a full theatre didn't scare Jared, but the thought of Fenix watching the show after two years definitely did. It made him nervous and anxious, and right now he could not afford any of those emotions, or he'd mess up his lines.

Maybe it wasn't even him.

Yeah, right.

Jared forced his traitorous mind back into the show. He had a costume change in about ten minutes. He'd know for sure then.

It turned out Fenix was indeed backstage. He was talking to Penn when Jared stepped off the stage to change his costume. Unable to take his eyes off Fenix, Jared just stood there like an idiot while the wardrobe guys helped him in his new costume, handing him a bottle of water. Penn was all smiles and Fenix was his usual charming self – laughing at what Penn was saying, touching his upper arm and nodding encouragingly.

Jared didn't want to feel jealous. But he did, and he hated himself for it. It was childish, unreasonable, and completely out of line, but all Jared wanted to do at that moment was stomp over to them, rip Penn away, and kiss Fenix in front of everyone. Claim him as his.

Forcing himself to look away before he got lost in his overwhelming thoughts, Jared took a step back and turned towards the stage, getting ready to go out again. Adam had just stepped off stage and his eyes immediately fixed on Fenix and Penn, much like Jared's had. His deep, brown stare was pure, melted fire. Only, his deadly glare was focused on Fenix.

"I thought you liked his brother?" Jared said when he approached his friend. Adam startled and shook his head.

"I do," he grumbled and stepped past Jared to take the bottle of water he was immediately offered.

"So why are you looking at Fenix like you wanna burn him alive?"

"Because Fenix going up in flames would be a great service to humanity. And besides, we'll have a chance to see if he can live up to his name," Adam said as he unscrewed the cap and took a few big gulps of water.

Jared narrowed his eyes at him in clear warning. They might not be together anymore but he'd hurt anyone who intended to harm Fenix. Adam caught the meaning behind Jared's narrowed eyes and gave him his trademark you've-got-to-be-kidding-me look. Jared didn't have time to deal with any of that right now – he had to be on stage in about a minute. With one last look in Fenix's direction – he has giving Penn a goodbye hug – Jared turned his back on everyone and took his place on the stage edge.

The show had to go on. Everything else could wait.

Jared walked into his flat and kicked the door closed – his hands were busy carrying the shopping bags. He'd realised that morning that his fridge was almost empty, so instead of accepting Adam's invitation for a night out, he'd gone to Marks and Spencer's and gotten food to last him a week. Adam had been unhappy that Jared was 'ditching him' yet again, but when Jared pointed out that he was hardly ditched – he had at least five people tagging along – Adam had smirked and walked out of the theatre. And besides, Jared knew his friend was going to go on a hunt for a quick fuck, and he was not in the mood for Adam's shenanigans.

Jared set on putting away the groceries and making dinner. He switched on the digital radio he kept in the kitchen and started humming to a well-known pop hit as his mind wondered.

Every single day for the past two years he had yearned to hear Fenix's voice when he came home at night. At first, Jared had thought that it was a normal reaction – they'd been living together for over a year before Fenix left. It was a natural instinct, a habit even, to want to talk to him when he was alone in the home they'd shared.

But the need didn't faze out after a few months. Not even after a few years. Jared still, to this very day, craved to hear Fenix's voice next to him. Craved to share his life with the man, to make plans for the future, to tell him how much he loved him, and how much he missed him. The sudden pang of need that slammed into his chest made him lose focus for a second and he cut his finger as he was chopping vegetables for the salad. It wasn't a deep cut but it immediately started bleeding. Jared swore, rinsed his finger under the tap, and wrapped it in a kitchen towel. He took a plaster from the first aid kit he kept in one of the drawers, put it on over the cut, and spread his hands on the counter taking a deep, calming breath.

This had to stop.

He could not go on like this.

All he wanted was Fenix, back in this flat, back in his bed, and back in his life. And he knew Fenix wanted that, too. Not just because he'd told him, but because Jared had seen the haunted look in Fenix's eyes that night at the Tonys. Jared knew their separation had been just as hard on Fenix, if not harder.

Jared fought the impulse to pick up the phone and call Fenix, to beg him to come back home. He should make that decision with a clear head, not when his love, his *need* for the man was clouding his judgement.

His phone rang, startling him. Jared hurried to the living room and saw the phone on the coffee table, Fenix's name illuminating the screen.

It was like he'd read his mind.

"Hi," he said as he picked up after a short hesitation.

"Hey," Fenix's soft, perfect voice sounded in his ear. "What are you up to?"

"Just cooking dinner."

Fenix hummed but didn't say anything. They fell silent for a while, listening to the other breathing.

"Jared..." Fenix began. Jared had to sit down – his knees almost gave out hearing the yearning in Fenix's voice. "I wanted to tell you something," he said, and then paused. Jared made an encouraging noise, but didn't trust himself to speak. He had to bite his lip, hard, to stop himself from blurting out something irrational. Something he really wanted to say... "I never stopped thinking about you, replaying every single moment I spent with you in my head. I think that's what kept me somewhat sane during the past couple of years. Remember when you told me that you didn't want to waste the time between meeting someone and gathering the courage to say you've loved them since the moment you saw them?"

How can I forget?

"Well, I don't want to waste the time between telling you how sorry I am that I left, and getting back together. I know I said I'd give you time and wait for you, but I don't want to waste another fucking second that I could be spending with you. I've already wasted two years that I can never get back and I promise, if you let me, I'll try to make up for that. I'll make you happy..." Fenix's voice wavered and he stopped talking, breathing heavily.

Jared's chest was about to explode. His heart swelled, his hands started shaking and tears streamed down his face. The man he loved was begging him to take him back, to make him happy, and he'd be damned if he said no. Whatever else life had in store for them, he had to take a chance. He had to be with Fenix again.

"Come home, baby..." Jared managed to say, his voice hoarse and sounding alien to his own ears. "Come home."

CHAPTER TWENTY NINE

FeNix

Fenix didn't need another invitation. The moment Jared had uttered the words 'come home' in a desperate, husky voice, Fenix had started packing. Less than an hour later, he was knocking on Jared's door, his heart hammering in his chest like it was about to bounce out.

He'd dreamed of this moment so many times.

Jared opened the door, breathing heavily like he'd run to get it. He was wearing sweats and an old t-shirt, his hair was all over the place, his cheeks flushed and his eyes alight with joy. He looked fucking gorgeous.

Mine.

And he was Jared's, too. Always had been, always would be.

They didn't speak. Fenix stepped in and dropped his bags on the floor, his eyes never leaving Jared's. Jared leaned in to close the door and their cheeks brushed. It was the slightest contact, but it sent an electric current down Fenix's body. He couldn't be away from Jared any longer.

Fenix turned his head slightly at the same time Jared turned his, their lips colliding. Their bodies moulded against each other, pulling clothes out of the way. Fenix started pushing Jared backwards, leading him further into the apartment, as he pawed at his clothing, wanting nothing between them. They left a trail of tshirts, jeans, pants, and socks as they made their way to the bed, still kissing, still unable to let go of one another even for a second.

Fenix pushed Jared down on the bed and fell on top of him, kissing his jaw, nipping his chin, licking his lips... He couldn't get enough. Jared ran his hands all over Fenix, reacquainting himself with his body, moving eagerly as if he wanted to touch everything all at once. Fenix groaned and started pumping his hips into Jared's, the friction smooth with their precome. Jared moaned, deep and loud. He squeezed Fenix's ass, hard enough to leave finger prints.

"I love you," Fenix whispered, surprised his voice still worked. He leaned back and looked seriously in Jared's eyes, letting him know he really meant it and it wasn't a heat of the moment thing. "And I'm never leaving you again."

Jared swallowed, his Adam's apple bobbing up and down.

"I love you, too. And I won't let you leave ever again."

Fenix's world exploded like a colourful firework display.

They made love all night. Urgent and desperate at first, then gentle and slow, until one of them screamed and begged for release. They fell asleep in each other's arms, their limbs tangled together, and their hearts beating as one. Again.

"So, I guess we're gonna have to cancel that magazine feature after all?" Jared said as he spread some butter on toast the next morning. Fenix was busy loading the coffee machine on the other side of the counter. God, he'd missed this. Jared and him, doing normal, boring stuff, like cooking or watching a stupid reality show or just pottering around the house. "Fen?" Jared said, turning to fully face him.

"Sorry, got distracted," Fenix apologised, grinning sheepishly, trying to remember what Jared asked him. Oh yeah, the interview. "No, I don't think we should cancel. Cat already went out of her way to get us in with such short notice, I think we should take advantage of the publicity. We could revise what we're going to tell them about us," Fenix finished with a wink.

"You mean, you want to go public? Tell the press we're back together?" Jared asked.

"Yeah. Don't you?" Fenix frowned.

"Of course I do... I'm not sure that's going to rid us of the photographers, though."

"The photographers can go suck a dick for all I care," Fenix said and shrugged, turning back to the coffee that was brewing nicely in the pot, filling the kitchen with a lovely smell.

Jared laughed and didn't comment any further. Fenix threw him a look over his shoulder, still unable to believe he was really here. That he was here *to stay*. That Jared had let him in his life again so easily.

He wondered how long it would take before he stopped being amazed at that. Before he got used to this again.

Fenix wasn't sure. But what he was absolutely certain about was that he was never going to take it for granted.

The *Entertain Me* office was in a non-descript building on Earl's Court. Fenix and Jared were immediately recognized by the receptionist and escorted to the studio on the third floor. A tall, lanky man in his early thirties spotted them as they entered the photo studio and headed in their direction, smiling.

"If it isn't the infamous Fenix Bergman and Jared Hartley," the guy said as he approached them. He shook their hands in turn. "So nice to meet you guys. You've thrown all my staff into fangirl mode today."

"Nice to meet you too, Michael," Fenix said politely.

"I can see someone's done their homework. I never told you my name."

"Yeah, Cat's been raving on and on about you for the last two days. Your name kinda stuck."

"I see," Michael laughed, and, throwing his arm over Fenix's shoulder, led him further inside the studio, waving at Jared to follow them.

Half the studio was set up as the main photo area which was mostly white right now, with lots of equipment around it. On the left were the make-up and wardrobe areas where a lot of people were walking around, busy with preparing everything they'd need for the photo shoot.

Michael introduced them to a girl named Sarah, who took charge of them, leading them to the make-up chairs to be 'prepared'. Fenix frowned – he'd done photo shoots before and knew that the preparation was never pain-free.

After more than an hour of poking, combing, moisturising, and styling, both Jared and Fenix were let out of their chairs and pointed in the direction of the rails full of clothes. Jared stood close to Fenix as Sarah showed them some pre-approved choices. Fenix's pulse raced and his mind could not absorb any information other than the fact the Jared was standing closer to him than necessary, and Fenix could *feel* the heat of his body.

They both chose clothes they'd wear themselves – Jared picked a pair of distressed designer jeans that hung low on his slim waist and a t-shirt that said 'Happy Ending'. Fenix opted for skinny jeans and a long V-neck t-shirt with an abstract, green tiger at the front. The photographer, Richard, instructed them to act naturally. Easier said than done. How were they supposed to act naturally when they were surrounded by a dozen magazine staff staring at them? Their surroundings consisted of white walls, huge lamps, shades and other photographic equipment that resembled an operating theatre.

They looked at each other awkwardly, before Jared started laughing. Fenix didn't know if Jared found the whole situation funny or not, but his laughter was infectious, and Fenix started laughing too. They could hear people around them giggling as well, while Richard started snapped pictures with record speed.

That seemed to relax everyone, and soon Jared and Fenix were posing like the pros they were, joking with the staff and each other, adding props like hats and glasses to their attire, and even simulating some of the dance moves they had to do for their shows. Fenix used Jared as a support dancer and Jared lifted him up as Fenix jumped in the air, bearing his weight effortlessly, and lowering him to the floor easily. Everyone clapped while Fenix's heart threatened to beat out of his chest under Jared's touch.

Soon, Richard announced they had more than enough shots for the feature and, after putting their own clothes back on, Jared and Fenix were led to another room for the interview. It was in stark contrast to the previous room – it was much smaller and quite cosy. There were several sofas and chairs, a coffee table filled with snacks and hot beverages, and Lorde was playing quietly on the surround system. Michael was already waiting for them, going through a notebook with what Fenix assumed were notes for the interview.

"Sit down, guys," Michael said, gesturing towards a cream leather sofa opposite him. "I got some sushi and sugar-free snacks delivered – I know you both watch what you eat. Help yourselves. There's coffee, green tea, water," he finished, and both Jared and Fenix filled a plate with sushi. Fenix was starving, and by the looks of it, Jared was too.

Michael kept the small talk going while they ate, politely waiting for them to finish their food. Then, he offered them cups of coffee, before he took out his phone and activated the voice recorder.

"So, Fenix, you're back in London. How does it feel after two years on Broadway?" Michael asked, leaning back in his chair.

"It feels great to be back. I've always had a soft spot for London and I couldn't be happier when I got the chance to play in a West End show. It was my first big break and it happened right here. Everything happened here. If it wasn't for London, I'd never be who I am today. I'll always think of this city as my home," Fenix said, casting a sidelong look at Jared who was thoughtfully studying his cup of coffee.

"That's great to hear. London certainly loves you, too. Your return to the West End caused quite the turmoil. There were speculations about why you suddenly decided to come back to Queen Victoria. You just won a Tony and can perform anywhere you choose."

"You're right, I can perform anywhere I choose. And I chose Queen Victoria," Fenix replied with a wink. He knew Michael would not be diverted so easily – after all they were here to talk about Jared and Fenix's relationship. That was what everyone was interested in and what would fuel the gossip columns for months.

"Why Queen Victoria, Fenix?" Michael asked directly.

"I was nostalgic, I guess."

"Jared, are you glad Fenix is back?" Michael asked, changing his tactics.

"Sure. Fenix is one of the best performers I've ever seen. Any theatre would be lucky to have him," Jared said, grinning. Fenix laughed out loud, unable to hold it in anymore. He quite enjoyed the cat and mouse game he played with the journalists. But maybe they should take pity on Michael. He seemed like a nice guy. And besides, if Michael complained to Cat about them, after she pulled so many strings to get them in, Fenix's balls were a goner.

Michael sighed and tapped on the phone screen to pause the recorder.

"Guys, come on. We all know why you're here. I don't know about you, but I don't have time for games. Cathleen told me you wanted to let everyone know you're friends and aren't holding any grudges. Are we going to cut to the chase or are we just wasting each other's time?"

"Yeah, about that," Fenix began and Michael groaned. "Things have... evolved," he said and raised an eyebrow.

"How?" Michael asked impatiently.

"We're not going to claim we're just friends... because we're not. I moved in with Jared last night and we're back together."

Michael was taken aback by this statement and leaned back in his chair, frowning.

"Are you sure about this?" he asked after some consideration.

"That I moved in with Jared? Pretty sure. My toothbrush is in his bathroom and all."

"No," Michael rolled his eyes. "That you want me to print it?"

"We just want the speculations to end. If we come out and say the truth, hopefully the press will lose interest and get off our backs," Jared said.

"OK. That's cool," Michael said. He reached to start the recorder again, but paused before his finger touched the screen. "I'm happy for you," he added sincerely and pushed the red button again. "What everyone wants to know is, how are things between you, guys? You were in a serious relationship before Fenix moved to New York, and now that he's back... Are you back together?"

"Yes. We are back together. I came back here for Jared and we've worked things out."

"That's good news, congratulations. But, how did you manage that in such a short time? Fenix, didn't you only come back a few days ago? Were you guys in touch before that?"

"No, we weren't," Jared said. "We were hurt and sad and angry, but not with each other. We both made bad decisions and we had to bear the consequences. In the end, what we have together is worth fighting for. It's more than the theatre would ever be able to give us."

"Are you really not mad at Fenix for leaving, Jared?" Michael asked.

"No," Jared said honestly. It was obvious he wasn't going to elaborate on the details any more. They knew what had gone down between them, knew it wasn't anybody's fault, knew it could have been different if they *both* had tried harder. "I love him," Jared said and looked at Fenix with such an open, loving expression that Fenix's heart melted.

Michael laughed, satisfied with their answers and sensing he wasn't going to extract any more personal information. Changing the subject, he asked Fenix about his Tony award, his Broadway experience, and if the audience could expect something new from *Poison*. They chatted some more about their musicals, and when the interview ended, Michael walked them out and told them they were welcome to come back and be featured in the magazine any time.

CHAPTER THIRTY

Jared

"You never told me what happened that night of the Tonys. When you called me," Jared asked as he and Fenix lay curled together on their bed after making love. Jared couldn't stop touching Fenix – he ran his hands all over his smooth skin as they talked.

Fenix didn't answer immediately and, even in the dim light, Jared could see a slight blush covering his cheekbones. He was biting his lip, not meeting Jared's eyes.

"Fen?" Jared said, suddenly alert and worried. He tucked a finger under Fenix's chin and raised his face to look into his eyes. They were the same haunted blue as when Jared had seen him make his acceptance speech. "You can tell me anything, love. I won't judge you or love you any less. I don't want you to feel like you need to have secrets from me."

Fenix nodded and swallowed a few times before speaking.

"After the speech, when I went backstage, I was holding the Tony, and I'd never felt more lost. I knew I needed to be fucking ecstatic. I'd done it. I should be proud and happy. But I wasn't, and..." he paused to take a few breaths. Jared didn't push him to continue before he was ready. "I just wanted the pain to stop. So I went to the bar and ordered shot after shot until I was numb. There was a group of four guys there, at the bar. One of them came to congratulate me, so he bought me more drinks. Soon his friends joined him and we all drank until way past midnight. It felt good. *I* felt good. So when they offered me to go with them, I did."

A cold shiver ran down Jared's spine. He had a suspicion what was coming next but schooled his face into a blank mask so that Fenix wouldn't be discouraged to continue.

"I don't remember much of what happened after that. I woke up in a luxurious hotel room, in a huge bed with all four men sleeping around me. I smelled of sex and alcohol and... other people. I barely made it to the bathroom before I puked my guts out. Fortunately, none of them woke up and I managed to sneak out undetected. I called you when I got home. I needed to hear your voice. Needed you to pull me up because I'd hit rock bottom that day, Jared. I knew I couldn't go on like this or that was what my life would turn out to be."

Jared's heart was beating frantically. He was so angry. His protective instincts were going into overdrive. It drove him insane that he couldn't do anything about it. He wished like hell Fenix hadn't gone through that, he wished for a thousandth time that they'd never separated, he wished they'd chosen each other instead of their jobs. Jared pulled Fenix closer when he'd finished talking, wanting to take away the memories of that night. Thank god he didn't remember much.

"I'm so sorry you had to go through this, love," he said, and then kissed him deeply. "You should have called me sooner. You should have come back sooner."

"I wasn't sure if you'd still want me."

Jared shook his head incredulously, but decided to drop the subject. There was no point in dwelling on the past. They could never change it. What was important was that they were together now. That was all that mattered.

Jared didn't have a show the next day and Fenix didn't start his promotional interviews and appearances until the end of the week. They had the whole day together, so they decided to take it easy – have breakfast at home, watch some movies, maybe go out for dinner. The plan had been going well until forty minutes into 'The Hangover 3' when Fenix was already bored out of his mind. Jared could feel him getting restless next to him.

"I hate this clock," Fenix said, glaring at the clock on the opposite wall.

"I know," Jared replied without missing a beat.

"How can you stand the constant ticking? It's been driving me nuts ever since I walked in here."

"I don't mind it. I don't even hear it anymore, got used to it."

"Why would you even buy it? It's not an antique, it's not a designer piece, it's not even pretty!" Fenix insisted. Jared didn't answer, pretending to be watching the film intently.

"Who needs a clock on the wall nowadays anyway? We should get one of those cool projector clocks and get rid of the annoying ticking..."

"I got it to remind me you don't live here anymore!" Jared snapped and immediately regretted it.

Despite the sound coming from the TV, the silence in the room was so thick that the damn ticking felt like someone was hammering nails in a tin wall.

"What?" Fenix asked quietly.

"I know how the ticking, or any repetitive, mechanical sound annoys you. So when you left I bought the clock to remind me that you're not here. As long as it ticked on the wall, you were not coming back."

Jared could feel Fenix's harsh breathing next to him. He was so close and yet he didn't touch him. He didn't speak. Jared felt him stand up and followed him with his eyes, curious to see what was going on. He caught Fenix's fuming expression before he took the distance to the clock in a few angry, long strides, took it off the wall, and walked out of the front door without bothering to put his shoes on. Jared's mouth was hanging open – he could not believe what he was seeing. Where was he going?

He ran to the window overlooking the back yard of the building and saw Fenix stomp to the huge rubbish container and chuck the clock inside. Turning on his heel, he walked calmly back to the entrance of the building and, a minute later, waltzed back in as if nothing had just happened.

"There," he said with an innocent smile, flopping back on the sofa.

Jared shook his head, deciding against asking for explanation. The message was loud and clear – Fenix was back, so the clock had to go.

It was a beautiful day and Fenix definitely needed a change of scenery, so they went out and strolled around London, enjoying each other's company. The streets were full of people taking advantage of the hot August day and the short London summer.

"I'm starving," Fenix said suddenly, looking around. They'd come all the way to the Southbank. "Let's find somewhere to eat," he added, grabbing Jared's hand, tugging him along.

They found a lovely Italian restaurant with a terrace overlooking the Thames. Nobody seemed to recognise them as they were seated at their table, which was a relief. It had been a great day and Jared didn't want to have to deal with any intrusions. Not today.

"Do you even remember when was the last time you had such a long break?" Jared asked as he seasoned his *tricolori* salad.

"I don't think I've had such a long break ever since I got *Poison*. Frankly, I think I need it."

Jared nodded. Everyone in the theatre business was used to the gruelling schedule and they rarely complained. But they were only human – everyone needed a good, long break from time to time.

"Are you excited about going back on stage?"

"Yeah. I can't wait for you to see the show. It had a little makeover," Fenix said and grinned.

"It did?" Jared was genuinely surprised. *Poison* had been a huge hit for so long, and the producers usually went by the mantra: 'Why fix it when it ain't broke?'

"Mhm," Fenix hummed through a mouth full of food. "There are two new songs and an incredible new final scene. I'm not sure how they're going to pull it off with the health and safety issue though..."

"Health and safety issue?" Jared echoed

"You'll see," Fenix said with a wink. "We start dress rehearsals next week. The rest of the cast, staff, and equipment should arrive over the weekend."

Jared tried coaxing more information out of Fenix for a while longer, unsuccessfully, when his phone rang. Casting an apologetic look at Fenix, Jared answered.

"Hey, what's up?"

"You wanna grab a beer?" Adam asked. Jared could hear a loud rustling sound.

"What are you doing?"

"Putting clothes on. You coming or not?"

"I can't. I'm already out for dinner."

"Alone?" Adam asked. The noise Jared could hear through the phone died down. He could just picture Adam standing completely still, half dressed, waiting for his reply.

"No."

"With who? All the people you know will be at the pub in fifteen minutes." The suspicion in Adam's voice was audible.

"Not all of them," Jared said, casting another look at Fenix, who was eating his meal, trying not to pay attention to the conversation.

"You've got to be fucking kidding me!" Another loud noise came from the other end of the line that sounded suspiciously like a shoe being hurled against a wall.

"Adam," Jared said, the warning clear in his voice.

"This is bullshit and you know it, Jared! Don't let him worm his way in your life again or I swear to god..."

"Don't say something you'll regret, Adam." Jared was getting fed up with this shit. Adam cared for him, he'd seen the devastation Fenix had left behind, but he had no right to tell him what to do. He certainly had no right to threaten Fenix in any capacity. Jared would not have it.

"Whatever. Do what you want. Just remember this – he'll leave again and I'll be the one on suicide watch. *Again.*"

The line went dead. Jared calmly switched the sound off and put his phone back in his pocket.

"Sorry. I should have gone outside to take this."

"It's OK. I know Adam hates me. He always has."

There was no point in denying it so Jared didn't even try. Fenix had probably heard the whole conversation anyway. Adam hadn't tried to tone down his frustration and keep his voice level.

"I hope you know we'll never get along. I'll never stop being jealous of him and he'll never stop hating me."

Jared nodded. He knew. He just hoped he wouldn't have to choose between them when he told Adam Fenix had moved back in.

CHAPTER THIRTY ONE

FeNIX

Loud banging on the dressing room door startled Fenix. He had just finished his dance work-out and was relaxing on the sofa, waiting for Jared who should be there any minute so that they can take a shower together. Fenix would never get tired of seeing Jared wet and soapy in the shower...

Bang. Bang. BANG.

Fenix rolled his eyes and decided he'd better open the door. Whoever it was, he wasn't giving up. Swinging the door open, he was stuck face to face with Adam. A very angry Adam. The man's black eyes could melt steel right now.

"Is Jared here?" Adam barked. Fenix thought that if the man clenched his teeth any harder, fillings would start flying.

"No. He should be here any minute though," Fenix replied. He took a closer look at Adam and saw he was clutching a magazine in his hand. "Oh," he said when he saw which magazine it was. "By the furious scowl you have going on I gather Jared didn't tell you?"

"No, he didn't," Adam snarled as he brushed past Fenix to walk inside. Fenix sighed and closed the door.

"What the fuck is he thinking? Declaring he loves you in front of the whole world a few *days* after you come crawling back?" Adam raged, not really at Fenix but to himself. He was pacing like a caged animal, his face twisted in anger and disbelief.

"I don't think this is any of your business, Adam," Fenix said flatly, starting to get angry himself. He got it – Adam was Jared's best friend, he was afraid Fenix would hurt him again, and he was looking out for him, blah blah blah. But the way he was acting was totally inappropriate.

"I don't care what you fucking think!" Adam erupted, throwing the magazine against the wall. "I know you're going to leave again because you're a fucking fame whore. The moment a better opportunity arises you're going to dump him again, but this time I won't be able to pick up the pieces. I barely managed it last time. So don't tell me this is none of my business!"

"I'm not going to leave. He's the reason I came back. You have no idea what I had to do to get back here." Fenix folded his arms defensively across his chest, glaring at Adam. "I could have stayed on Broadway and my life would have been much easier. I came back because I love Jared and I want to be with him," Fenix finished, his voice rising as he stepped closer to Adam and challenged him. If Adam thought all this macho bullshit he was trying to pull was impressing Fenix, he was very mistaken.

"Yeah, right," Adam huffed, and laughed sardonically. "I don't believe that for a second."

"I don't give a fuck what you believe. Both Jared and I are adults, capable of making our own decisions. You'd better back off," Fenix said through clenched teeth.

Adam stepped closer to him. Fenix had to tilt his head to meet his eyes. He didn't back down though, even though Adam towered over him.

"I wish you would disappear," Adam said with quiet menace. "I wish I could erase you from his mind and he never remembers you even existed."

"Why? So that you'd take my place instead?" Fenix shot back. Adam physically recoiled as if he'd been hit. Fenix took advantage of the fact that he'd struck a nerve and continued, "It doesn't matter if you wipe his mind blank. He'll never love you the way he loves me. That's the issue here, not me. And I think it's pathetic that you can't even admit that."

Fenix saw how Adam's face transformed from angry to hateful in a second. He took a step back, genuinely worried by the hate oozing from Adam's whole being. If the man had a gun right now, Fenix had no doubt he'd use it.

But Adam didn't have a gun. So instead he drew his arm back and punched Fenix so hard that the force of the collision threw him back and he fell in a heap on the floor, banging his head on the wardrobe. His ears started to ring, his vision going black around the edges. Fenix felt disoriented and his jaw hurt like hell. If Adam decided to strike again, Fenix would have no way of defending himself against the bigger man.

Fenix heard heavy footsteps around him and then the door slammed shut.

He felt like crying. Crying! Like a fucking baby!

Fenix tried to move his jaw, opening and closing his mouth, and was relieved it wasn't dislocated. But it hurt so badly. He still couldn't see well with his left eye and hoped the damage was temporary.

Gingerly, propping himself on the small coffee table, he pushed himself up and immediately regretted it when he felt dizzy. Sitting down on top of the coffee table and putting his head in his hands, Fenix hoped like hell he didn't have a concussion.

The door opened again and Fenix heard Jared walk in, talking on the phone. He kicked the door shut behind him and Fenix winced at the loud sound.

All talk and movement halted as Fenix raised his head to look at him. Jared had stopped mid stride and was gaping at him.

Making a quick excuse, he ended the phone call and moved towards Fenix.

"What the fuck happened?" Jared asked as he hurried to kneel in front of Fenix. He must have looked pretty bad because Jared stared at him like he was a moment away from welcoming death.

"Nothing, I'm fine," Fenix said, waving Jared off.

"The hell you are! What's going on, Fenix?" Jared persisted.

Fenix didn't reply. Knowing that he wouldn't be able to lie to Jared about it, but still biding his time, he saw Jared looking around the room as if searching for clues. He watched in horror as Jared saw the magazine Adam had thrown lying on the floor, conveniently opened on one of the pages of their spread.

Jared's face twisted in anger and he walked out of the room without another word.

"Fuck!" Fenix groaned, running his hands over his face, wincing at the sharp pain in his jaw. "I'm so sick of this shit," he murmured to himself, standing up to follow Jared. He had a very good idea exactly where he'd gone.

A few minutes later, Fenix approached Adam's dressing room and heard shouting. His head was still pounding, but at least his vision had cleared. Feeling confident he could take on another confrontation, Fenix inched closer to the door that was gaping open, taking in the scene in front of him. Jared was standing in the middle of the room, his posture stiff and ready for attack. Adam was sitting on the sofa, touching his newly split lip, glaring at him.

"You stay out of my life, of *our* life! You have no right to question my decisions," Jared barked at him.

"I can't believe you punched me over him! What, he needs you to fight his battles now? Since when are you the white knight saving the princess?" Adam shot back.

Fenix decided against letting his presence known. That was their fight. Adam had lashed out at Fenix because Jared hadn't been there. Maybe it was a good thing Adam had punched him – Fenix could bet Adam had fantasised about it for a long time. Now that it was out of his system maybe he'd leave them alone.

"There's no battle here," Jared spat out. "We don't need your approval. *I* don't need your approval. There's nothing to fight over – I love him and I want to spend the rest of my life with him. If you have a problem with that, feel free to never speak to either of us again. And I swear to god, if you ever touch him again I'll kill you," Jared said flatly as he turned to leave.

Adam kept his mouth shut for the first time in his life. Jared met Fenix's eyes and went to him, wrapping an arm over his shoulder and pulling him close.

"You OK?" he whispered, kissing his temple.

Fenix nodded and they left without looking back.

CHAPTER THIRTY TWO

Jared

Time flew by when the whole musical arrived in London. The cast had an immense amount of promotion and rehearsing to do, and Jared barely saw Fenix during the two weeks before opening night. Most days they met only in bed at night, but Jared wasn't complaining. He knew it was all part of the job.

Jared had also tried to coax some information from Fenix on how he'd managed to convince the producers to move back to London. Fenix had promised to tell him everything after opening night. Jared had no idea why but decided against dwelling on it.

It didn't really matter. Fenix was *here*.

Jared still couldn't believe Adam had punched Fenix. His friend was impulsive and hot headed, but he'd never been cruel and violent. After their fight, Adam had apologised, but things hadn't been the same since. They both kept their distance. Jared was sad their friendship had taken such a nose dive, but he would not tolerate *anyone* treating Fenix like that.

Jared sighed and turned off the water. A hot shower had been exactly what he'd needed. It relaxed him after the show and calmed him before Fenix's big night. *Poison* was about to premiere on Queen Victoria's stage in an hour. Fenix had been shaking with nerves all day even though he'd been playing that role for almost four years.

Again, Jared wasn't allowed to watch *Poison*'s dress rehearsals. Fenix had been very secretive about it, mentioning some new special effects and a couple of new songs, but nothing else. Jared was excited and couldn't wait to see it. He shaved, styled his hair, got dressed in black slacks and a button down shirt, and walked out the door with a huge smile on his face.

Just like the last time he'd seen *Poison* open at Queen Victoria, Fenix had insisted on him watching the show from the Dress Circle instead of backstage. Jared took his seat – no Adam to sit beside him this time – and waited.

The audience hummed excitedly around him, but the moment the lights dimmed and Fenix's voice came through the sound system, everyone quieted down and watched mesmerised as the show started.

Fenix had been right – it was bigger, louder, and better. Jared couldn't take his eyes off Fenix – he'd gone out early that morning, claiming he had an appointment at the hairdresser's before rehearsals, and Jared hadn't seen the result until now. Fenix's long, blond hair had been cut shorter at the sides, while the rest was tousled in a messy, uneven style. The eye make-up he wore on stage was bolder too – the simple black eyeliner had been exchanged for black, sparkling eye shadow that covered most of his lids.

Fenix was striking.

He was wearing his usual tight, leather pants that could be easily mistaken for leggings, and a black t-shirt. When he started singing and moving, Jared wished the show would never end. He could watch this gorgeous, talented, amazing man perform on stage till the end of time.

Jared had seen the show so many times that even the smallest change was noticeable to him, but there were a few quite significant ones. What made a huge impression on him was a new song – a ballad – that Fenix performed while three barely-dressed women danced around him, touching him seductively. It was the part where his and Joy's character had separated, and Fenix's character had started sleeping with as many women as possible, often all at the same time.

Wanting... waiting....burning...
Walking towards the pleasure.
Sensing it... smelling it... tasting it...

Fenix's low, seductive voice started singing in a slow, sensual rhythm as the women weaved around him. Jared instantly got hard. That song was sexy on its own, but Fenix singing it brought it to a whole new erotic level.

Finally reach it. Touch it. Want to grab it, squeeze it, feel it
all at once.
But touch it slowly, softly, gently...
Enjoying every piece of it, every single part.
Burning... playing... feeling...

Oh, god! Jared was so turned on. Right then, Fenix was the epitome of sex.

Wanting... to stay there forever.
Never let go, never let it slip away.
Loving while tasting it... licking it...
Smiling... crying...

The song picked up in rhythm, as if depicting the culmination of a sexual act, and the more Fenix sang in that breathless voice, the more Jared's cock pushed uncomfortably against his zipper.

Pushing it hard... harder... harder...
Stop!
You're mine! Want you!
Stay with me, be with me, fly with me.
Slowing it down...touching it softly... gently...
Kiss me! Taste me! Hold me!
Hugging...   warming...   breathing......   calming...
whispering...
Tired of pleasure... sleeping.... dreaming.... of you.

Was he actually trying to make Jared come in his pants? A few times Fenix had met Jared's eyes directly, as if he was singing only for him. And that song... God, that song sounded so much like Fenix was describing their own love making.

Jared had a hard time concentrating for the rest of the show. He noticed a few more changes here and there, but the biggest difference, besides that fucking sexy song, was the final scene.

It started when the stage went completely black, staying like this for a few agonising moments. People around Jared started murmuring in confusion, but before they had a chance to brace themselves, the stage lit up again and water started falling along the back wall. It was pouring! A light mist started raining on stage as Fenix walked out, alone, dressed just in black leggings. His skin gleamed as droplets of water slid down his chest, his back, his arms...

He started dancing like Jared had never seen him before. He looked so composed, so relaxed, and so... free. After a few minutes, the water sliding down the back wall of the stage erupted in fire and the whole audience gasped simultaneously. Jared was amazed – it was incredible! How had the theatre even allowed that? And how the fuck did that fire burn in water?

Fenix started singing and tiny drops of fire, *fucking fire*, began raining on him. He didn't seem to mind which meant it was not actual fire, but it looked so real.

Speechless.
Telling me everything without a single word.
Speechless.
Invisible.
Seeing him in everything, in my own reflection.
Invisible.
Strong.
Giving me all the tender love I'd ever need.
Strong.
Serious.
Joking, laughing, smiling. All the time. With me.
Serious.
Strict.
Teaching me how to break all the rules.
Strict.
Special.

Wow. The combination of the vision Fenix was in those tight leggings, his voice, his movement, the water, the fire... It was incredible.

When the song drew to a close, the lights dimmed, the fire disappeared leaving just the water and the rain. Fenix dropped to his knees, arched backwards, supporting himself with one arm extended to the floor behind him and tangling his other hand in his wet hair. He breathed heavily as he kept his pose, his chest heaving up and down, until the lights dimmed again and the curtain fell.

There were a few seconds of stunned silence. Nobody moved. Nobody even breathed.

And then the theatre erupted in applause. It was so loud and enthusiastic that Jared could feel the walls vibrating.

The lights in the hall came back on and people started standing up, applauding and whistling until the whole cast, including a very wet and sexy Fenix, appeared on stage and bowed deeply.

CHAPTER THIRTY THREE

Jared

Jared kissed Fenix deeply, he couldn't help it. They'd made love three times that time after *Poison*'s premiere and Jared still couldn't get enough. The man was intoxicating. Jared thanked life, fate, god – whoever was responsible for bringing Fenix into his life. He felt like the luckiest man on earth.

"I love you so much, Fen," he whispered as Fenix curled around him, burying his head in the crook of Jared's shoulder.

"Love you, too," Fenix said against his skin, his lips brushing the sensitive spot where Jared's pulse beat erratically.

"Those new songs... Wow! They were amazing, Fen," Jared said for the first time tonight. They hadn't managed to get much talking in, besides Jared telling him how much he loved the show and pouncing on him first in the dressing room, then again at home. Twice.

"You really like them?" Fenix asked, raising his head slightly to look into Jared's eyes. Was it him, or did Fenix look a bit sad?

"Of course I did, love," Jared said and smiled, brushing his thumb over Fenix's chin. "That first one almost made me come in my pants! You were so hot... And the final one – the whole production was incredible! I couldn't believe what I was seeing. The song was so touching, but combined with the water and the fire and you, almost naked, it was breathtaking."

Fenix grinned and leaned down to kiss Jared again.

"How did you do that, by the way? The fire?" Jared asked.

"It's not real fire. It's some synthetic pyro-effect they developed in Japan. It was a pain in the ass to get all those special effects on the show," Fenix explained, rolling his eyes as if having water pouring down the stage wasn't such a big deal. "I wrote those songs," Fenix said quietly, almost shyly.

"What? Really?"

"Yeah... Wrote them for you."

"Baby..." Jared didn't know what to say. He choked up, remembering the songs, replaying the lyrics in his head. They were for *him*. "I... I don't know what to say."

Fenix looked at him with that same sadness again.

"What's wrong?" Jared weaved his fingers in Fenix's hair and pulled him down for another leisurely kiss.

"Remember I promised I'd tell you how I managed to convince the producers to move back here?" Jared nodded. "I threatened them I'd pull out of the show and they wouldn't have their award winning star anymore. But that wasn't enough. Thanks to Joy's big mouth, they knew I was writing songs and choreographing some dances, but I refused to use any of them in the show. Those two songs and the final dance scene, which, by the way, was also inspired by you, were the condition. I had to sign the rights over to them. Now, they can use them even if I'm not in the show anymore."

"That's ridiculous! How could they ask that from you?"

Fenix shrugged.

"I'd have given them anything they wanted to come back here."

Jared pulled him into a hug again and they kept silent for a few moments.

"I'm sorry," Jared whispered.

"I showed them a few things, played a few songs for them, and it's like they knew these were the ones I loved the most. The ones that were special. So they took them away."

"They can never take them away from you. You wrote them for *me*. You can sing them to me when we cook dinner or when we shower together," Jared suggested with a smile. Fenix laughed, some of the sadness evaporating from him. "Or, on our fortieth anniversary..."

Fenix looked at him sharply, hope and joy shinning in his eyes.

"You mean that?"

"Yeah. I do."

The next day, Jared and Fenix were relaxing in their dressing room after Jared's show and before *Poison* was about to start when Jared's phone rang.

"Hello?" he said, not recognising the number.

"Um... hello. Is that Mr Jared Hartley?" a woman asked uncertainly.

"Yes, that's me."

"My name is Judie Mallory. I'm sorry Mr Hartley, but I'm calling with some bad news."

Jared's heart started hammering in his chest as he leaned forward in his seat.

"Bad news?" he echoed, trying mentally to account for everyone he knew. Was someone hurt?

"Unfortunately, yes. Your mother... She passed away."

The room started spinning around Jared and he managed to keep his balance only because he was sitting down.

"When?" he asked dryly.

"Five days ago. The funeral was today."

"Five days? Why didn't you call me sooner?" Jared asked sharply, barely keeping his control.

"Because she specifically instructed me not to."

Jared felt like someone had stabbed him in the chest. His own mother hadn't wanted him to come to her funeral. Even in death, she didn't want him.

"Why are you calling now?" he managed to ask through the lump in his throat. Fenix moved to sit next to him, silently offering support even though he didn't know exactly what was happening.

"Because they'll be reading the will tomorrow, and as her sole living relative, you should be there."

"Where?" Jared asked shortly.

Judie told him the address and the time, and they said their goodbyes.

"I can't believe this," Jared said to himself. Fenix draped his arm over his shoulders and pulled him close.

"What's going on?"

"My mother is dead," Jared said flatly.

"Oh my god! I'm so sorry, baby. When's the funeral?"

"It was today," Jared said, turning to face Fenix. "She'd requested that they didn't call me before that. She didn't want me there."

Fenix didn't say anything, but Jared could feel the disapproval radiating from him. There was nothing either of them could do. Pauline Hartley was gone, and she hadn't managed to find it in herself to love him.

"I have to go for the reading of the will tomorrow."

"I'll come with you."

"It's probably going to be an overnight trip, Fenix. Colchester is two hours away and the reading won't start till 4:00 pm. I don't know how long it's going to take, but I'll probably stay there instead of catching some late train back. You won't be back in time for your show..."

"I don't care about the fucking show," Fenix said angrily. "Your mother is dead. Even if she was a heartless bitch, I know you're hurting. I'm coming with you. End of discussion."

Jared stared at Fenix, trying to convey the gratitude and love he felt for him with a single look. He needed Fenix there with him because he knew he was going to fall apart. He was lucky and thankful Fenix knew that without Jared spelling it out.

"I'm going to find Oliver Lowe, the director, and let him know they'll be using my stand-in tomorrow," Fenix said, and then gave Jared a quick kiss. "I'm sorry," he said against Jared's lips, and he knew what that meant: I'm sorry she couldn't love you; I'm sorry you lost your hope she'll ever love you; I'm sorry I can't fix it for you.

Jared nodded as he waved Fenix away to go sort it out, while he lay back on the sofa, refusing to dwell on the question he'd been pondering ever since he'd last spoken to his mother: why?

The next day, Jared and Fenix sat side by side at *Shaw, Reed and Webster*'s office as Earl Shaw himself read the will. Pauline Hartley had left everything to her church. No surprise there. Jared's mother had always been a devoted Catholic, but her dedication to the church had turned to almost an obsession after his father's death. Ultimately, she had chosen her faith over her only child, even in death.

Not that she had much. She had the house that had been paid off before his father had died, a few thousand pounds savings, and some personal possessions. Jared didn't care about any of that. What he cared about was that his mother hadn't even mentioned his name in the will. It was like she didn't even have a child.

As if reading Jared's thoughts, Fenix took his hand in his and squeezed. They hadn't talked a lot during the two hour trip, but

Fenix had been there, and that meant the world to Jared. He needed him there, needed to feel that Fenix would drop everything and support him when Jared needed it the most. It reassured him that Fenix had really meant that he was here to stay, that his career was not above his relationship with Jared anymore.

After the reading, Jared stood up and, followed closely by Fenix, went to Earl Shaw's desk, ignoring everyone he passed by.

"Excuse me?" Jared said politely and Shaw raised his eyes to meet his. "I'm Jared Hartley, Pauline Hartley's son." Jared extended his hand and Earl Shaw shook it.

"Of course. How can I help you, Mr Hartley?"

"Is there something my mother might have left for me? Not in her will, but like a letter or a note?" The hope in his voice made Jared disgusted with himself, but he clenched his teeth and ignored it. For now.

"Unfortunately, no, Mr Hartley. Everything Pauline wanted to say she said in her will."

Jared nodded and turned to leave because the pity in Earl Shaw's eyes was making him want to punch the wall.

Fenix put an arm on his shoulder and they headed for the door, ignoring the stares and whispers from the few other people in the room. Jared didn't know any of them – they were probably his mother's friends from church.

They hadn't made two steps into the hall outside the office when a woman's voice called after them.

"Mr Hartley!" Both Jared and Fenix stopped and turned. A slim, blonde woman, probably in her sixties, and a tall, equally slim man wearing a priest's shirt, were walking out of the office and heading in their direction. Jared had seen them inside but otherwise didn't know them. "My name is Judie Mallory. We spoke on the phone?" the woman said nervously. Jared nodded, but didn't extend a hand or offer any pleasantries. He was past that. He just wanted to go home. Judie cleared her throat, glanced at Fenix and continued: "And this is Father Joseph."

"Nice to meet you, Mr Hartley. I'm so sorry for your loss," Father Joseph said, offering his hand.

"Nice to meet you, too. This is my partner, Fenix Bergman," Jared said, shaking the priest's hand. Father Joseph offered his hand to Fenix, although he didn't smile when Fenix took it. He nodded curtly, while Judie pursed her lips disapprovingly.

"I wanted to ask you something," the priest said, his dark eye concerned. "Are you planning on contesting the will?"

Jared was so taken aback by the straightforward question that he must have looked appalled. Father Joseph continued hastily, "I don't mean to pry in your personal business. You're free to take your time and do as you wish. But I'm asking because I need to know what to prepare for. Our church doesn't have a lot of money for lawyers and legal fees, but if you decide to contest the will..."

"I won't contest anything," Jared said sharply, unwilling to listen to the priest's rambling anymore. "My mother hadn't spoken to me in ten years. She adopted you and your church as her family. If she wanted to leave all she had to you, then so be it. I don't want something my mother wasn't willing to give me."

Jared was surprised at how emotional he suddenly felt. He didn't want to show these people an ounce of his true self. He wanted to put on a perfectly blank face and get this over with. Fenix stiffened beside him, touching his hand with his pinkie finger to show him he was there, as if sensing the storm brewing inside Jared.

"Your mother loved you, you know. In her own way," Father Joseph said kindly.

Jared wanted to rip his head off. The priest had no idea what he was talking about. He had no idea how much his mum's rejection had hurt.

"Yeah? And what's 'her way', exactly?" Fenix said, taking a small step in front of Jared as if to shield him. "Was she proud of him? Did she see the amazing person her son had become? Did she support him, was she there for him when he needed her the most? Did she even call on his birthday?" Fenix paused, unflinching, as they gaped at him. "No. She did none of that. She hid like a coward behind her faith. So get off your high horse and don't try to tell Jared his mother loved him because she sure as hell didn't."

Fenix turned on his heel and grabbed Jared's hand, tugging him along. They managed to walk out of the building without any more interruptions. Jared couldn't wait to get out of there. He felt suffocated. Tired. Sad. Angry. All he wanted was to go home and forget this day had ever happened. His mother was dead, but she'd been as good as dead to him for over ten years, so Jared had somewhat overcome that sense of loss. Today he got closure. Confirmation that his mother had really stopped loving him, even in death.

Tomorrow he could start healing.

"Let's get the train and get out of here. I can't be here anymore..." Jared began, but Fenix was already walking towards the station.

"I know. I can't be here either," he said, frowning.

"Thank you. For what you did back there. If you hadn't stepped in I'd have exploded all over them. It wouldn't have been pretty."

"I know, baby. I could feel you trembling next to me," Fenix said, and suddenly stopped, taking Jared's face in his hands. "I love you, OK? And I will never stop loving you." He kissed him lightly and smiled, his pale blue eyes shining with such adoration that, at this moment, Jared had no doubt Fenix meant it.

CHAPTER THIRTY FOUR

Fenix

When Adam found out about Jared's mother, he pushed all his personal views aside and came running to support his friend. Fenix couldn't help but respect the man for that. Their friendship had been strained since Adam had punched Fenix, even though he tried to make amends, apologised, and even managed to look remorseful. Despite that, Jared never seemed to fully forgive him. Fenix's relationship with Adam had never been great, but after that night they both had enough and stopped fighting. Adam had probably gotten it out of his system, and as far as Fenix was concerned, there was nothing to fight about. He didn't care if Adam liked him or not. He was Jared's partner, and he was here to stay – Fenix knew that, hopefully Jared knew that, and everyone else could go fuck themselves.

Jared truly appreciated Adam's support as well as the fact that he proved to be a real friend despite everything. Fenix was certain Jared would have had a harder time coming to terms with his mother's death and her ultimate rejection if Adam hadn't been there for him. All of their friends had been great – quietly standing by Jared and showing him he was indeed loved and accepted.

Soon, Jared began to heal.

He smiled again for no reason, started cooking almost every night while Fenix relaxed on the sofa after his show, and stopped waking up in the middle of the night, unaware of where he was.

December came and went in a blur. It was the busiest period of the year for the West End, and both Jared and Fenix had back to back shows all month, with the exception of Christmas Eve. They'd declined their friends' invitations for dinner and drinks, choosing to stay at home instead. They were both exhausted and were looking forward to a quiet night in.

"Fen, seriously, it's fine. I'll chop the veggies. Get yourself a glass of wine and go sit down to watch *Love Actually* or something," Jared said and tried to shoo Fenix away from the chopping board.

"I want to help," Fenix said stubbornly, refusing to budge.

"But you're not helping, love. I'm not making vegetable mash, I'm making roasted vegetables, and I need them to be chopped in big chunks, not grated," Jared gestured towards Fenix's chopping board in exasperation. Fenix smirked and leaned in, catching Jared's lips with his.

"I love it when you go all Gordon Ramsey on me," Fenix murmured against Jared's mouth. "It's hot. Makes me wanna mess up all your ingredients."

Jared laughed and snuck his arms around Fenix, pulling him closer for a deeper kiss.

"That's not hard," Jared replied when their mouths separated. "All you have to do is *be* in the kitchen."

Fenix swatted his arm, squirmed away from his embrace, and continued chopping the vegetables. Jared shook his head and went to check on the roast. But he was still smiling and that was all that mattered to Fenix.

They ate in the living room in front of the TV and exchanged presents at midnight. Fenix had gotten Jared the Tissot watch Jared had fallen in love with earlier that year, and had the back engraved with what he was starting to think of as 'their poem':

To hearts which near each other move
From evening close to morning light,
The night is good; because, my love,
They never say good-night.

Fenix had asked the jeweller to engrave it in a spiral and make a heart with F+J in the middle. Jared loved it and, even though he tried to hide it, Fenix saw his eyes misting over.

When Fenix opened his gift, he saw it was a study-at-home course in Swedish.

"I hate to break it to you, baby, but I'm already fluent in Swedish," Fenix said with a smile, knowing there must be something more to the gift. Jared smirked.

"I know, love. It's for me. I want you to teach me."

"Why?" Fenix asked, genuinely bewildered.

"Because I want to be able to say a few words to the locals when we go in January," Jared said triumphantly and pulled out an envelope from behind his back, presenting it to Fenix. There were two plane tickets to Stockholm inside, as well as hotel bookings and itinerary. The theatre closed for two weeks in January after the gruelling schedule in December, and Fenix could not think of a better way to spend their holiday.

"Wow! That's... I don't know what to say. Thank you!" Fenix wrapped his arms around Jared and rested his head on his shoulder. That was the best gift he'd ever received. He'd mentioned to Jared once that he'd been to Sweden as a child and he had fallen in love with the country. Fenix had wanted to go again for some time, see it through an adult's eyes, but there was always something more important that came up.

"You're welcome," Jared whispered against his hair. "I don't think they have all the dirty words you shout during sex in the course, though. You'll have to make a list of those and teach me yourself."

"Let's go have your first lesson, then," Fenix said, standing, and offering Jared his hand to pull him up.

"Are there going to be rewards for excelling students?" Jared asked as he padded after Fenix towards the bedroom.

"Oh, yeah," Fenix said, turning to wink at Jared. "But there's also going to be punishment if you don't do your homework on time," he said seductively.

"Looking forward to it, Mr Bergman," Jared replied, and their laughter followed them up the stairs before they collapsed on the bed.

Fenix's show on New Year's Eve ended ten minutes before midnight. While the audience applauded and the cast bowed, a voice on the speakers informed everyone that there will be a countdown in a few minutes and everyone was welcome to stay and celebrate with the cast. Behind the curtain, people were busy rearranging the decors, putting up *Happy New Year* banners and loading the confetti machines.

A minute before midnight, the curtain went up and the audience started cheering. The whole *Poison* cast was on stage and Fenix had to be with them, even though all he wanted to do was run into Jared's arms backstage. He could see Jared standing on the edge of the stage, watching him and smiling.

Ten, nine, eight...

The countdown began and Fenix's heart started beating faster.

Seven, six, five, four...

Fenix ran off the stage and collided with Jared just as the counting reached one and the hall exploded in cheers, whistles, and confetti. Jared hugged him and kissed him, and whispered 'Happy New Year' in his ear. Fenix had never felt happier.

Their first week in Sweden was fantastic. Jared had booked a nice hotel in Stockholm and they went sightseeing, visited most of the fourteen islands the city was built on, took long walks in the Royal National City park, and enjoyed the fresh air, good food, and beautiful scenery. Fenix felt like a child again, remembering walking hand in hand with his mother during one of her rare breaks. At the same time, Fenix discovered so many things that hadn't made an impression on him as a child, like how friendly and open the locals were or how, for some reason, it felt like coming back home.

Jared had learned some words and phrases with Fenix's help, and he was very proud when he could order their meal in the restaurant or request room service. He beamed like a child every time he said a sentence correctly and Fenix rediscovered his mother's tongue through Jared's enthusiasm.

Their second week began in Malmö – Evelyn's home town. The weather was milder – the city was in Southern Sweden and it was breathtaking. Fenix felt so relaxed, so happy and fulfilled during those ten days, like he'd never felt before.

Four days before they were scheduled to go back to London, Fenix's phone rang while he and Jared were having lunch in a cosy cafe in Malmö city centre, before heading out to an ice skating rink.

"Hey, Cat. How are you?" Fenix said as he picked up.

"Not good. You need to catch the next plane to New York, Fenix. We have a problem," Cat said in a brisk, business-like voice.

Fenix's blood ran cold. He met Jared's eyes across the table and frowned.

"What's going on?" he asked his agent.

"I'd rather not discuss it over the phone. But it's big."

"How big?"

"End-of-your-career big," Cat said with a heavy sigh. She paused and Fenix could imagine her rubbing her fingers across her forehead in concentration. "Look, I don't mean to be a bitch, Fenix. But trust me on this. You need to get here as soon as possible or this whole thing will blow up and we won't be able to stop it."

"I'll be there as soon as I can," Fenix said and disconnected the call. Jared was looking at him with concern. Fenix hated that he had to break it to him that their perfect vacation was over.

"Cat wants to see me in her office as soon as possible. She didn't say much, but apparently something big is going on and we need to face it right now. She said my career depended on it."

Jared took Fenix's hand across the table and squeezed.

"Let's go back to the hotel and pack. We'll book the tickets online," Jared said without a moment's hesitation, and leaving some money to cover the bill on the table, stood and tugged Fenix behind him.

CHAPTER THIRTY FIVE

FENIX

They managed to book a flight for the next morning costing an extortionate sum of money. Fenix tried hinting that Jared didn't have to come and spend all this money, but Jared had glared at him as he'd keyed in his credit card number, and the subject was dropped.

Fenix hadn't slept at all that night, worrying what could have happened. He couldn't manage to doze off on the plane either – he kept thinking, trying to remember any insignificant detail, *something* that would lead him in the right direction. All he came up with was someone he'd fucked during the two years he'd spent on Broadway had come out with a confession story or some other nonsense, and Cat was trying to stop it from going into print. Fenix could imagine that could be harmful to his image, but career threatening? He was single at the time, so there was no scandal there. Everyone knew he was gay so they couldn't cash in on that either.

What could it be?

"Fen?" Jared said quietly next to him. Fenix turned to face him and tried to smile. "You've been thinking about this pretty much nonstop for the past twenty four hours. Try to relax and get some sleep." Jared pushed Fenix's hair out of his face, caressing his cheek in the process. He tugged Fenix closer, wrapping an arm around him. "Whatever it is, we'll deal with it, OK?" Jared said, kissing the top of Fenix's head when he rested it on his shoulder.

Fenix nodded weakly and closed his tired eyes. Jared was with him. He'd be OK.

That was his last thought before he drifted off to sleep.

Fenix felt a bit more like himself as he and Jared walked into his agent's office. The few hours sleep he'd managed to get on the plane had done wonders for his mental state.

"So what is it?" Fenix asked as he and Jared sat down next to each other in Cathleen's office. She took the chair opposite them. Her expression was grim and she had dark circles under her eyes as if she hadn't slept well either.

That was bad.

"Someone contacted me yesterday saying they have a video of you. They said they were going to sell it to the highest bidder unless you pay them half a million dollars," Cat said bluntly.

Both Fenix and Jared gaped at her.

"A video?" Fenix managed to say at last. "A video doing what?"

Cat glanced nervously at Jared before she spoke.

"Getting fucked by four men at the same time."

Fenix ears started ringing.

No.

This could not be happening.

He ran a shaking hand down his face, trying to think, but failed miserably. A hand snuck around his shoulders and he turned to meet Jared's concerned eyes.

"Fen? Are you alright? You look like you're going to pass out," Jared asked.

Jared.

Jared was going to see him getting fucked by four men.

Jared was going to witness the worst night of his life.

"We have to stop this, Cat," Fenix said desperately.

"I know, Fenix!" Cathleen exclaimed as she stood up. She started pacing around the room, her features drawn in concentration. "We can't let the world see this or your career is over."

"I don't give a fuck about the world or my career!" Fenix yelled. Both Cathleen and Jared looked at him sharply. He sighed and leaned back on the sofa, his head resting on the back. "I don't want Jared to see it." Shame and humiliation like he'd never felt before overwhelmed him, and he couldn't stop the tear that slid down his cheek.

"Cathleen, will you give us a minute, please?" Jared asked quietly. Cathleen nodded and exited the room.

"Baby?" Jared said. Fenix couldn't face him. "Look at me, love," Jared asked gently. The moment Fenix met his eyes and saw the kindness and concern there, he started crying harder, unable to stop the agony inside him from spilling over.

Jared hugged him and rocked him, whispering calming words while Fenix cried. When the tears dried, Jared let go of him, wiped down his eyes and his cheeks with a tissue, and kissed him softly.

"Listen to me," Jared began, holding Fenix's face between his palms. "I knew about this, remember? You already told me. Leaving you hadn't crossed my mind then, and it certainly doesn't now. I'll support you whatever you decide to do, OK? If you wanna pay them off, I'll mortgage the flat and we'll pay them. If you decide to tell them to go fuck themselves and tomorrow the whole world sees the video – fine. I'm still not going anywhere. We're in this together, Fenix."

Fenix nodded, but couldn't force any words out. His throat had completely closed off. Jared's support in that moment meant more to him than anything.

"It was the worst night of my life, Jared," Fenix managed to stay at last. "The night I thought I had nothing left to live for. I don't want you to watch it, I can't live with myself if you see me like that..."

"Shhh," Jared whispered. "I won't watch it, I promise."

A knock on the door interrupted them and Cathleen walked in with a handsome man in tow. He was tall and muscled and wore a stern expression on his face. His dark eyes scanned the room automatically before he sat down next to Cathleen.

"This is detective Trey Griffin with NYPD. We're very close friends and I trust him implicitly," Cathleen said meeting Fenix's worried eyes. Fenix relaxed after that statement – if his agent trusted that man, then so would he. Cathleen didn't use the term lightly. "I think we should hear his opinion on this, Fenix. I told him the gist of the story already."

Trey Griffin shook hands with both Fenix and Jared as Cathleen spoke.

"There are a few ways to handle this, but I'd like to see the video before I advise you any further," Griffin said.

"See the video? You actually have it?" Fenix's voice rose in horror.

"They sent me part of it, yes."

"Have you seen it?"

Cathleen nodded. Fenix hid his face in his hands, too ashamed to even look her in the eyes.

"They'll contact me by the end of today for an answer, Fenix. We don't have any time to waste. Trey should see the video and we should decide what to do as soon as possible."

Fenix nodded and stood. He took Jared's hand and tugged him towards the door.

"Watch it. We'll be outside."

They sat on the sofa in the foyer, glad that Andy, Cathleen's assistant, was busy typing on her computer and didn't pay them any attention. Fenix could feel Jared's tense body next to him. He felt awful that his moronic behaviour was coming back to haunt him. To haunt *them*, because Jared was in this with him. As much as Fenix appreciated that, he couldn't help but feel guilty.

"Hey," Fenix said quietly, touching Jared's upper arm. "You OK?"

Jared looked at him and frowned.

"I'm not OK," he said through clenched teeth. "I want to find those bastards and kill them with my own two hands. How could they do this to you?"

Jared trembled with silent rage. Fenix's eyes softened as he spoke:

"It's my mistake, Jared. As much as I'd like to blame it on someone else, it's my responsibility."

"We all make mistakes, Fen! That doesn't mean that someone should take advantage of you, ply you with alcohol all night, film you without you realising, and then try to sell the footage to the highest bidder! Fucking useless, greedy motherfuckers! If I could get my hands on them for just a minute..." Jared visibly shook with fury and his eyes blazed in a dark blue storm.

"Hey, baby, calm down, please. I... I feel shaken enough because of all this, I need you to be calm for me or I'll completely fall apart."

Jared exhaled loudly and his shoulders sagged. He nodded and wrapped Fenix in his arms.

Fifteen minutes later Cathleen invited them back in her office. Detective Griffin was frowning. He didn't waste any time and started speaking as soon as Fenix and Jared took their seats opposite him.

"Did you drink that night, Fenix?" Griffin asked. Fenix nodded. "How about drugs?"

"No."

"Are you sure?"

"Yes!"

"How well did you know those men?"

"I've just met them an hour before..." Fenix trailed off. The detective nodded, as if his reply was what he'd expected.

"Is it possible that one of them slipped something in your drink?"

Fenix thought about it for a second. Was it? He'd been so out of it already that it would have been easy to drop a pill in his glass.

"I guess."

"Do you remember exactly what happened that night?" Griffin continued asking questions like a true professional.

"I don't remember anything between drinking with them in the bar and then waking up in a hotel room, puking my guts out."

The detective nodded thoughtfully before he spoke again.

"Without a toxicology report we can't be certain that's what happened, but I'm pretty sure they drugged you. Your pupils are abnormally dilated, your body is slack, and you kept mumbling incoherently. Also," Griffin glanced nervously around, "you were not aroused at all during the footage I saw."

Fenix turned red in an instant. God, was this ever going to end?

"What are you trying to say, detective?" Jared asked. Fenix wished the ground would open up and swallow him whole.

"I think Fenix has enough cause to press charges."

Fenix looked sharply at the man as if he'd gone mad.

"Charges? For what?"

"Rape."

Fenix shook his head vehemently.

"I remember when they asked me if I wanted to go with them. I said yes!"

"But you don't remember anything after that? If you were just drunk, you may have come to your senses and left before things got out of hand. Or at least noticed they were recording you. But I think that choice was taken away from you, Fenix. I think those people drugged you and then raped you and filmed it. Why would they film it otherwise? Why would they come after you if it was just about the sex for them? In my personal opinion, I think you were targeted."

Fenix pondered that for a few silent moments – was it really possible? He'd fucked so many people during those two years, word may have gotten around that he was an easy lay. And the fact that he had no recollection of that night worried him – he'd been drunk before and he'd always remembered at least parts of what had happened. Total blank was very strange indeed.

"What are the options if that was the case?" he asked the detective.

"You could press charges. I don't suppose you have the names of those men?" Fenix shook his head. "That would make things a bit more complicated. Their faces are not clearly visible in the video, and it might take time to identify them. But still, if you press charges based on that video, we can start an investigation and try to find those men. If we don't, it'll get filed under 'unsolved' and all evidence will be stored in a box in the basement."

Fenix blinked a few times, trying to make sense of what the detective was saying. Sensing his confusion, Trey Griffin continued.

"If anyone tries to sell and upload that video online, they'll be messing with evidence for a rape case. Those people are trying to make money. If they can't get anyone to pay for the footage, they'll drop it. There's no point in uploading it online for free – the trouble they'll get into will outweigh the gain."

"I'll make sure nobody touches that video with a barge pole. Trust me, just hinting the word 'rape' and 'investigation' will scare everyone off. If it doesn't, the word 'lawyers' will," Cathleen added.

"If I press charges and you start the investigation, won't that get public? Won't it get the media even more interested?" Fenix asked.

"I'll take on the case personally and do my best to keep it under the radar. My superiors will have access to the files, but nobody else. I doubt it'll get blown up out of proportion," the detective said.

Fenix wasn't convinced.

"Look, our best bet is opening the case and filing the video under evidence. I don't have much hope we're going to find those men since their faces are not clearly seen. Let me talk to them when they call. I'll explain what they'll be getting into if they sell the video or upload it online themselves. Hopefully that'll scare them off," Griffin said.

Fenix nodded in agreement. He caught the 'there are no guarantees' meaning of 'hopefully', but there was nothing he could do, was there?

"How long is the statute of limitations on sexual assault?" Jared asked.

"Five years," the detective replied shortly.

"So in four years they could come back and we won't be able to stop them?" Fenix asked.

"Technically, yes. If that happens, you can always hire good lawyers and sue. But let me be honest here – the video is disturbing. It's not erotic in any way. It clearly shows four men taking advantage of you. Even without the rape charges, no reputable media, or even the gossip rags, would want anything to do with it."

Fenix winced at the detective's words and felt Jared's arms sneak around him. If it wasn't for Jared, if he didn't have his support, he'd have been a wreck right now. He'd have completely fallen apart.

"OK, let's do this," Fenix said, trying to sound confident even though he was anything but.

"You'll have to come down to the station and I'll personally take your statement. I'll do everything I can to keep this confidential," Trey Griffin assured him.

Just then, the phone rang. Everybody froze for a second before the detective stood up and strode purposely towards the phone.

"Hello?" he said as he picked up. He listened for a couple of seconds, then said in an authoritative voice, "This is detective Trey Griffin with NYPD. I'm here with Mr Bergman who has filed charges for rape. That video you're trying to get paid for is officially evidence in a rape case. It's being analyzed as we speak and I'm certain the facial recognition software will do its job, and I'll be knocking on your door shortly." He paused and listened for a few more seconds with a bored expression on his face. Jared got up and took the few steps separating him from the detective quickly, silently asking for the receiver. The detective passed it to him with a raised eyebrow.

"Listen to me, you worthless piece of shit," Jared snarled. "This is Jared Hartley, Fenix Bergman's partner. If you're doing all this to hurt him, which I doubt because you're probably a greedy bastard, let me tell you that you won't succeed. His friends and family, and *I*, will stand beside him whatever happens. He will not lose his job because he's brilliant at what he does and you can't change that. Nobody will buy your fucking video because it's obvious you took advantage of a vulnerable person. But if someone does, the police and our lawyers will be after you so fast you won't have time to say 'scumbag'," Jared barked and disconnected, throwing the receiver back on Cathleen's desk.

"Did you just hang up on the blackmailers?" Cathleen asked and raised an eyebrow.

"Yes. I'm sick of this," he said, his voice suddenly sounding tired. He walked back to the sofa and sat down next to Fenix, taking his hand in his. "I don't want you to sit here and feel threatened by these useless assholes anymore, Fen. You know as well as I do that in this business anyone could turn against you and stab you in the back. We did what we could. Let's go to the station, make the statement, and catch a flight back home. Whatever happens tomorrow, we'll deal with it."

"OK," was all Fenix managed to say, feeling exhausted himself. He'd reached a point, after the initial shock and embarrassment of the discovery had worn off, where he didn't care anymore. Jared was right – they'd done everything they could. It was out of their hands.

Cathleen hugged him before they left and whispered: "Don't worry, Fenix. Jared is right. Whatever happens, we'll face it head on and I'll help you any way I can." She kissed his cheek and they walked out, following detective Griffin's lead to the station.

CHAPTER THIRTY SIX

Jared

Jared watched *Poison*'s final scene backstage, thinking he'd never get tired of seeing Fenix on stage. As the water rained on his bare chest and Fenix moved with such elegance and grace, Jared's gut clenched as he realised, yet again, how much he loved that man.

Six months after their trip to New York, the video was still nowhere to be found. No magazine, newspaper, blog, or TV show had covered the story. Cathleen had been vague when Fenix had asked about it shortly after they returned to London, and Jared suspected she might have had to do some damage control.

Detective Griffin had been right – he hadn't managed to identify the men in the video and it was filed under unresolved cases, and stuck at the back of the queue. The video was still evidence and would be for another three and a half years. After that, it might come back to haunt them, but Jared couldn't bring himself to worry about it right now.

Right now Jared had been offered an extension to his contract that expired in two months, and he was seriously considering declining. Adam had also mentioned the other night that he might retire from the stage and take on producing. It had always been his passion, ever since he singlehandedly produced *Of Kids and Monsters* almost ten years ago.

Jared's passion was directing and working with kids. He was so tired of the stage, of musical theatre in general. But he'd love to work with kids in some way.

The final notes of the song sounded, Fenix dropped on the floor as the rain beat mercilessly on his body, and the stage went black. The audience exploded in applause and Fenix ran backstage, taking the towel Jared had waiting for him. He gave him a quick kiss and dried himself off before running on stage again to bow with the whole cast.

Later that night, Fenix raised his head off Jared's chest to look into his eyes, saying,

"I have a meeting with the producers tomorrow."

The nightlight cast an eerie glow on Fenix's face, making his features seem even more beautiful. Jared caressed his cheekbones with the pads of his fingers, and tugged his bangs behind his ear.

"They'll probably want me to sign the new contract," Fenix continued.

"Yeah, it's that time of the year," Jared said. "I got offered a new contract today too."

"Did you sign it?"

"No."

"Jared, I've been thinking for a while," Fenix began nervously. "I want a real life with you. A life where we don't get followed by the paparazzi when we go out to eat or see a new show, or where I have to look over my shoulder all the time because someone might decide to stab me in the back. A life where we get weekends off and normal working hours and more than a two week holiday once or twice a year. I want a house and a yard and a dog," Fenix paused as if unsure whether to say what was coming next. "And kids. I'd like to have kids with you, a family."

Jared's heart was about to explode with joy. He leaned down and kissed Fenix, long and hard, until they were both panting and ready for round two.

"I want all that too, love," Jared said as their lips separated. "I've been thinking about it for a while, too, but I wasn't sure if you were ready."

Fenix beamed at him, so happy and open and genuine that Jared couldn't help but kiss him again.

"I've been thinking of moving to Malmö," Jared said.

"You want to move to Sweden?" Fenix asked incredulously.

"Yes. It was beautiful there. And they have an up and coming musical theatre scene. I bet any show would be more than happy to hire you as a choreographer, or whatever you decide to do."

"What do you wanna do?"

"I'd like to open a dance and drama studio for kids of all ages. I was also thinking about directing, but I'm not sure I want to get involved in the theatre again. Not yet, anyway. But I'd love to work with kids."

Fenix's grin hadn't left his face when he said,

"I'd love that."

"What part?"

"All of it. The moving to Malmö, the dance and drama studio, maybe even choreographing a show..."

"Yeah?"

"Yeah."

"We can sell the flat and we'll have more than enough money to buy a house and maybe even a smaller property for investment. I'm also going to get royalties from *Of Kids and Monsters* while it's on stage because I've co-written it," Jared said.

"I have some savings," Fenix added. "We can buy the studio with it and get it started. I'm sure with your passion, it'll quickly grow into something profitable."

"So we're really doing this?"

"We're really doing this."

They stared into each other's eyes, looking for doubt or hesitation, but found neither.

In two months, Jared found himself watching Fenix's final performance backstage. If judging by his own last show the day before, Fenix must be feeling quite emotional. Even though they were both ready to take on the next phase of their lives, it was still overwhelming to say goodbye to the stage.

The audience knew it was Fenix's final performance in *Poison* and the standing ovation in the end lasted a while. Just as it started to die down, a voice on the sound system announced,

"Ladies and gentlemen, please take your seats. We have a surprise planned for you tonight."

People started murmuring among themselves but eventually quieted down. Jared's heart was pounding in his chest, his knees almost giving out. Just before Fenix came backstage, Jared ran to his hiding place as he had rehearsed that morning. He saw Fenix frown and look around, searching for Jared and looking baffled about what was going on.

Music started playing, and the *Poison* cast along with the *Of Kids and Monsters* cast appeared on stage, dancing and singing to Fall Out Boy's *The Phoenix* just as they had rehearsed. It had been incredibly difficult to plan this without Fenix ever finding out, but with Joy's, Ned's, and even Adam's help Jared had managed to keep it a secret.

Jared saw Joy hurrying off stage to get Fenix, who looked very confused. That was Jared's cue. The moment Fenix was dragged on stage by Joy, the audience erupted in applause. Jared walked slowly after them. The singing and dancing ended and the performers lined at the end of the stage, whispering and giggling. Jared stopped in front of Fenix and took his hand in his before he spoke.

"Fenix, I wanted to do this here, tonight, because this has been our home for the past five years. All these people," he gestured towards the performers, "and everyone who came to see our shows every day, are our family. I know you love the stage and that, even though you want more out of life, you'll still miss it every single day. I know this, because I will too."

Fenix nodded as his eyes welled with tears. Jared prayed that he'd be able to keep his voice steady through this and not cry.

"You once told me that dance is like life – there are good moments and bad moments; moments when you sprain your ankle, but you have to go on, even when it hurts like hell; moments when the applause goes for such a long time you feel like a god; moments when you nail the move you've been practising for a week and you feel invincible; moments when you're scared as hell to even cue up the music. But just like life, dance goes on whether you like it or not. It flows in your veins."

A tear slipped down Fenix's cheek and Jared wiped it away with trembling fingers. He was deaf and blind to everything around him. All he could see were Fenix's crystal blue eyes, shining with love and so much hope.

"I'd like to ask you to dance with me, Fenix. To marry me and spend your life with me," Jared said. He fell on one knee, producing a small, velvet box with two rings inside. "Will you?"

"Yes! Of course I will!" Fenix exclaimed and helped Jared up, taking the rings and putting one on his finger and one on Jared's. They hugged and kissed through their tears as the people around them applauded, whistled, and cheered.

EPILOGUE

FeNiX

Eight years later

"One, two three, one two three, and hold," Fenix counted as the little girls around him danced to his instructions in their little pink tutus. He eyed them critically, trying to hold back his smile as he watched their cute faces drawn in concentration.

"Feet a bit further apart, Lina," he said as he knelt down to correct Lina's posture. "That's better," he said, meeting her beautiful, blue eyes, so much like his.

"Thanks, Mr Bergman," Lina said officially.

Fenix grinned proudly.

"You know you don't have to call me Mr Bergman, right?" he whispered so that the other girls wouldn't hear.

"I know. But I don't want them to think I get any special treatment just because you're my Daddy," Lina replied stubbornly.

Fenix shook his head and stood up – like father, like daughter.

"OK, girls, one more time. One, two, three..." he started counting again and the girls continued dancing around him.

Looking at them, Fenix thought how much his life had changed during the past eight years. He and Jared had moved to

Malmö and bought a beautiful house – one with a large yard just like Fenix wanted. They set up the dance and drama studio out of nothing and it was so successful that they were thinking of opening another one to be able to accommodate the huge demand.

They also had their beautiful little girl Lina with a surrogate. Viktoria was the most wonderful woman, and five years after she had given birth to their daughter, she'd agreed to do it one last time for them, and was currently pregnant with their second child. She was due to give birth to a boy any day now, and both Jared and Fenix had been ecstatic. Jared had wanted their second child to be Fenix's, like Lina, but Fenix had been adamant that Jared should get his own mini-me.

Movement outside the glass door of the dance studio caught Fenix's attention. Olivia, one of the other dance instructors, was waving at him, beckoning him to come to the door.

"That's it, girls, you're doing great. Keep going," Fenix said as he headed towards Olivia.

"Jared called. Viktoria is in labour. You need to get to the hospital now, Fenix. He said things were progressing fast."

Fenix's heart did a somersault. Their baby was about to be born. A beautiful little boy just like Jared. He grinned at Olivia, went back inside the studio, and wrapped Lina in his arms, carrying her outside with him.

"Daddy", she squealed. "We talked about this."

Fenix laughed and put her down as they exited the studio. Olivia gave him the thumbs up and went inside to finish his class for him.

"Listen, gorgeous, Dad is in the hospital with Viktoria. She's having your baby brother right now. We have to hurry or we'll miss it."

Lina's eyes got huge and she grabbed Fenix's hand, pulling him towards the front door. They called a taxi and headed to the hospital, Fenix in his dancing leggings and, thank god, a t-shirt, and Lina in her pink tutu.

Two hours later, as Fenix stared at Jared who was holding their son, and Lina as she gently patted the baby's head, beaming with joy, he could not imagine his life being any more perfect.

Even if the whole of Broadway applauded him every single night.

This right here, his family, and his quiet, relaxed lifestyle, was everything Fenix needed to be happy.

Jared glanced at him and waved him closer, giving him the baby to hold. Fenix took him and was surprised at how small he was. He'd forgotten babies were that small – after all, their daughter was nearly six and was getting bigger by the second.

"Hey, Alec. Welcome to the world," he said quietly, caressing the baby's cheek.

Jared pulled him closer and snuck an arm around his waist while hugging Lina with his other arm.

"I love you," he whispered in Fenix's ear.

"I love you, too," Fenix replied. "All of you," he added, looking at his husband and his children, silently counting his blessings.

THE END

ACKNOWLEDGEMENTS

I started writing DANCE on a whim after seeing a great West End musical. While watching the show, the story of Fenix and Jared hit me so hard, I could feel it flooding my brain and taking down all the writer's block walls I'd had up for months. Nothing about this novel was planned – I was actually supposed to be writing 'Colour Me Inside', the third book in my 'Heartbeat' series. I never expected to get the urge to write a MM romance book, even though I've been an avid reader of the genre for a long time. I had no budget for it, no time in my schedule, no contacts in the genre. But the desire to write was back, after it had completely evaporated for several months, so I decided to go for it and write what I really wanted to instead of what I was supposed to. When I told my friends and family I was writing this book, they were all so supportive and encouraging. People offered their help without expecting anything in return and I'll forever be grateful for that.

Kameron Mitchell edited this book and put so much effort in making it as good as it could possibly be. He praised my writing, occasionally, but more often than not criticized it and made me re-write so many paragraphs that my head was spinning. I'm hugely thankful for that, and for all the times he was just a text away when I needed him.

Midian Sosa endured all my meltdowns while I was writing, and all my nervous freak-outs when the book was ready for beta reading. She beta read it, proofread it, gave me feedback, encouraged me and helped in any way she could.

Charmaine Butler who beta read and proofread, and was the first person to finish reading the book. She was the first person to give me positive feedback and stop me from pulling my hair out while waiting for people's reaction. Oh, and she's an excellent cherry pie maker.

Kathryn Grimes was one of the first people I told about writing DANCE and she welcomed the idea wholeheartedly, giving me the thumbs up. She also beta read, and gave me invaluable feedback.

Veronica Bates, who also beta read and loved the book, saying the things I needed to hear when I was riddled with self-doubt. You know me so well, V.

Kelly Schwertner who got to experience the MM romance genre for the first time when beta reading DANCE – seriously, she didn't even know what MM stood for! I was very nervous what she'd think of it, and when she texted me to say how much she loved it, I was so relieved! Thanks, Kelly, for giving my book a chance and I hope that won't be the last MM romance book you'll read.

Kellee Fabre who beta read and wrote such a lovely, sweet review that made me grin like an idiot.

All those people supported me and my work, no questions asked. I'm so lucky to have such people in my life. Thank you!

I've written about love at first sight before, and I'll continue to write about it in the future because I truly believe in it. It's real – I know, because I've lived it. I still am living it. My husband and I met eleven years ago and have been together ever since. He endures all my crazy while I write, all my tears, all my ramblings about books and characters and series and covers... He's my lobster and I love him.

My little boy who is such a lovely, smart, funny person and inspires me every single day.

All the bloggers, readers and reviewers who took the time to read the book and give me feedback – thank you, guys!

ABOUT THE AUTHOR

Hi, my name is Teodora and I live in London with my husband Ted and my son Jason. I've been writing ever since I can remember, but it became my full time job in 2010 when I decided that everything else I've tried bores me to death and I have to do what I've always wanted to do, but never had the guts to fully embrace. I've been a journalist, an editor, a personal assistant and an interior designer among other things, but as soon as the novelty of the new, exciting job wears off, I always go back to writing. Being twitchy, impatient, loud and hasty are not qualities that help a writer, because I have to sit alone, preferably still, and write for most of the day, but I absolutely love it. It's the only time that I'm truly at peace and the only thing I can do for more than ten minutes at a time - my son has a bigger attention span than me. When I'm procrastinating, I like to go to the gym, cook Italian meals (and eat them), read, listen to rock music, watch indie movies and True Blood re-runs. Or, in the worst case scenario, get beaten at every Nintendo Wii game by a six-year-old.

CONTACTS

www.facebook.com/teodorakostovaauthor

www.teodorakostova.blogspot.com

t.t.kostova@gmail.com

@Teodora_Kostova

ALSO BY TEODORA KOSTOVA

IN A HEARTBEAT

Stella

"I've been in and out of hospitals for the past ten months. I've had half my liver removed and even though this time the doctors are very optimistic that they've removed all of the tumours, they can't be sure. In another three months they want me here again for a check up. Right now I feel better than I've ever felt. I know the damn thing is gone, at least for the moment. Despite that, I can't make any plans for the future, not yet. I need to go somewhere

where nobody knows me, where I can relax and maybe even forget about all this. Where I can meet people who don't think of me as the girl who lost her father and her brother in a car accident, and who has cancer. I want to have fun, even if it's for a couple of months."

When Stella decides to visit her estranged cousin Lisa in Genoa, she has no idea Italy will give her a new reason to live.

Max

"Her gaze locked on a scene so beautiful, the picturesque beach paled in comparison. A lifeguard emerged from the water, his orange trunks stuck to his legs and water dripping all over him. He shook his head to get rid of some of the water in his hair and Stella felt as if everything started developing in slow motion – tiny drops of water slid from his neck down his broad chest and muscular arms, along a weaving tattoo on his right shoulder, and continued downwards towards his chest and washboard stomach, finally getting lost in the waistband of his trunks. A part of another tattoo peeked over his trunks on his left hip, the other part hidden under them. It was a total Baywatch moment."

Their love is epic. But there are too many things keeping them apart.

"How could you keep this from me, Lisa? If you had told me the first day I met him, I would have avoided him like the plague. Nothing would have happened between us."
"I kept your secrets, too, Stella."

Are Max and Stella strong enough to fight not only for their love, but for their lives?

THEN, NOW, FOREVER

THEN

"Gia had let Beppe into her life so easily, as if it was the most natural thing in the world. She'd held him when he'd hurt so badly he'd thought he might die; she'd talked him down when he'd been so angry he'd considered doing something he'd regret for the rest of his life.

Gia had saved his life.

At least once he needed to be strong for her.

This right now, this moment, was theirs. It belonged to them, not to abusive or dead fathers, not to guilt, regret or sorrow, not to the